EVERYTHING CAN CHANGE

Brian Kemper

ISBN: 1507555229
ISBN 13: 9781507555224
Library of Congress Control Number: 2015910026
CreateSpace Independent Publishing Platform
North Charleston, South Carolina

In Memory of Michael, Sean, Kurt, Otis, and Wes

PROLOGUE

When I was fourteen years old, on Christmas Eve in 1989, my eighteen year old sister, Jesse, gave me my first CD: Don Henley's *End of the Innocence*. Jesse's gift was borne out of necessity, rather than any sisterly thoughtfulness or love. She had received the CD earlier from an aunt, who, for all we knew, had received the CD as a gift from someone else. Jesse did not want the CD. She was a fan of Depeche Mode, The Cure, The Violent Femmes, and, of course, Prince; in the 1980's, there was an unwritten law in Minnesota that teenage girls had to like Prince. Luckily for her, she had not yet bought a present for me, so re-gifting the CD became a win-win situation for her. At least, it was, until she realized I couldn't listen to the CD in our house unless I used her Sony Discman.

The CD had not been one of the gifts on my Christmas wish list. At the time, I was not a big music fan. In fact, I only owned one cassette, and that was the audio recording of the first *Star Wars* movie. I have always been a bit of a geek; a fan of science fiction, fantasy, horror, and superhero stories. As a result, my list consisted of things like the *Indiana Jones* movies on VHS, books by Stephen King, Raymond Feist, Stephen Donaldson and Robert Jordan, and superhero t-shirts.

It was my first CD, though, at a time when CDs were relatively new, so it was still a big thing for me. After my family of four had finished unwrapping presents - - none of which included any *Indiana Jones* movies - - I went to my bedroom with Jesse's Discman and listened to the CD a couple of times. After a while, I decided I liked it.

Over the next three or four months, I listened to the *End of the Innocence* constantly. After Jesse and I had our third fight over my use of her Discman (only three days after Christmas), my parents bought me my own Discman. I took it and the CD everywhere I could, listening to the music while I was reading or as I fell asleep at night. Out of all the songs on that CD, I probably listened to *New York Minute* the most. I had a fascination with New York City at the time, and the song seemed to sum up life, especially in the City (well at least to a small-town boy like me) perfectly.

If you had asked me at the time what the song meant, I would have told you that it was about how, in an instant, a person's life could change from great to horrible, and that we need to appreciate what we have. At 14, I had never had such an experience, but that didn't stop me from believing that I "understood" *New York Minute's* lesson.

Of course, at 14, I was certain that I would be one of those lucky ones who would never have to experience that lesson first hand.

CHAPTER ONE

I stared out of the office window as the afternoon sun bathed the New York City skyline. The June sky was bright blue with a few snow-white, billowy clouds floating in it. The clouds were the type that resembled objects or animals, like elephants or regal lion heads. A commercial jet flew past one of the clouds on its descent into La Guardia Airport. I followed its path, as it flew behind the Chrysler Building, which sparkled in the sunlight. The Chrysler Building was my favorite building in Manhattan, and after living in New York City for six years, I was still in awe of it. I loved the stainless steel tower and its Art Deco styling. On each side of the tower, seven concentric sunburst patterns rose upwards giving the building a futuristic, yet classic look that, in my opinion, epitomized New York City. Whenever I looked at it, I couldn't help feeling inspired and hopeful.

The plane soon flew out of view, and I reluctantly turned my eyes to the office's occupant: Elizabeth (not Liz, not Beth, and certainly never Lisa) Jennings, who was reading a file that I had given her a few minutes before. Elizabeth was a short woman with a brunette bob haircut and thick rimmed glasses. When I had met her two years before, I instantly realized that she was the spitting image of Velma from the Scooby Doo cartoons. That is if Velma wore expensive suits instead of a frumpy orange sweater and brown skirt.

Elizabeth was sitting behind a tan L-shaped, faux-wood platform desk. Various law books including *Black's Law Dictionary* and *Basic Trial Advocacy* were on a bookshelf on the wall above the desk. A laptop computer sat on the desk next to neatly organized stacks of papers and files.

Elizabeth's office was virtually identical to the offices used by all associate attorneys at Garrick Knight Scott & Grant, the large and prestigious law firm for which we both worked. Like all of the other associates, Elizabeth had added her own personal touches, such as her diploma from Harvard Law School and photographs of her hiking in various locales. Elizabeth was unmarried and, to my knowledge, was not dating anyone so I assumed that she went hiking with two guys, a girl and a talking dog.

"Good job with the outline, Jack," Elizabeth said, after she finished reviewing the file. "And this Ramstein case that you found. It's perfect." Elizabeth and I were both in the litigation department. At that time, in 2003, Elizabeth was a sixth-year associate and I was a third-year. We were preparing a motion to dismiss a large class action lawsuit brought in New York state court against our client, National Mutual Insurance, a gigantic property and casualty insurance company. The case was essentially a breach of contract case, similar to most of the cases that I had handled in my three years as a lawyer. The plaintiff, Richard Kopf, claimed that National Mutual had underpaid him for damage covered by his auto insurance policy. Mr. Kopf also claimed that National Mutual had systematically underpaid millions of other policy holders as well. It wasn't a "sexy" case. No movies starring George Clooney would be based on the case, nor would any episodes of television shows produced by Dick Wolf or David E. Kelley.

However, the case was important to Garrick Knight, and therefore to Elizabeth and I, because Mr. Kopf was seeking hundreds of millions of dollars in damages for himself and for those policy holders allegedly injured by Garrick's actions. National Mutual had not been satisfied with the law firm that previously handled its cases, and had retained Garrick Knight to represent it in the matter. The partners at Garrick Knight, including Mike Goldman, the senior partner of the case, had accepted it, knowing that it would bring in millions of dollars in legal fees for the firm. If the case was defended successfully, National Mutual would likely hire Garrick Knight for future cases, and more money would pour in.

As the senior associate on the case, Elizabeth was responsible for carrying out the day-to-day management of the case and supervising my work. I was responsible for doing the legal research and writing the first draft of the brief. While doing the research, I had found the Ramstein opinion, an obscure Massachusetts case reported in a law journal five years earlier, in which a judge dismissed a lawsuit that was virtually identical to the one brought against National Mutual.

"Yeah, it is good," I said. "I just wish it was from a New York court. Hopefully, the judge will see that the law is the same in New York." I wondered, not for the first time, how to trick Elizabeth into saying "jinkies;" perhaps, if I said "zoinks."

"I think we'll be able to convince him," Elizabeth replied. "Let's discuss timing." Elizabeth was smart and ambitious, as were all of the attorneys who worked at Garrick Knight, including myself. I worked fairly well with her, but she could be a little intense. Although given the fact that she would be up for partner in a year and a half, her more severe nature was understandable.

"Today is June 5th," continued Elizabeth, "and the motion has to be filed on the 20th. I know that we discussed having a draft ready for the client by the 17th, but since this is their first case with us, they want to see the brief by next Friday, the 13th. So, Mike told me that he wants to see a draft by next Wednesday." *Ruh-roh!* I thought. That was not good news. "That means I will need the draft by Monday morning. I hope that you don't have any big weekend plans."

My heart dropped. I did have some plans with a friend, Kyle Robinson, and his wife, Rachel. Kyle was a fifth-year associate at Garrick and one of my closest friends. We had planned to take Friday afternoon off and spend the weekend on the Jersey Shore at a summer house that Kyle and Rachel had rented with friends. I had been looking forward to the trip for weeks.

"Nothing major," I lied as I started to calculate what I would need to do to finish the draft by Monday morning.

"Okay," Elizabeth replied. "Mike wants the brief at twenty pages or less. I'll write the introduction, which will be no more than three pages. That gives you seventeen pages for the rest of the brief. Do you think you can do that?"

Just barely, I thought. "Yeah, I think so," I said. "If you don't mind, I was thinking of working at home tonight."

"That's fine. I know that you will get the work done," replied Elizabeth. "It's why Goldman wanted you on the case."

"Thanks," I said, enjoying the compliment, until I remembered the change in weekend plans. Disappointment replaced elation.

"You're welcome. Let's talk tomorrow morning and you can give me an update." I nodded my head. "Have a good night." With that, Elizabeth turned back to her laptop.

"You too." I stood up and left Elizabeth's office. My office was to the left, but I turned right. I had to break the news to Kyle and I didn't think he would like it any better than I did.

⚔

At 6:00 pm on a Thursday night, or on any weekday night for that matter, Garrick Knight's offices are quite busy. The administrative assistants had left for the night, but virtually all of the attorneys, including the partners, and paralegals would be there late into the evening. Many would grab dinner at the office cafeteria and eat at their desks. After dinner, they would sit in their offices, in conference rooms or in file rooms, staring at their computers, or reviewing documents. The main lights in the hallways and common areas would stay on until ten at night, but many of the offices and conference rooms would stay lit long after.

Like lawyers at every law firm, everyone was concerned about their billable hours. The more time they spent working, the more time they could bill. For partners, more hours billed meant more money in their pockets. For associates, more hours billed meant a better chance to become partner, which in the long run meant more money in their pockets.

When I arrived at Kyle's door, he was busy typing on his laptop. Kyle kept his office tidy, although it was not as orderly as Elizabeth's office. Kyle also had a radio on his desk which he often used to listen to Yankees and Jets games. Pictures of Rachel and his two year old daughter Megan were on his desk and bookshelves. Next to the radio, Kyle had placed a photo of himself and Don Mattingly that he had from a fantasy baseball camp he attended a few years back.

Kyle had curly black hair and was four inches shorter than I am. Like many others at Garrick, including myself, his skin was pale and he was a little overweight from working long hours with little exercise. His yellow tie was loosened and his blue business shirt was open at the neck. Not for the first time, I acknowledged that Kyle's work attire was more stylish than mine, but I attributed that to his wife, Rachel, rather than Kyle's own personal sense of style.

Kyle turned from his computer and saw me. "Smalltown, how are you doing?" he asked.

I originally met Kyle during my first week at Garrick, when I was assigned to a case representing a famous talent agency, a case

Kyle had been working on for two months. When we met, Kyle asked where I was from, and I made the mistake of telling him that I grew up in a small town in Minnesota. From that time on, Kyle called me "Smalltown." Sometimes, he would call me "Ritter," and, very rarely, "Jack." In retrospect, I was glad I hadn't told Kyle that I grew up in a farm town.

Kyle was the quintessential New Yorker. He was loud and brash, and busted my balls all the time, especially when the Yankees beat the Twins. However, he was also very intelligent, funny and loyal, and was the closest thing I had to a mentor at the firm. Kyle often provided me advice that helped me stay sane as I worked the late hours required at Garrick.

"Okay," I said as I sat in one of the two chairs in front of his desk. "How are you doing?"

"I've been better," Kyle answered. "We just got word that the Qualtech trial has been scheduled to start in the second week of August and it will probably last a month. That means trial prep starts next Monday."

"That sucks," I said.

"Well, more reason to enjoy this weekend, right?"

"Unfortunately, I don't think I'm going to make it," I said, and then quickly described my meeting with Elizabeth.

"Shit," Kyle said, shaking his head. "Goldman should have pushed back on the client. You could have had a couple extra days."

"You know he wouldn't do that," I said. "National's a new client and he wants to keep them happy. He wouldn't rock the boat at the start of the relationship."

"Yeah, you're right," Kyle replied, and then pointed his finger at me. "You shouldn't have agreed to be on this case in the first place. You've got enough other cases, and you've been working your ass off for the last six months. You should be taking a break instead of working on another case."

Kyle had a point. During the previous three months, I had been working virtually around the clock, including weekends, on a summary judgment motion on a different case for another client. In fact, I had worked at least ten hours every day in May, except for Memorial Day. We had finished the motion at 2 a.m. on Memorial Day, and I walked out of our office building, just as some other people were leaving the bar across the street, including one couple whose display of affection bordered on the obscene. Jealous of their freedom, I took a cab home and spent the rest of the day in bed or on my futon watching television.

Because of that workload, I had planned to take time off from work during the first weeks of June and August. I didn't have a real vacation planned in June. I had hoped to hang around the City, catching up on television, books and movies, and spend the weekend with Kyle and Rachel in Jersey. However, two days after Memorial Day, Mike Goldman and Elizabeth came to my office and asked me to join their team on the National Mutual case. At Garrick, associates had a little flexibility in their case assignments. If an associate felt that he or she had enough work or had a vacation planned, they could turn down a new case assignment. As a result, I could have turned Mike and Elizabeth down with no repercussions. However, Mike explained how important the case was, and how it could be a career maker for me. He didn't promise that the firm would make me a partner in four years if I joined the team, but he made it clear that such an outcome would be more likely if I did. Ambition had swelled within me as I thought of the possibility. Assuming that I could keep my weekend plans with Kyle, an assumption that was reinforced by the original proposed drafting schedule, I agreed to work on the case.

"You may be right," I told Kyle. While I wasn't happy that I had to cancel my plans, I didn't regret the decision to work on the case. "But this is a big case. This could be huge for me."

"I get it," Kyle said, "but you need to be careful. If you keep working like this, without a break, you're going to burn out. You need to take time for yourself every now and then."

"Don't worry," I reassured him. "I've got a week's vacation planned for the first week in August. I'll be heading home for my ten year high school reunion. I'll be fine."

"Aright, but I wish you were coming this weekend," Kyle said, as he picked up a Nerf baseball and started tossing it in the air. "Rachel's high school friends, Allie and Sophie, will be there, and I like them, but I don't enjoy spending an entire weekend alone with three women. Plus, Rachel was thinking you and Allie would hit it off."

"I don't know. I've met her, and she is cute ..." *But not my type*, I thought.

"You two haven't *schtupped* already, have you?" asked Kyle, with a grin. Like many New Yorkers, Kyle frequently peppered his speech with Yiddish terminology. During my time in the City, I had learned a few words myself. *Schtup* was my favorite, and not just because it represented one of my favorite activities. I loved the sound of it. It was a perfectly ridiculous word for sex.

"No, I never *schtupped* Allie," I replied. "Why would you think that?"

"Well, you've *schtupped* so many of Rachel's friends, it's hard to keep track."

"I have not *schtupped* many of her friends."

"What about Kim?" he asked.

"Okay, she and I *schtupped*." I said.

"And Robin?"

"We had a bit of a kiss and a cuddle in that booth at Chumley's, but we didn't *schtup*."

"'Kiss and a cuddle,'" Kyle said with a smirk. "Where I come from, they call that second base."

"Which phrase do you think women like better?"

"Good point," he conceded. "Alright. What about Susan?"

"Rachel's sister?" I said defensively. "I never touched her."

Kyle laughed. "I know. I just like giving you shit."

"Keep that up and maybe I won't let you guys set me up anymore." I bluffed. In the past two and a half years, both Rachel and Kyle had set me up with a few single women they knew. The date with Kim over a year before had led to a short, two month relationship. The other attempts had not panned out.

"Well, we can't have that," said Kyle. "You work too much to meet women on your own, so if you don't hook up with Rachel's friends you'll never have sex again. And then who will I live vicariously through?"

"I didn't know that my sex life was so important to you."

Kyle ignored the comment. "Plus, if you're not going to let Rachel set you up, she's not going to let me hang out with you anymore."

"And why is that?"

"Rachel is like any other woman in a committed relationship," Kyle explained. "She has a compulsive need to set up her single friends. She's like a germaphobe, but it's not germs that make her antsy. It's single people."

I laughed. "Or maybe she's just like you and she wants to live vicariously through stories of her friends' sex lives."

"Hey, that's my wife you're talking about," said Kyle, sternly, and he threw the Nerf baseball at me. As I caught it, his face broke into a huge smile. "Seriously, I wish you were coming with us."

"I know. So do I," I looked out Kyle's window, which faced east and gave him a decent view of the East River and Queens. "Tell you what; the brief is due on the 20th. I'll take off the July 4th week, and I'll come to the Shore then." I threw the Nerf baseball back to him.

"Deal," he said, catching the ball.

"Well, I should get going if I want to get work done tonight," I said. "I'll see you tomorrow before you leave."

"Sounds good, Smalltown. Good luck tonight."

"Thanks," I said, standing up. "See ya."

The various Garrick Knight legal departments, such as the litigation, intellectual property, and corporate departments were located on seven different floors in the 57th Street building. On each floor, the attorney offices and conference rooms were located along the perimeter, so that each room had a window view. The administrative assistants and paralegals were located in cubicles in the interior area.

Along the office walls on each floor were various prints, paintings and photographs, each portraying New York City in various ways and time periods. Garrick Knight was formed in New York City in the 1930's, and, in 2003, was one of the oldest and most successful law firms in America. Over the years, the firm had opened a number of other offices, both in the United States and in Europe and Asia, but the New York office remained the firm's headquarters. The art in the New York office celebrated that fact.

I looked at some of that art as I walked to my office, which was located on the west side of the 30th floor. My window didn't face any cool landmark. Instead, I could only see the brick façade of another office building located next to our building. Still, I was luckier than the first-year and second-year associates, who were doubled up in their offices.

While my office was not as organized as Elizabeth's and Kyle's, it wasn't a mess either. Files and papers weren't stacked neatly, but they were stacked and each stack was organized by case. Like Kyle,

I had a radio next to my laptop, although, when I listened to the radio, I listened to talk shows on WNEW. Next to the radio, and attached to some speakers was my newest, favorite possession: an iPod that I had bought three months before. It had taken me almost that long to burn all of my CDs, numbering over two hundred, onto my home computer, but it was worth it. Once the music was transferred my iPod, I could listen to it wherever I went. The music represented a variety of genres, from Alien Ant Farm and Annie Lennox to Van Morrison and Weezer. The majority of the music though, was from the 1990's, a mixture of alternative, power pop, grunge and rock music.

I didn't have any personal pictures in my office, but on one wall hung two framed movie posters from the first *Star Wars* and *Superman* movies. As I grew older, and despite playing college football, I had retained my geek interests. I bought new comic books every Wednesday; watched TV shows, like *Farscape, Buffy the Vampire Slayer* and *The X-Files;* and read sci-fi and fantasy books, like *Harry Potter* and the *Song of Fire and Ice* series.

Looking at the posters, I smiled as I recalled a conversation that I had had a couple of months before with another third year associate, Hal Allen. Hal had asked me whether the posters were meant to be inspiration to me. When I asked him why, he pointed out that both Luke Skywalker and Clark Kent were both farm boys who left their farms for a larger world, where one became the savior of a galaxy, and the other became Superman. He noted that, while I wasn't a farm boy, I had left the Minnesota farm country for New York. I told him that I hadn't consciously made that connection, but sub-consciously, who knows?

I sat down at my desk and quickly checked my e-mails to see if there were any important messages. Finding none, I shut down my laptop and started to pack up. My telephone rang and the Caller ID screen displayed the work telephone number for Sarah

Danvers, a current friend and former girlfriend. I had met Sarah in my first year of law school when I had waited tables part-time at a restaurant in Hoboken, New Jersey. Sarah had also been a part-time waitress, working full time as an unpaid intern at an advertising agency. We started dating about two months after I started work at the restaurant. The relationship lasted a turbulent and passionate six months. After Sarah broke up with me, she quit her job at the restaurant, while I spent weeks listening to break-up songs like Dire Straits' *Romeo and Juliet.*

We didn't see each other again until three years later, when, by coincidence, we both attended the same party on the Upper West Side. It was an awkward meeting, but after a few drinks, we were reliving old times and catching up on our lives. Sarah had become a full-time employee of the advertising agency, still single and lived five blocks from me on the Upper East Side. I offered to share a cab with her that night and she accepted. We also ended up sharing her bed.

We had a great time that night, but the next morning, we both realized that another relationship would not work, so we decided to remain friends. Over the next two years, about once or twice a month, we would have dinner, hang out at a bar or a party, or watch a movie together. On a few occasions, when neither of us was seeing anyone, we would have sex. As Sarah put it, we were "buddies," because "friends were friends, but buddies get to sleep with each other." After hearing that pronouncement, I never used the term "buddy" to refer to a male friend again. The last time we had slept together was the previous December, right after she broke up with her boyfriend, Dean, one of the biggest jackasses I had ever met.

I hit the speakerphone button, and said, "Jack Ritter." I almost always answered the phone as if I did not know who was calling, even when I thought I recognized the number. During my first year at the firm, I didn't answer the phone that way. I answered a call that I thought was from a law school buddy, by saying "Wassup?!!" The call was from a partner who was calling from his home. The partner was not happy, and I learned my lesson.

"Hey Jack, it's Sarah," she said, in a light, bubbly tone. "How are you doing?"

"I'm okay, Sarah. How are you?"

"I'm good," she said. "Listen, my team just finished a huge project at work, and we're going out to celebrate at Culture Club." Culture Club was an '80s themed bar in Midtown. "Want to join us?"

At that moment, I desperately wanted to say "yes." I was really bummed about canceling my weekend plans, and I was not looking forward to another night of work. A night out with Sarah would go a long way to easing the disappointment and stress I was feeling. I also could use some of the female companionship that I thought I heard promised in Sarah's voice. Even a little kiss and cuddle would have been great. Other than Sarah, I had not kissed, much less *schtupped*, anyone in the past eight months. I had gone on a few first dates, and two second dates, but that was it. I was in a drought, and I wasn't happy.

Talking to Sarah, though, I knew that I had no options. In order to finish the draft by Monday morning, I had to work that night, and every night until it was finished.

"Ah, Sarah, it sounds like fun, but I have a big brief due on Monday. I'll be working on it tonight, and all weekend."

"That's too bad," she said, her voice full of disappointment. "I haven't seen you in a month. I've missed hanging with you."

"I know. I've missed hanging with you too. I've been really busy lately, and haven't seen much of anyone."

"Well, if you change your mind, you know where to find me. Good luck with the brief."

"Thanks. Have a good night," I said, with a sigh. *The drought continues*, I thought as I hung up the phone. I packed my laptop and my files into my computer bag, and grabbed my iPod. As I left my office, I donned my earbuds, selected the shuffle option, and pressed play. *Semi-Charmed Life* by Third Eye Blind started as I walked out the door.

CHAPTER TWO

My spirits lifted a little as I stepped out of the building that housed Garrick Knight's offices. The weather was still beautiful. The sun was shining and the temperature was around sixty-eight degrees. It was the perfect weather for walking to my apartment, which was located about two and a half miles away on 90th street. The sidewalks were still packed with people, but not as many as there would have been two hours before. As I started walking east, an attractive brunette in a red cocktail dress smiled at me as I passed her. The dress hugged her curves nicely, and she knew it. I smiled back, and my spirits lifted a little more.

No matter how many years pass by, walking around New York City remains one of my favorite things to do. Almost every time I do it, there is a part of me, the part that will always remain a small town Minnesota boy, that marvels at what he sees, and asks "How did I get here?"

I originally grew up in Oak Lake, Minnesota, which is located in the middle of dairy and turkey country in central Minnesota. Oak Lake was and, in many ways, still is very similar to the town in the movie *Footloose*. In Oak Lake, though, dancing is permitted, and no one burns books; at least not in public. With less than three thousand people, the majority of which are German Catholics, and the rest Swedish Lutherans, Oak Lake is the antithesis of New York. Its tallest structures are the water tower and the two grain elevators. The tallest building is the three story Oak Lake State Bank that was built before Prohibition, which was known in Oak Lake as the First Great Depression.

When I grew up, Oak Lake was probably no different than any other small town in the Midwest, if not America. Its residents were polite and religious. It had no movie theaters or any five-star restaurants. If you went out for the night in Oak Lake, most likely you were going to a friend's house, one of the two restaurants or four bars in town, or, in the summer, to a softball game in the park. It was safe, slow paced, and, to me, more boring than anything, except fishing (which made me a bit of a pariah amongst the rest of the Oak Lake residents who loved fishing, especially if ice was involved).

Therefore, as I grew up, I wanted nothing more than to leave Oak Lake. At some point in my teens, I decided that New York City was where I wanted to be. Many of the people I knew, including my family, thought I was crazy. They all had the same small town distrust of large cities, which along with movies like *The Warriors*; *Death Wish*; and *Fort Apache, The Bronx,* made them believe that New York was overrun with prostitutes, pimps, drug dealers, rapists, murderers, and perhaps worst of all, Yankee fans.

I had a different view of New York. To me, New York was fast-paced, exciting, and, perhaps most importantly, a challenge. For as long as I could remember, I knew I was smart. Long before girls were interested in me, and before I became good at sports, my intelligence was the one thing I had going for me. However, being smart in Oak Lake wasn't good enough for me. I wanted to prove to myself and the world that a small town Minnesota boy was as smart as anyone else. Sometime around the time I received the *End of the Innocence* CD, I decided that New York was the best place to prove how smart I was. I'm only a little embarrassed to admit that my decision was probably heavily influenced by the show *Family Ties* that year, when Alex P. Keaton, perhaps TV's most famous smart kid, moved to New York to make it big.

During my senior year in high school, I applied to several Ivy League schools, thinking that they would provide the best stepping stone to a life in the Big Apple. To my great joy, I was accepted by my first choice, Yale, which had recruited me to play football. Unfortunately, my parents couldn't afford the tuition, even with the financial aid package that Yale offered us. Instead, I went to St. John's College, a great Division III school located a half hour from Oak Lake. Despite the setback, though, New York City remained my goal.

I worked hard throughout college, and decided on a career in law. During my senior year, I again applied to Eastern schools, this time, law schools in New York City itself. Again, I was accepted by my first choice: New York University School of Law. Like Yale, it was an expensive school. My financial situation was worse, though, because I, and not my parents, would be paying for my education. Despite the costs, it was my dream, so I took out student loans that could have paid for one of the nicest homes in Oak Lake, and went to New York.

During the first month after I arrived in Manhattan, I was overwhelmed. The City was too much: too many people, too many choices, too many noises, and too much to learn, both in school and out. Once I gained my footing, though, I started to thrive. I came to enjoy the variety that New York offered, in food, people, or things to do and see. I tried to experience as much of New York as I had time for or could afford.

During my free time, usually only on weekends, I would take long walks, exploring the various neighborhoods in Manhattan:

Greenwich Village, SoHo, Tribeca, East Village, Chelsea, Kips Bay, and so on. Despite the fact that they were all part of the City, they each had their own feel. Soon, walking became my favorite way to experience the City. Wandering through the City was how I ran into Matthew Broderick on the street in 2000, and how I appeared as an extra in a crowd on an episode of *Law & Order* in 2002. I especially loved walking around on my favorite day of the year: "Spring Saturday," that first warm Saturday in spring where the City sheds the cold, and women don their spring and, often skimpy, summer clothes.

After I started working at Garrick Knight, I had less free time for my walks; to compensate, I would walk to and from work any time the weather and time allowed. During my breaks, I would take ten minute walks around Midtown. After a while, I realized that walking cleared my mind, and I could focus better on work. In fact, walking helped my focus so well, that, whenever I am puzzled by a knotty situation, my first instinct is to walk around, even if it's just to pace around the room.

On that June night, I spent the time during my walk home thinking about the brief, rather than appreciating the City and the evening. Before I knew it, I had arrived at my apartment building on 90th street. My one bedroom apartment was on the third floor of a four floor walk-up building. The apartment had only four rooms: the small kitchen, the small living room, the small bedroom and the small bathroom. After I entered the apartment, I walked into the living room and placed my bag on the circular dining table. The table, like all of the other furniture in the room had been purchased at Ikea or similar stores where decent, affordable furniture was available. Of course, I had to assemble the various items myself.

I threw my keys onto my black wood desk that sat against the wall next to the window that faced 90th Street. A framed poster from the movie *Thunderball* hung above the desk, and a framed poster from *Blade Runner* hung over my black wood futon. I walked over to the dark wood entertainment stand (another Ikea purchase) that held my stereo, television, DVD player and Xbox. I plugged my iPod into the stereo and Collective Soul's *The World I Know* poured out from the speakers.

From there, I went to my bedroom and changed into some comfortable clothes: a red Daredevil T-shirt and a pair of dark brown cargo shorts. Like the other rooms, the bedroom was reasonably clean. I am not by nature a tidy person, but I kept the apartment clean on the off chance that I brought a woman home some night. Of course, at that point, calling that possibility an "off chance" was like calling a high school musical "off Broadway."

When I was done changing, I went to the kitchen where I made a quick call to a nearby sandwich shop for delivery of a cheesesteak and fries. I then poured a Maker's Mark and Diet Coke into a low ball glass with ice. With my drink in hand, I went back to the living room to set up my laptop and research on the table. When the deliveryman arrived twenty minutes later, it was 8:15 PM, and I had started writing the brief.

⊱⊰

Around 11:30, my phone rang. The last few remnants of my dinner lay on a plate on the table. My glass held the last of a second Maker's Mark and Diet Coke, and the iPod was playing *Lover, You Should Have Come Over* by Jeff Buckley. I was frustrated and tired.

The brief was not going well. I had finished a little more than half of what I had planned, and I was struggling with my writing. With each sentence, my mind strained to find the best words and the order in which to put them, and each attempt was worse than the last. I knew what was wrong, but I did not know how to fix it.

To a large degree, writing a legal brief resembles doing algebra. In algebra, you solve equations, and you have to "show your work" by providing each iteration of the equation until you reach the final equation. In a brief, the writer also has to show his work when making his argument. He has to provide providing each legal point in the chain of logic, citing the precedential rules, analyzing those rules, and applying those rules to the current case. If the writer skips a point, the reader may not be able to follow the logic of the argument.

I had shown my work in the parts that I had written, but the work was missing the extra piece that every brief needs in order to persuade the judge. If you've shown your work, you're ninety percent of the way to that goal. Getting that last ten percent, though, that's the bitch, because what's needed varies with the reader, the case and the arguments made. The writer needs to appeal to something in the judge, whether it's their sense of fairness, compassion, justice or even humor. One brief I had read in the past referenced *Alice in Wonderland* to point out the absurdities of the other side's argument. As can be imagined, it's easier for experienced lawyers to provide that "something extra." It's much harder for younger lawyers, like those only three years out of law school. It is even harder for those lawyers when they are tired and frustrated.

When my phone rang the first time, I was debating whether to continue writing for a couple more hours or to get a good night sleep and start again early in the morning. After the second ring, I answered the phone. "Hello?"

"Hey Jack, it's Sarah. How's my favorite lawyer?"

"I'm okay." I stood up and started to pace the room. "How's Culture Club?"

"It was good. We did a lot of dancing." She sounded a little drunk; her voice wasn't slurred, but it had the energy that comes with a solid alcohol buzz. "You should have joined us. How is the work going, by the way?"

"Not as well as I had hoped. I was just taking a break when you called."

"If you're taking a break, why don't you come over to my place for a drink? I've been drinking margaritas all night, and I'm not ready to go to sleep yet."

At the moment, I knew that Sarah was offering more than a drink. Sarah had the habit of becoming particularly amorous after drinking tequila, and she knew that I knew it. Given the dry spell that I was in, my answer should have been easy. In fact, a second after Sarah's question, there should have been a hole with my outline in my front door. At that moment, though, the answer wasn't so clear.

I wanted to go. In fact, there was nothing I wanted more. Yet, there was this loud voice in my mind that said that if I didn't continue working on the draft, I would not be able to finish it by Monday. That voice reminded me that handing in the draft late would be seriously detrimental to my career. It was the voice of my father reminding me of responsibilities. As a result, when I should have been saying "I'll be right there," I was trying to find the best way to say "no."

"That sounds tempting, but I don't know," I said. "I was thinking of going to bed and getting up early to work."

"Come on. You lawyers don't go to work until ten in the morning, and you'll have tomorrow and all weekend to get your brief done. Just come over for one drink. I'll make it worth your while." She said that last part in a sultry voice that made it very clear that it would be worth my while.

Yet, even that was not enough to convince me. I was about to decline and offer my apologies when I heard Kyle's voice in my head telling me that I had been working too hard and that I needed to make time for myself. He was right. Plus, if he ever found out that I turned down sex, he would never stop busting my balls for it.

"Okay," I said. "I'll be right over."

"Awesome! I'll be waiting."

"See you soon."

I hung up and saved my work on the laptop. I debated briefly whether to change into some better clothes, but remembered that seduction wasn't necessary. Instead, I brushed my teeth and put on some deodorant. When I was done, I looked in the mirror and assessed myself. I was about fifteen pounds overweight, but at my height and build, the extra weight didn't look too bad. I thought I looked pretty good. I turned off all the lights, and walked out of my apartment. As I walked away, there was only one voice in my head, and it was repeating "I'm gonna get laid."

Less than ten minutes later, I was standing at Sarah's door, after she had buzzed me into the building. I paused there for a few seconds, trying to think of a witty entrance line, but the only thing in my head was the "How you doin?". *Derivative*, I thought, *but it would have to do.* I knocked three times.

"Come in," I heard Sarah say. "It's open."

I opened the door, and immediately saw Sarah standing five feet away. Suddenly, the blood rushed from my brain southward, stopping me from coming up with a line, much less uttering one. Sarah stood there, with her right hand above her head, leaning on the wall and her left hand on her left hip. She was nude except for a pair of red high heel shoes, which increased her height three inches, putting her at almost six feet. Her curly shoulder length hair, which was sometimes brunette, but now was a dirty blonde, framed her twinkling hazel eyes and her devilish smile. I stood there speechless, as my eyes drank in the sight of her beautiful curves and pale skin.

"What took you so long?" she asked, in a mock pout. "I almost started without you."

I walked over to her, closing the door on the way. When I reached her, I could smell that she was wearing my favorite perfume, the kind she always wore when she wanted to drive me crazy. I kissed her with the intent of curling her toes and leaving her breathless. When we broke the kiss, I couldn't see the effect the kiss had on her toes, due to her closed toe shoes. However, she was a little out of breath. *Mission accomplished*, I thought.

She looked into my eyes with a smile on her face. "Take me to bed, Jack," she said.

So I did.

A respectable time later, we were laying on her bed in a post-coital bliss. The floral print covers and sheets, and about a dozen or so throw pillows were lying on the floor. My head was on one of the few real pillows, and my right arm was wrapped around Sarah. Her head was on my chest, and her right hand was tracing circles on my stomach.

I didn't need a mirror to tell me that my face wore one of those goofy smiles that I always had after sex. If it had been pointed out to me at that moment, I wouldn't have cared. The sex had been great. Of course, it had been so long since I had it; my judgement could have been off. One thing I knew for sure was that I felt great, as if a heavy weight that I had unknowingly carried had been lifted off of me. I had forgotten about my brief, my job, and virtually everything else in the world. I was content.

"Wow. That was great," I said.

"Mmmm," Sarah purred.

"But I do believe that a drink was promised," I said dryly.

Sarah gave me a soft jab to my ribs, muttering "Smartass."

"Oof," I said. I reached down and brushed the small of her back with my right hand. "By the way, great touch with the high heels."

"Thanks. Nothing says take me to bed like a good pair of 'fuck me' pumps."

"The lack of clothes helped, too," I noted. "So do you want to take the shoes off?"

"God, yes," Sarah said, and she sat up and took off her shoes quickly. "Oh, that feels so much better," she said, when she finished.

When she settled back down next to me, I asked, "So any special reason for the booty call tonight?"

She turned to look at me, her lips set in a little smile. "Well, when I called you this afternoon, I was hoping that you would come out with us, and that we would end up here. But then you chose to stay home rather than come out with me ..."

"Clearly, I was a moron."

"Yes, you were," she said, the light dancing in her eyes. "Anyway, when I was at the club, I was talking to one of one of my co-workers, and she couldn't stop talking about her new boyfriend. Apparently, they just started having sex, and they're having it all the time. And, while she's a pretty reserved woman at work, apparently, shots make her very talkative and uninhibited."

"They tend to do that," I said, as I grazed my fingertips down her side.

"So, she couldn't stop talking about how amazing her new boyfriend is. She was telling us stories, and she was pretty graphic, too."

"Yeah? Did she use the word '*schtup?*'"

"No," she said, puzzled. "Why?"

"Never mind; inside joke. How graphic was she?"

"Well, I'm not going to repeat it, but let's just say she talked about the things his big rooster would do to her cat."

"Why, Ms. Pot, the things you say about Ms. Kettle," I said, with a grin.

"Hey," Sarah said, and gave me another soft jab to the ribs. "There's a time and place for things. I may say things in the heat of passion in my bedroom, but I'm not going to say the same things in public with my co-workers."

"Good point," I conceded. "Please continue."

"Long story short, she kept going on about her sex-capades, and they were getting me a little hot and bothered."

"They're having an effect on me as well."

"I can see that," she noted, as she moved her hand further down my body. "So, there I was, getting randy at a bar, and then she asks me if I've been having any great sex lately. Of course, since I'm not seeing anyone, I had to say no."

"When's the last time you were with someone?"

"It was with you, back in December."

"What a coincidence. That was my last time as well."

She giggled, as her left hand continued to explore my nether regions. "So there I was, frustrated and as horny as hell, so I decided right then and there, that I would be calling you when I got home."

"Well, I'm glad you did," I said. "So, the dating scene hasn't been treating you well?"

"I've had about three first dates in the last two months, and that's it. I do have a blind date set up for next Friday, but …" Sarah's hand suddenly stopped on my right nut. "Jack, what is this?"

I didn't notice that the tone of her voice had changed. "Given your familiarity with my anatomy, I'm surprised that …."

Sarah raised her head and looked at me. Her face lacked any sign of playfulness. "Stop. I'm being serious. There's a lump on your right testicle."

I lay there stunned. Sarah moved her hand as I reached down between my legs to check myself. Sarah was right; there was a hard lump on the outside of the testicle. It felt like a rock had been implanted in it.

"Fuck," I said. At that moment, deep down, I knew it was cancer. I had heard too many stories about people who were diagnosed with cancer after finding lumps where they didn't belong. Too many of those people had died.

"You never noticed it before?" Sarah asked, with concern.

"No." I thought that it couldn't be cancer; I was too young. *But if it is, am I going to die?* I thought, suddenly frightened. *I can't; I haven't lived yet. I want to get married and have a family.*

Sarah was persistent with her questions. "Do you know when the last time you felt yourself there?"

"No." I suddenly wondered whether I had lumps elsewhere. I sat up and quickly checked my other testicle. It felt normal.

"So you don't know how long it's been there?"

"No," I said, and stood up from Sarah's bed. "Sarah, I should get going." I started to look for my clothes on the floor, looking under each of the throw pillows. *Why the fuck do women like throw pillows*, I thought in frustration.

She stood up from the bed and walked around to me, putting her hands on my shoulders. "What? Why?"

"I need to figure this out, and I need to be alone to do that." I explained. I saw my underwear and shorts under a different two feet away and reached down to pick them up..

"So, you're going to go back to an empty apartment, and sit up all night worrying? Jack, just stay here with me. You'll feel better. I have some Tylenol PM to help you sleep, and we don't even have to talk."

"Sarah. I'm freaked out here, okay?" My tone was harsher than I intended. "Thank you for the offer, but I just need to be alone right now." I quickly put on my underwear and pants, and started to look for my shirt.

"Okay, you're freaked out." Her tone also suggested that I was being an asshole, which I probably was, but I was the one with the possibly cancerous tumor. "I can't imagine what I would do in your place. I think you should stay, but if you need to go, I understand." Again, her tone suggested otherwise.

"Thanks." I found my shirt, and put it on.

"But you have to promise me some things," she said.

"Sure." I found my socks and shoes and put them on.

"First, I'm going to give you some of the Tylenol, and you have to promise to take it when you get home."

"Okay."

"Second, you need to call me tomorrow when you get up. I want to hear how you're doing."

"Agreed."

"Third, you need to have a doctor check that tomorrow."

"I was thinking the same thing." I said.

"Okay, wait here while I get the Tylenol." Still naked, she walked out of her room to the bathroom. When she came back, she gave me the bottle. "Here. Call me tomorrow okay?" She gave me a tender kiss.

"I will. Thanks." I left Sarah's apartment, and headed to the elevator, my stomach in a knot and questions and fears swirling in my mind. I knew that sometimes lumps are benign. *Maybe the same was true in my case? Maybe it's a cyst, and not a tumor?*

I walked home with those and other thoughts in my head. By the time I arrived at my apartment, a little after 1:00 AM, I realized that Sarah was right. I wouldn't be able to sleep the way my thoughts were churning. After I stripped down to my boxers, I poured myself two fingers of Maker's Mark and took two Tylenol PM pills. That was not part of the recommended directions on the Tylenol bottle, but, as I told to myself, I needed the sleep.

Lying in bed, five minutes later, I thought about the night. One moment, I was happy in bed with a beautiful woman, who was happy to be with me. A moment later, I was more scared than I had ever been in my life. Suddenly, the chorus of *New York Minute* played in my mind: *In a New York minute, everything can change.* At that moment, I understood fully what those words meant. With those words on repeat in my head, I said a prayer for my health and for some sleep. I tossed and turned for a while, often reaching down to feel the lump. Eventually, thanks to the whiskey or the pills, I fell asleep.

CHAPTER THREE

I woke up at 9:30 AM the next morning. I was lying on my back in my queen-size bed, the blue quilt my Mom had made for me years before covering my lower body. I was very drowsy and disoriented. I had forgotten to turn on my alarm before I had gone to bed, and had slept past my usual wake-up time. "Damn," I said, as I shook off the lethargy. I reached down to touch the lump, to see if the previous night was just a bad dream. It was still there.

What am I going to do? I thought. I needed to make an appointment with a doctor to have the lump examined, but I didn't know any doctors in New York. Like most twenty-somethings, I assumed my health was always fine, so I hadn't had a physical in the past six years. Plus, even if I had a primary doctor, I wasn't sure whether I should see him or some cancer specialist. There was also the question of finding a doctor that was in-network with my health insurance company.

Work! I suddenly remembered the National Mutual brief. I hadn't thought of it since the moment I had made the decision to go to Sarah's apartment. I had wanted to be at work by 9 AM so that I could get an early start on the National Mutual brief. *Should I go to work and worry about the lump after I'm done with the first draft?*

My indecision lasted for two, maybe three seconds. *No.* The most important thing was my health, so I had to see a doctor as soon as possible. Plus, I probably wouldn't be able to work on the brief until I did that; I would be too worried about what the lump may or may not be. At that moment, I knew that I wouldn't make the Monday deadline. I would have to call Elizabeth and tell her that something was happening; I just wasn't sure how much to tell her. I did not want her or the rest of the firm to know about my condition.

What am I going to do? Suddenly, it occurred to me that Kyle could help. He would know how to deal with Elizabeth, and he once told me that his uncle was a doctor on Long Island. I just had to decide whether I wanted him to know about the lump. A second later, I stood up from my bed, went to the living room where I had left the phone, and called Kyle at work.

"Kyle Robinson," he answered.

"Kyle, this is Jack."

"Smalltown? I was just thinking about you. I'm looking at the box score from the Twins game last night. Looks like the Twins took it in the nuts."

God, he could not have chosen worse words. "They weren't the only ones," I mumbled. I quickly continued before he could respond. "Listen, I need your help with something that's come up. It's pretty personal, so I need you to keep it private."

"Sure, what's the problem?"

"I found a very hard lump on my right testicle last night."

There was a moment of silence on the phone. "Jesus Christ, Jack," Kyle said. "How are you doing?"

"I've been better." As I spoke, I found myself touching my right nut, feeling the lump. I checked the other nut again to make sure there was no lump on that one. It occurred to me that I had not touched myself so much since puberty.

"I bet. What can I do?"

"Well, first, I need to get it checked out, but I don't know if I should see a regular doctor or if I should go to a specialist. Your uncle's a doctor, right? Can you give him a call, and see what he recommends?"

"Will do. I'll call him as soon as we're off the phone. What else do you need?"

"I need your advice about work. I'm supposed to work on this brief, but I don't think I can do that until I see a doctor."

"I agree."

"So I'm thinking that I should call Elizabeth. I think we may need an extension on the brief, but I don't know how much of an extension we need. Also, I don't know how much information to give her. I want her to know it's serious, without telling her everything. I'd like to keep this as private as possible."

"I'll handle Elizabeth," Kyle said. "I'll tell her that something serious came up and you have to see a doctor and that you don't know when you'll be done with the draft. We'll let her decide what she wants to do."

"Thanks," I said, feeling relieved. "Once you hear from your uncle, can you call me on my cell?"

"I will. I'll talk to him first and then get back to you. Listen, Jack, try not to think about it too much okay?"

At that moment, I realized that, since I mentioned the lump, Kyle had been calling me 'Jack" -- not 'Smalltown' or 'Ritter.' He was really worried about me. "I'll try," I said, without a lot of conviction.

"Alright, I'll call you soon."

I hung up the phone, and put it down. I picked it up again two seconds later and called my administrative assistant, Carol, to let her know that I would be out of the office for personal reasons.

Once that call was over, I let out a sigh. I had taken care of my two most immediate worries, scheduling an appointment and handling work. I felt a little relieved, but then my mind went back to the lump on my body and what it meant. The swirl of thoughts started up again. I decided to call Sarah to divert my mind.

"Jack?" She answered, after the first ring.

"Hey, Sarah." I responded.

"How are you doing? Were you able to sleep last night?"

"Yeah, the Tylenol you gave me did the trick. You were right. If I hadn't taken them, I probably would have been up all night. Thank you."

"You're welcome."

"Also, I'm sorry that I bolted so fast last night."

"Jack, there's no reason to be sorry."

One of the best pieces of advice my father ever gave me was that the best time to apologize to a woman was when she said that there was no reason to be sorry. Wise man, my father. Apologizing made me feel better, too. Justified or not, I had been a dick to Sarah.

"That may be so, but I'm sorry, anyway." As I apologized, I walked into my living room, and looked out the window. Like the previous day, the sun was shining, but there were more clouds in the sky than there had been the day before and they were darker.

"You're forgiven," Sarah said, gently. "So, are you going to see a doctor today?"

"I hope so." I quickly told her about my call with Kyle.

"That sounds good," Sarah said. She sounded a little rushed. "Listen, I'm sorry, but I have to head to a meeting with my boss. Call me after you see the doctor, okay?"

"I will."

"Good. I'll be thinking of you. Bye."

I hung up the phone, and started to pace the room, wondering when Kyle would call. I realized that pacing and worrying wouldn't be useful, so I went to my bathroom to take a shower. While I was showering, I tried to keep my hand from touching the lump, but my fingers kept finding their way there as if pulled by a magnet.

Ten minutes later, I was dressed and Kyle called. "Jack, hey, it's Kyle. Sorry, it took so long."

"That's okay. Did you talk to your uncle?"

"Yeah, he said that you need to see a urologist. One of his med school classmates, Charles Cross, is an excellent urologist and he's in Midtown, near Grand Central. My uncle called him and he set up an appointment for you at 2:30 today."

"Wow, that's great," I said, happy, but surprised, that his uncle had taken that extra step. "Tell your uncle thanks for doing this. All I was hoping for was a name."

"Anything we can do to help you, Jack." Kyle gave me Dr. Cross's address and telephone number. "While my uncle was setting up the appointment, I called Elizabeth. After I told her what's going on, she said that she would call the other side and get an extension. She also told me to tell you that she hopes everything works out, and that you should not worry about work."

"Great," I said. I made a mental note that I would have to buy Kyle a bottle of scotch to reward him for his help. "Thanks a lot, Kyle. You've taken a lot off my plate."

"You're welcome. Once your appointment is over, I want you to give me a call, okay? No matter what the news is."

"Sure. I promise." Kyle and I ended the call. I felt my stomach rumble. Now that I had a plan of action, I was a little less worried, and could think about other things, including breakfast. My appointment was in four hours, and I had some time to kill, so I decided to eat at my favorite diner, the Blue Moon Cafe. I grabbed my iPod and headphones, and walked out of my apartment.

⟫⟨+ +⟩⟫

At 2:30 p.m., I was sitting in Dr. Cross's waiting room. The hours before the appointment had moved slowly, my thoughts consistently on the lump. After breakfast, I had spent the time walking through the City. I had arrived at Dr. Cross's office, which was near Grand Central Station, about a half hour before. After I had filled out the requisite health and insurance forms, I sat waiting for a nurse to call me. Two other men sat in the waiting room, each one at least twenty years older than me.

The magazines on the coffee table were the standard fare for doctor's offices, something for (presumably) everyone: *People*, *Sports Illustrated*, *Cosmopolitan*, *Men's Health* and Women's *Health*, and a variety of others. *Cosmopolitan* advertised "10 Amazing Sex Tips to Drive Him Wild In Bed," while *Men's Health* promised "A Six Pack in Ten Minutes." Having played competitive sports for almost half of my life, I knew that promise was pure equine excrement.

"Jack Ritter?" inquired a matronly nurse, standing by the receptionist. I stood up and followed her to a room, which contained an examination table, a sink, a rotating chair and various medical illustrations of the male and female urinary systems. Once there, the nurse checked my height and weight, and drew some blood into test tubes filled with a gel-like substance. As she left, she asked me to undress and put on a patient's gown.

Dr. Cross came in shortly after I finished putting on the gown. He was tall and thin, like a long distance runner, and in his late forties. His gray hair was cut close to his skull. He was wearing a white lab coat, a yellow tie, light blue French cut shirt with gold cufflinks, and tan chinos. His silk tie, cufflinks, and expensive leather Gucci shoes suggested that urology was a very rewarding specialty. He gave me a reassuring smile, and said, "Jack Ritter? Nice to meet you, I'm Charlie Cross." After we shook hands, he went on. "So I heard that you found a lump on your right testicle?"

"That's right."

"Okay, let's take a look." He had me lie back on the examination table, and reached under my gown. He slowly felt the lump. He was gentle, but firm. His touch was much different from Sarah's touches the night before. "Yep, it's right there. Let me check the other one." He felt the other testicle and then, using both hands, felt the rest of my pelvic and stomach area. As he did the exam, he asked me a variety of other questions, such as whether I had noticed any other lumps or felt unusual back or stomach pains. He also asked me questions about my family history, such as whether anyone had ever suffered from cancer. His questions only required one word answers, most of which were no.

After his examination, he stepped outside the office and pulled in an ultra-sound machine. I had seen enough television shows and movies that demonstrated its use on pregnant women, so I was familiar with the device. Being a man, though, and, thus, incapable of having children, I had never expected to be on the receiving end of it. After applying gel to my scrotum, Dr. Cross gently rubbed the ultrasound wand on the lump, and watched the ultrasound monitor. He then printed out pictures, which he place in a manilla file folder.

"Okay," he said, when he finished. He handed me a paper towel. "You can use this to clean up. When you're done, why don't you get dressed, and then we'll talk in my office across the hall, okay?"

I nodded my head and he left the room. I wiped the gel off, and quickly put on my clothes. Dr. Cross's office was exactly across from the examination room, and when I entered it, Dr. Cross was sitting behind a big, dark oak desk, writing in a folder with a gold Mont Blanc pen. The oak book shelf behind him matched his desk and was filled with diplomas and awards. Throughout the office, Dr. Cross had hung or place pictures of him and various New York politicians, athletes and celebrities. He looked up when I walked in.

"Jack, please take a seat," he said, pointing to one of the two dark brown leather seats in front of his desk. When I did, he continued. "Jack, I have some bad news." I swallowed, and nodded my head. My hands gripped the arms of the chair. "Based on my experience, I believe that the lump you found is a malignant tumor. I'm afraid that you have cancer."

It's one thing to believe that you have cancer, but it's another to hear a doctor actually confirm it out loud. At that time, the only word scarier was AIDs. The only thought in my head was simple. *Cancer? Fuck.*

"Jack, this is going to sound stupid but if you could choose a type of cancer to have, testicular cancer is it. The survival rate right now is 95%, especially if it is caught early. And I believe we caught it early, because I didn't feel any other lumps or abnormalities. Plus, you haven't had any pain or other side effects suggesting that you have tumors elsewhere."

He paused, probably to give me a chance to speak. I was still too stunned to do anything but listen.

He continued. "So, next steps. We're going to get the results from the blood tests on Monday to confirm my thoughts."

The fact that they needed a test to confirm it was cancer gave me hope that Dr. Cross was wrong. I suddenly found myself able to speak. "How will you do that?"

"We're going to test the blood to see if it contains certain proteins that would indicate that you have cancer."

I felt a small spark of hope light up inside me. "So, if the blood doesn't have the proteins, does that mean the tumor is not malignant?"

"It would suggest it, yes," Dr. Cross agreed. "I wouldn't get your hopes up, though, Jack. I'm 99% sure that the lump is cancerous."

Hearing Dr. Cross's words, the hope inside me dimmed, but didn't completely die. "Okay, but will the tests show if the cancer has spread?"

"No, unfortunately not. Right now, we can only worry about the lump, and to address that, you'll need surgery to remove your testicle."

"Remove?" I was shocked again. For some reason, I had never considered that I would lose the testicle. *Does that mean no kids? No more sex?* "You can't remove the tumor without removing the testicle?"

"No, we can't." He stood up and walked around his desk to sit on the chair next to me. He continued to speak, and as he did, his tone changed. He had previously spoken like the physician he was, clinical and distant. He now spoke with the reassurance and warmth of an uncle. "It's natural to be upset by the news. I want to you to know that you'll still be able to have sex and even have children. I've done this surgery many times, and all of my patients have had full sex lives afterwards. Also, if you are worried about your appearance, we can implant a prosthetic testicle. It's the same type of implant as a breast implant, and will look like a testicle."

Hearing about the loss of one of my balls had put me back into silent mode.

"I recommend that you have surgery as soon as possible," Dr. Cross said after a couple seconds of silence. "Testicular cancer is a fast moving cancer, which actually makes it easier to cure. I have operating privileges at New York University Medical Center, and, while you were dressing, I scheduled the procedure to take place next Thursday morning."

I felt a wave of panic rise through me. Dr. Cross must have seen it on my face. "I know this must seem sudden," he said. "What you should do is to spend time with friends and family this weekend, and try to not think about the tumor. On Monday, I'll get the results, and call you. Afterwards, if you want a second opinion, I'll give you the name of a colleague. For now, I'll keep the surgery scheduled as is, but if we need to change it, we can do that later."

"When would we know whether the cancer has spread?" I asked. "Would you be able to tell during the surgery?"

"Maybe, but probably not. After the surgery is over, we'll do some tests to see whether it has spread."

"And if it has?"

"You'll be seeing an oncologist, a doctor that specializes in treating cancer, after the surgery. He can outline the next steps, but even if it has spread, Jack, the survival rate remains around 95%."

I sat in silence, trying to process the information I heard.

"Jack, I know this is scary," Dr. Cross said. You probably have a million fears running through your head. But the methods of treatment now are much better than they were 25 and 30 years ago. Back then, testicular cancer was pretty much a death sentence. But now, we have the chemotherapy drugs that kill the cancer. I can't promise it is going to be easy, but with the right attitude, your chances of getting through this are incredible."

"Okay." I said. Hearing Dr. Cross's words, I was a little comforted, but only a little.

"Do you have any other questions?"

"Um, is testicular cancer common for someone my age?" I thought that testicular cancer was a cancer like prostate cancer that I wouldn't have to be worried about until I was older.

"Yes, the age range for this is 18 to 35. We don't know what causes it. Sometimes it's hereditary, but in your case, since you have no family history of cancer, that's obviously not true for you. Do you have any other questions?"

"Not right now," I replied. Dr. Cross stood up, and I followed suit. When he held out his hand, I shook it.

"If anything comes up, we can discuss it next week. I'll give you a call with the test results on Monday, and we'll go from there. Try to take care of yourself this weekend. "

I nodded and then left his office. I stood on the sidewalk facing 42nd Street and Grand Central Station, and watched the traffic go by.

Cancer, I thought. *Fuck.*

CHAPTER FOUR

I stood on the sidewalk, my mind reeling from my visit with Dr. Cross. I was having trouble processing the news, so I stared north-east at Grand Central Station, and then beyond at the Chrysler Building that loomed above to the right. Unfortunately, looking at my favorite NYC building did not alleviate any of the feelings I had, so I turned back to look at Grand Central Station.

At the top of the façade of the Station, there is a clock with three statues above it. Before that moment, I had never really looked at the statues and did not know who they were meant to represent. I stared closer at them, in particular, at the statue in the middle. The statue was of a man standing, a winged helmet on his head. His right arm was outstretched to the west and his left hand was holding a caduceus staff. When I was in elementary school, I had read everything I could find on Greek and Roman mythology, so I knew that this statue must be Hermes, the messenger of the gods in Greek mythology or Mercury, his Roman counterpart. Other than his helmet, the statue was naked, his genitals obscured by a cloth. I thought grimly that, barring some disaster, Hermes would always have two testicles under the cloth; something that would not be true of me soon.

I suddenly became aware of the bustling crowd passing on the sidewalk around me. I felt the eyes of some upon me, as they passed. I was probably quite the spectacle; a distraught man clearly losing his composure. I backed up against the building and tried to process the facts that I had cancer and that part of my physical manhood would be amputated. For whatever reason, I had never considered that one of my balls would have to be removed. Now, the realization brought me close to breaking down in the middle of the busy sidewalk filled with people. I could feel tears threatening to burst from my eyes. I wanted to sit down and let it all out. *What am I going to do?*

Move, I told myself, and I began walking north. I refused to be one of those people who creates a scene in public. Walking would help me keep my composure. As I walked, I remembered my promise to call Kyle.

"Kyle Robinson's office," said his secretary Colleen, when she answered my call.

"Colleen, hey, it's Jack Ritter. Is Kyle available?"

"Hi Jack, I think he's on the phone but he told me to let him know when you called. Just hold on a second." She put me on hold. Not for the first time, I thanked God that our firm's telephone system did not play Muzak.

Kyle answered after ten seconds of silence. "Jack, it's Kyle. What's the news?"

I stopped walking, and stood next to the side of a building. "It's not good. He says that it's likely cancer, and that he has to remove the testicle."

"Shit," he said, the anger and sadness apparent in his voice. "I'm sorry, man. How are you holding up?"

"To be honest, just barely." I said, the last part softly.

"Okay, head to my apartment," Kyle directed. "I should be there in about 15 minutes. We can discuss stuff then."

"Kyle, I can't do that." I said, my voice gaining some volume. "You have work, and you and Rachel are going to Jersey tonight."

"No arguments," he said, firmly, but still gently. "Get to my apartment. And don't worry about Rachel and me. After you called this morning, I spoke to Rachel, and we both agreed to put off Jersey for the night. You need some people around you. My parents picked up Megan last night, so it will only be the three of us."

"Kyle, I …," I paused, unsure what to say. The emotions that I had been holding in demanded release in response to his gesture. "Thank you."

"You're welcome. By the way, Elizabeth called me to let me know that the opposing counsel agreed to a ten day extension, so you don't need to worry about the brief this weekend."

Finally, some good news. "Great. Thanks Kyle."

"You're welcome. I'll see you soon."

Grateful for Kyle's friendship, I resumed walking uptown. Kyle and Rachel owned an apartment on 65th Street between First and York Avenues. Their apartment was about a half hour walk from where I was. After a few moments of walking, I remembered that I had promised to call Sarah after the appointment.

"Sarah Danvers."

"Sarah, it's Jack."

"Jack, did you see the doctor?

"Yeah," I answered, my voice wavering. "He said its cancer."

"Oh, Jack. I'm so sorry," Sarah said, softly and sympathetically. "How are you feeling?"

"Not good." I told Sarah what Dr. Cross had said about the tumor, the surgery and the blood tests. As I was finishing, a car horn and a swearing taxi driver interrupted me. The taxi was trying to get through the intersection, but the people in front of me were in the crosswalk, blocking his way. I decided to wait on the corner.

"Jack, where are you?"

"I'm on 42nd Street, near Grand Central. I'm headed to my friend Kyle's apartment. He and his wife Rachel are going to hang with me tonight." The pedestrians cleared the crosswalk, and the taxi driver, still shaking his head, passed through.

"That's a good idea. Have you called your family yet?"

"Not yet," I said. I had forgotten that I would need to speak to my parents and Jesse. I almost started crying at the thought of telling them. "I'll call them when I'm at Kyle's place."

"That makes sense," Sarah said. "Listen, I'm going out tonight but if you need me to stop by later, just let me know."

"I'll think about it, but you should have fun tonight. I'll be okay with Kyle and his wife.

"Okay, but I'll call you later to check in on you, alright?"

"Sure."

We said our goodbyes, and I hung up. I took a deep breath to steady myself. It was 2:30 p.m., and I knew it was going to be a long day. The walk sign ahead turned green, and I started walking to Kyle's.

Before I knew it, I was knocking on the door to Kyle's apartment. The shock had worn off during the walk. I was still pretty devastated from the news, but I had accepted my condition as reality, and had started to think about what was to come.

When the door opened, Kyle was there. He had changed from his business casual Friday attire into a pair of black shorts and a blue U.S. Open golf shirt. He looked sad. "Come on in, Jack," he said. I walked in and he gave me a quick hug.

I walked down a short hall and into Kyle's living room. Kyle and Rachel had purchased the three bedroom apartment two years before. I had been to the apartment for parties or dinners at least once a month during that time. I had even babysat Megan on a couple of occasions when I didn't have plans and Kyle and Rachel needed the help. I enjoyed being there; it had a nice homey feel. Because they owned the apartment, they could paint the walls, and not leave them white like my walls were. The living room walls were painted fallow which complimented the dark beige three cushion couch, coffee table and two darker chocolate brown sitting chairs. I sat down on the couch.

"Rachel's going to be here soon." Kyle walked into the kitchen, and returned a minute later with two lowball glasses filled with scotch. He sat down on the other side of the couch and gave one to me. "I figured you could use this. It's not five yet, but there is an exception for times like these."

"Thanks." I took a sip of the scotch, and felt the whiskey burn its way down my throat. Kyle loved scotch, and while I preferred bourbon, I could tell that whatever brand this scotch was, it was a good one. "And thanks for inviting me over."

"Hey, no one should have to go through this alone. So, tell me what Dr. Cross said."

I described my visit to Kyle. I kept it simple and brief, if only to maintain my composure. The more I talked about what was happening, the more out of control I felt.

"So, we'll know for certain on Monday," I said, when I had finished the story. "I guess there is still a chance that it may not be cancer."

"There may be a chance," Kyle replied, "but you're going to be better off if you prepare for the worst. I spoke to my uncle before I left work, and he said that if Dr. Cross thinks you have cancer, you have cancer."

"Did you talk to him about the surgery?"

"I did. Urology and oncology are not my uncle's specialties, but based on what he knew, he thought Dr. Cross was doing the right thing."

I took another drink of the scotch. The bite from the alcohol was still there, but slightly less painful. The last time that I drank scotch was at an Oscar party Kyle and Rachel had held in their apartment the previous March. I drank far too much that night, and had a massive hangover the next day. I learned that when you are drinking scotch, and you reach the point where it loses its bite, it is time to stop drinking.

"Jack, I know this sucks," Kyle said, interrupting my thoughts, "but you need to look at the bright side. The survival rate is incredibly high. I mean, Lance Armstrong had testicular cancer, and it spread to his brain, and he still survived. And, if the cancer hasn't spread, all you need to deal with is the surgery."

"I know. Right now that's what I'm counting on."

We sat there for a while, each sipping our glasses of scotch until Kyle broke the silence. "Can I ask, how did you find the lump?"

"Technically, I didn't."

"What?" Kyle said, with a confused look on his face.

"Sarah did," I said, and told him how she found it.

"So let me get this straight," Kyle said, when I finished, a small grin on his face. "The reason you found the tumor was because a chick was getting you ready for a second round of *schtupping*?"

"Pretty much."

His smile grew. "You know, you are lucky."

"Really?" I asked, sarcastically. At that moment, I thought the only luck I had was bad.

"Well, you hadn't felt the lump before, but it must have been there for a least a little while, like days or, maybe, even weeks. And you found it because you hooked up with a girl, after what six months of no sex? Maybe if you didn't have sex last night, you never would have found the lump or discovered that you had cancer until it was too late."

I thought about what Kyle said. There was some logic to it. "Yeah, I guess."

"Plus," he said with a grin, "you're lucky that Sarah even found it. I mean, if I ever have a lump on one of my balls, Rachel won't be the one to find it. She hasn't touched my balls in years."

I have to give Kyle credit. He made me laugh, at a time when laughter seemed impossible. I took another drink of the scotch and noticed that it was almost gone.

"Do you want another?" asked Kyle.

"Sure."

Kyle took both our glasses and walked to the kitchen. He returned a minute later, with two full glasses. "Do you want to call your family?" Kyle asked. "You can take the phone into our guest room."

"No, I need some more liquid courage before I call them." My Dad and Mom, Ed and Adelaide Ritter, owned a hardware store in Oak Lake. On a Friday afternoon, they both would be at the store until 6 p.m. or so. "I'll call them soon."

"Okay."

We sat in silence for a while, drinking our scotch. I was a quarter of the way through mine when I heard the front door open. Rachel, a tall blonde, the same height as Kyle, walked into the living room. She wore a blue dress suit and white blouse, and carried a leather computer bag. Rachel was also a lawyer, and worked part time at Walters, Franklin and Matthews, another law firm in town. When she saw us, she dropped her bag, and said. "Hey Jack, Kyle told me the news. I'm so sorry." She came over and gave me a hug. As long as I have known Rachel, she's always reminded me of my older sister. On a number of occasions, she even acted as if she was my older sister. At times, that attitude was very annoying. At that moment, though, it was very comforting. "How are you doing?"

"I'm okay, all things considered."

Rachel looked at me with compassion. "You're lying, but that's okay. It's okay to feel like shit. You're entitled." In addition to her older sister attitude, Rachel often was blunt.

"Thanks for letting me hang out here," I said. You didn't have to cancel your plans for the Shore, but I appreciate that you did."

"Jack," Rachel replied, "we're happy to do this. Jersey's not going anywhere. And tonight it was more important to be here with you."

"What about Allie and Sophie?"

"They went down by themselves. They'll be fine alone. Hell, they'll probably prefer to have the house to themselves for a night." She paused for a second and looked at a smiling Kyle. "Get your mind out of the gutter. It's not like they're having naked pillow fights."

"Hey, who has the dirty mind? Kyle said, somewhat defensively but from the smile on his face, Rachel was not too far off. "I wasn't the one who brought up the naked chicks."

"Anyway," Rachel continued, ignoring her husband. "It's only for a night. I told them that things came up and we couldn't make it tonight, but that the three of us will be there tomorrow."

Rachel's comment took me by surprise. I hadn't even thought about what I was going to do over the weekend. "Ah, I think I'll stay here tomorrow," I said. "I don't want to ruin everyone's weekend."

"Don't be silly," Rachel said, dismissing my comments. "You're not going to ruin the weekend. We're going to help you have a good weekend, or at least make sure that you are not having a miserable one."

I tried to think of some arguments that would convince Rachel and Kyle to head to the Shore alone. I looked at Rachel's face, though, and I knew that arguments were hopeless. I sighed, and said "Okay." I wondered whether Kyle ever won any arguments with her. Based on my experience with them, I decided that the best he ever did was to reach a draw.

"Now that that's settled," Rachel continued, "I need to change into some comfortable clothes. Kyle, why don't you see if there is any baseball on?"

"Yes, dear." Kyle replied. Rachel walked out of the room, and Kyle looked back at me. "Don't worry. I guarantee you that a weekend at the Shore will be better than a weekend here alone."

I shrugged, and watched as Kyle turned on the TV, and changed the channel to the YES Network. Highlights from the Yankees' trouncing of the Cincinnati Reds the night before were playing. We watched in silence for a while, which surprised me, because Kyle was never one to remain silent for long, especially when he was watching the Yankees. I assumed that he was respecting my privacy.

After the highlights were over, Kyle asked, "So, are you just worried about your survival chances, or you bothered by other things?"

I thought for a second. "It's a bunch of things, I think. Given what the doctor said about my odds, I'm not really too worried about not surviving. The thing that worries me most is the surgery."

"Makes sense," Kyle said.

"I mean, I just can't get it out of my mind. I know Cross said the surgery won't affect me sexually, but what if he's wrong, or there's a mistake, and I can't have sex anymore? I mean, I'm a guy, I like sex. A lot."

"Yes, I believe that's been well documented," Kyle said, with a small grin.

"And then I think, let's say that the surgery goes fine and I can have sex, but when a chick sees or feels that I have one testicle, they get turned off? What if they think that I'm not a real man?"

"Sorry, if I'm intruding." I turned my head to the right and saw Rachel standing in the entry to the hallway to the bedrooms. I wasn't certain how long she had been standing there. She had changed into a yellow blouse and white shorts. "Jack, you don't have to worry about that. Most women I know wouldn't care about something like that. In fact, most women probably would never even know that you had only one testicle. I mean, I haven't touched Kyle's balls in years. He could lose a testicle tomorrow, and I wouldn't know unless he told me."

Kyle and I looked at each other, and he started laughing while I managed a slight smile.

"What? It wasn't that funny," Rachel said with a confused look.

"I'll tell you later, dear," Kyle said, and gave me a wink.

"Rachel, I understand what you're saying," I said. "I'm just having trouble believing it."

"Jack," Kyle said, "is there some sort of implant that they can put in so no one knows?"

"Yeah, the doctor said that they have prosthetic testicles that are similar to breast implants. But I'm not sure I like the idea of something fake in there. Implants leak. They rupture. When this surgery is over, I don't want there to be any reason to have surgery down there again. I haven't decided yet, but I don't think I'll do that."

"Okay, but whatever you decide to do," Rachel said, "we just want you to know we won't think any less of you."

I looked at Kyle and he nodded.

"And if any woman thinks differently," said Rachel, "she's not a woman that you would want to be with anyway."

"Thanks," I said, hiding the fact that I was not convinced. My glass was empty, and I decided that I had had enough scotch for a call with my parents. "I should call my parents. Do you mind if I call them from your guest bedroom?"

"Go ahead," said Kyle. "Feel free to use the phone in there."

I stood up and turned right to the bedrooms. I stopped, and then turned back to Kyle and Rachel. "Guys, again, thanks. I'm not sure how I would be doing if I was handling this alone."

Rachel looked at Kyle for the response. Something seemed to pass, unsaid, between them. Kyle took a second and then said. "Jack, we're friends. This is what friends do. We're going to be here for you no matter what happens."

"Thanks."

"You're welcome. And good luck with your calls."

The Robinson's guest room was a nice room, about the size of my bedroom. The walls were painted blue, and the room had a King size bed, and a white wood desk and chair in it. A computer monitor, keyboard and mouse sat on the desk, and a gray Dell desktop computer was placed beneath it. On the wall above the bed, Kyle and Rachel had hung a oil painting of a large white flower. There were pictures of Kyle, Rachel and Megan throughout the room. I sat down on the bed and I called my parent's store. It was 3:15 p.m in Oak Lake.

"Hello?" Mom answered. I had hoped to speak to Dad first. It would have been easier on me to give the information to him, instead of Mom.

"Mom, hey, it's Jack. Is Dad there?"

"He's in the back. Do you need to talk to him?"

"I need to talk to you both. Is the store busy?"

"Nope, it's empty. What's going on?"

Good, I thought. I knew Mom wouldn't take the news well, and I didn't want people seeing that. "I've got some bad news." My voice started to waver, and suddenly all of the emotions I had bottled up spilled out. "Uh, last night I found a lump on my right testicle. I saw a doctor today, and he said that it's testicular cancer."

Mom was silent for a second. When she spoke, her voice was barely a whisper. "This isn't a joke, is it?"

Although I can be a smart-ass with people, I've never played a joke like that on Mom, or anyone else for that matter. "No, it's not, Mom. This is real." I heard her start to cry. "We're waiting on blood tests to be certain, but he's pretty sure."

"So what does that mean?" She said, slowly and softly.

"It means I have to have surgery on Thursday morning to remove the testicle. After that, what comes next depends upon whether the cancer has spread."

Mom started to cry harder. Hearing Mom weep pushed me closer to breaking down. "Listen, Mom, the doctor says that this type of cancer is 95% curable, and that he thinks we caught it early. If we did, and the cancer hasn't spread, that will be it. My life will be back to normal."

"And if it has spread?"

"We haven't discussed that yet, but the doctor said the survival rate is still very high." I told her the information Kyle had given me about Lance Armstrong.

I heard some noise in the background and then Dad ask "Addy, what's wrong?"

"Ed," Mom said to Dad. "It's Jack. He says that he has cancer."

"Jack?" Dad's voice came on the line. At that moment, I heard something in his voice that I had never heard before. I had seen Dad happy and proud, as well as angry and disappointed. Until that moment, I had never heard or seen him act afraid. "What's going on? Your mother is saying that you have cancer?"

I told Dad about the lump, the diagnosis, and everything else.

"The surgery is on Thursday?" Dad asked, when I finished. "Do you know what time it's at?"

"The doctor just said the morning. He didn't give me a time. I'm sure he'll tell me on Monday when he calls with the test results."

"Okay," Dad said, "well, then your mom and I will be flying in on Wednesday."

"Dad, that's not necessary." My parents did pretty well for themselves in Oak Lake, but still I knew that buying tickets six days before the flight would be pretty costly for them. "I'm going to be fine and I have friends here with me."

"Jack, I'm not going to sit here, half a country away, while my son goes through surgery without any family around," he said, his voice strained, but stern. "Your mom and I are coming."

"Okay," I said. After a pause, I said, "Thanks, Dad."

"You're welcome. How are you doing?"

"I'm okay," I said, my voice cracking again. "I'm scared, obviously, and worried, but I'm at a friend's apartment, and he and his wife are keeping an eye on me."

"Good. Have you talked to Jesse?" My sister Jesse lived in Plymouth, Minnesota with her husband Rick Studeman, and their children Libby, who was six, and Belle, who was four.

"Not yet," I admitted. "Listen, Dad, I'm drained. Can you or Mom tell her? I promise I'll call her tomorrow."

"Okay, we'll tell her, but if you don't call her tomorrow, she's going to call you. Have you told your firm yet?"

"I haven't spoken to anyone yet," I said, "but my co-worker told the senior associate I'm working with that a serious medical issue came up. I'm going to go in on Monday and will talk to a partner then."

"Okay."

Suddenly, a thought occurred to me. "Dad, one more thing. Can you and mom keep this as quiet as you can, at least for now? I really don't want anyone but close family to know about this." I knew that this type of information could fly through Oak Lake. Oak Lake residents did not need a twenty-four hour news service or the internet to get instant updates about its residents. It had a built-in rumor mill, and usually Mom was plugged directly into it.

"Okay, Jack. I'll talk to your mother. We'll try to keep it quiet for now."

"Thanks Dad. Listen, I should get going."

"Okay, but your mom wants to talk to you quick. Just remember, you're going to get through this, okay?"

"Thanks, Dad." I heard him pass the phone to Mom.

"Hi Jack," Mom said, sounding a little better.

"Hey Mom."

"Sorry about that, I got a little carried away."

"That's okay, Mom. I was pretty freaked out too when I got the news. I still am, actually."

"Are you going to be okay this weekend? Do you have any of your friends around?" Ever since I was young, Mom has always been concerned that I spend too much time alone. Growing up, I often sat in my room, reading book after book. There were a number of times, when she would walk in and tell me that I needed to go outside and play with friends. One of her favorite sayings was "you have to be a friend to make a friend." As I grew older, and made a small group of friends, her comments dwindled. At least they did until I moved to New York, where, as she often reminded me during the first year in law school, I knew no one. When I told her about the friends I was making, her relief was palpable. I don't think it ever removed her fears that I was alone, though.

"Yeah, I'll be hanging out with my friends Kyle and Rachel at the Jersey Shore all weekend." I paused for a couple of seconds, and then added for effect, "I'll be fine, Mom."

"Okay." I could tell from her tone that she did not believe me. "I'll be praying for you, and we'll talk tomorrow?"

"Yes, I promise; I'll call. Bye." I said.

"Bye. I love you."

"I love you too. Bye." I hung up the phone. I had been keeping it together for a while, but suddenly tears started to flow from my eyes. I did not want to break down, so I shook myself and said aloud, "Enough." After some pacing around the room, with some deep breaths, I felt composed enough to join Kyle and Rachel in the living room.

⇒⟶ ⟵⇐

When I walked out into the hallway, I heard Kyle and Rachel talking in low voices.

"I just think it's something you should tell him." Rachel said. I was tempted to stay back to hear what they were talking about, but I was the guest in their house, and they were being such great friends. I couldn't eavesdrop on them, so I coughed and then entered the living room.

Kyle saw me, and said, "Hey Jack. How did the calls go?"

"Okay. I only spoke to my parents. I'm going to call my sister tomorrow."

"How did they take it?" asked Kyle.

"Pretty much how I expected. My mom was crying, and my dad was shaken up. It looks like they're going to come out on Wednesday for the surgery."

"Well, that's good," said Kyle.

I sat down on the couch next to Kyle. "Listen, I'm sick of talking about cancer. Can we talk about something else, for a while?"

"Sure." Kyle said, and he stood up and grabbed my glass. "How about another glass of scotch, and then later we'll order some Chinese."

"That works for me," I said.

For the rest of the day and night, we ate, drank and talked. We talked about our plans for the weekend, and we talked about what young lawyers always discuss when they are together: stories about who's sleeping with whom, partners who were making associates' lives hell, and other stories of life at large law firms. Rachel told an especially funny story about an associate at her firm who discovered her office mate demonstrating some advanced skills of oral persuasion on another associate in their office late one night. We did not talk about cancer, life or death, instead concentrating on stories to lighten the mood. It helped me for a little while.

Around 10:00 PM, I thanked Kyle and Rachel and said my good-byes. It was drizzling outside so I caught a taxi to my apartment. When I arrived home, there was a message from Sarah on my answering machine. She was checking in with me. I called her back on her cell, but she didn't answer. I left a message for her on her voicemail, telling her that I was okay, and would talk to her later in the weekend.

Although it was only 10:30 PM, a time that had not been my bedtime in years, I decided that I needed some sleep. I changed and went to bed. I was pretty drunk from the scotch and it did not take long for me to fall asleep. Before I did, listening to the sounds of the City in the summer, I prayed that the cancer had not spread, and reminded myself from time to time that the lump was still there.

CHAPTER FIVE

On weekdays, traffic in New York City is almost always a nightmare. If you decide that you want to leave the City for any reason (say for instance, because the traffic is driving you crazy), then traffic usually becomes a nightmare conceived by the love-child of Salvador Dali and Stephen King. Often the traffic exiting through the tunnels or over the bridges are backed up for a couple of miles, delaying traffic for over an hour.

On weekends, however, the traffic situation is usually better. The Saturday morning that Kyle, Rachel and I drove to the Jersey Shore was one such time. Although it was a summer weekend, most of the people with plans to spend the weekend on the Shore had left the night before. Many of those people that hadn't left changed their minds after seeing the light rain that fell Saturday morning. As a result, after we left Kyle and Rachel's apartment at 10:00 AM in Kyle's Audi, it didn't take us long to travel to, and through, the Holland Tunnel.

The rain matched my mood that morning. I was a little hungover from drinking scotch the night before, but even without the hangover, I would have been miserable. I was sad about my upcoming surgery, and feeling sorry for myself. I didn't want to be around anyone that weekend; I wanted to sit in my apartment all weekend by myself and mope. Before I left my apartment, I had considered calling Kyle to cancel our plans, but I knew that Kyle, and especially Rachel, wouldn't take no for an answer. They would have showed up at my door and dragged me out. In the end, I decided that I would just have to suffer through the weekend silently.

When we exited the Holland Tunnel, Kyle, who was driving the car, turned to me in the backseat. "Are you ready to have a fun time?"

"Sure," I said, without much enthusiasm.

Kyle saw my lie for what it was. "Okay, we'll have to work on that. Since we're in Jersey, I think our music should be one of Jersey's favorite sons. So, will it be Springsteen or Bon Jovi?"

"Springsteen," I said.

"Bon Jovi," Rachel said, at the same time. Rachel grew up in New Jersey, which must have had an unwritten law similar to the one in Minnesota, except New Jersey girls had to like Bon Jovi, instead of Prince.

"Since Smalltown is our guest," said Kyle, "we'll start off with Springsteen, and then listen to Bon Jovi afterwards." He put a CD in the car radio and the song *Lonesome Day* started. I knew then that Kyle was playing *The Rising*, Springsteen's album about 9/11. Suddenly, my thoughts turned to that day almost two years before.

Whenever I think about 9/11, in Kyle's car or even today, I always recall the same things. The day was beautiful, possibly the best day of the summer. I remember standing in the elevator at Garrick's office when I first heard about the attacks on the World Trade Center. I also remember leaving the office, soon thereafter, just after the South Tower fell. I walked home up Second Avenue with a sea of other people. The street itself was empty to give emergency vehicles quick access to the place that had become "Ground

Zero." I remember trying to reach my family on my cell phone, to tell them that I was okay. Everyone else had the same thought, so the phone lines were jammed. I didn't talk to family until three hours later when I received a call from Jesse, who was more freaked out than I had ever heard her.

I remember sitting at home that afternoon, and in the days that followed, either watching the unbelievable images on the television or listening to talk radio. One of my strongest memories from those days was walking around my neighborhood two days later. Garrick's offices were closed all week, so there was nothing to do but sit at home or walk around. People had posted pictures of their missing family members anywhere they could, seeking help in locating their loved ones. I remember standing on 86th street, looking at those pictures with tears in my eyes, when the wind shifted, and all of a sudden, I smelled the smoke from the wreckage at Ground Zero. I remember thinking that it was the smell of death.

I also remember the emotions everyone felt after 9/11. For the most part, we still felt them in 2003, and many years later. There was the sorrow at the deaths of so many innocent people. I didn't know anyone who died in the attacks, but after seeing the pictures on the City walls and hearing stories from that day, I felt a sadness that I had never felt before. I couldn't imagine how much sadder I would have been if I had lost someone close to me.

People were also afraid that there would be more attacks and more deaths in the future. That fear would grow after the news of anthrax being sent through the mail, and after an American Airlines flight crashed in Queens two months after 9/11.

Then, there was the anger, the anger that someone would not only dare to attack the U.S., but that they weren't stopped. It was an anger that people expressed in many ways, such as invading Iraq and refusing to drink French wine because France didn't support the invasion.

As I sat in Kyle's car, recalling those days after 9/11, the song *Into the Fire* started to play, and I remembered the most important thing, in my mind, to come out of the attacks. *Into the Fire* is a tribute to the firemen, police offers and other emergency workers who went "up the stairs, into the fire." In the end, 411 of those heroes died trying to save others. New Yorkers were devastated by the loss of so many first responders, but in the end, the actions of those men and women gave New Yorkers strength and hope.

Listening to the song in Kyle's car, I turned my head to stare, with tears in my eyes, at the City, at the hole in the skyline where the Twin Towers used to stand. Suddenly, I gained clarity. In times of trouble, many people turn to faith, to God, to give them hope and strength. For whatever reason, I've never been one of those people. Instead, I've often been inspired by other people, and the things they have accomplished in the face of adversity. What New Yorkers did on 9/11, and afterwards, in a situation that dwarfed my own, was one of those things. Their actions reflected a strength that I needed to emulate. Like them, I could not stop feeling my emotions, but I could refuse to let them control my life.

I wiped my eyes, and turned back from the City. "So, Kyle," I said, when I was ready to talk, "should we take a shot at a round of golf this afternoon?"

I saw Kyle stare at me in the rear view mirror. "You sure? You're okay with playing in some rain?"

"As long as it doesn't come down too hard, I think we should," I said. "It would be a shame to let a little bad weather ruin our day."

"Cool. Sweetie, you okay with that?" He said to Rachel.

"Sure, I'm sure Sophie, Allie and I can do some shopping or something else to keep us busy."

"Excellent," Kyle said. "Then afterwards we can grab some lobsters and bar food at the Parker House, and then maybe Jack can get lucky with Allie …," Rachel slapped his arm, but Kyle continued, "or a B&T chick …." That earned him another slap from

Rachel. "B&T" or "Bridge & Tunnel," is a name for people who do not live in Manhattan but who travel there, via the bridges and/or tunnels, usually to enjoy the night life. It was a term that Rachel, a Jersey girl, did not appreciate.

"Actually, Kyle, since we're in New Jersey now," I said, "we're the B&T crowd today."

"What are you, some kind of lawyer?" Kyle said, with a laugh. "Fine. So you can hook up with a nice Jersey girl, is that better?"

I smiled. "Let's just start off with some golf, and see what happens from there."

⇒⧾ ⧾⇐

Much later that night, Kyle and I were sitting with Rachel, Sophie and Allie in the basement tavern of the Parker House. The Parker House is a long-standing fun spot on the Jersey Shore. We had eaten our dinner (shrimp, lobsters, sliders and other bar food) there, at the outdoor Porch Bar. After dinner, we headed to the tavern in the basement. There were about six tables, all filled, and a small dance floor, with a DJ stand nearby. The DJ had been playing a mixture of current Top 40 hits, electronic dance music, and some old favorites. I swear I heard Neil Diamond's *Sweet Caroline* and Springsteen's *Born to Run* at least three times that night.

The dance floor was mostly empty though as the attention of the crowd was on the televisions, which played Game 6 of the NHL Stanley Cup playoffs. The New Jersey Devils were playing the Anaheim Ducks and had won three of the previous games. To the dismay of the crowd that night, the Devils were down 5 to 2 as the third period was coming to an end. Despite the score, the crowd was pretty lively, doing what many people in their twenties and early thirties do on weekend nights: be young, drunk and stupid.

I was feeling much better than I had been when the day started. Kyle and I had a good day of golf, the details of which I will not provide; the less said about my golf skills, the better. After golf, we had gone back to the house, where we prepared for the evening. While waiting for my turn in the shower, I spoke to my sister Jesse. Like my parents, she was concerned about me, and offered me her sympathy. Unlike the call to my parents, the call with Jesse didn't leave me near tears. When the call ended, I wasn't footloose and worry free, by any stretch of the imagination, but I wasn't feeling sorry for myself either.

My mood benefited from the night of drunken fun that we were having. Kyle and I had been drinking all night, including two rounds of shots. We were drunk, but not overly so. For most of the night, the girls spent the time in conversation with each other. Apparently, Allie had met someone the night before, and wasn't interested in me, which suited me just fine. Meanwhile, Kyle and I spoke about our job, movies and sports.

Around 9:30 or so, I was explaining to Kyle how it was that I, as a Minnesota native, did not really like hockey, when he interrupted me with a nudge. "Don't look now, but there's a blonde at four o'clock who has been checking you out."

Four o'clock was just over my right shoulder, so I could not look at her without being completely obvious, but Sophie and Rachel had a good view of her.

"Do you mean the blonde in the gold top?" asked Rachel, who had overheard Kyle's comment. "She's a hottie."

"And she's a got a great sense of fashion," said Sophie. If anyone would know that, it would be Sophie. She was a short brunette who was decked out in glitzy white and floral print dress. "I'm pretty sure her top is a Van Dyne."

"That's her," said Kyle. "Smalltown, take a look now, she's not looking over here."

I took a casual look over my shoulder at the woman. Rachel was right; she was a hottie. She was a blonde, with short hair, and appeared to be my age. As Rachel had said, she was wearing a stylish gold blouse with a V-neck that showed a blue turquoise necklace and an appropriate amount of her fair and freckled skin. She was sitting at a table with four other women. Before I turned back, she looked back at me, and our eyes met. When she smiled, it lit up the dark and smoky room.

"You should go over there and talk to her." Kyle said.

"Nah." The entire table gave me a variety of puzzled looks. "Don't get me wrong. I think she's attractive. I'm just not in the mood to hit on anyone right now."

It was a lame excuse, but I didn't want to say, "I'm not looking to meet anyone, since one of my nuts is being removed in less than a week." It looked like Allie was going to call me on the excuse, but, then, Rachel came to my rescue.

"He's probably still a little gun-shy after the Two Robins incident last summer."

"What 'Two Robins incident?'" Sophie asked, with a smile.

I appreciated that Rachel had changed the subject, but I wished she had chosen another story. Still, telling that tale was better than talking about cancer. "Go ahead, Kyle," I said. "You tell them the story."

"Alright," said Kyle, with a big simile. "So Smalltown and I were at a bar on the Upper East Side, and we were playing pool. Suddenly, this attractive woman comes up and asks him if they can play a game against us. She's clearly into Ritter, but he's clueless, and tells her that she has to put her name on the chalkboard. She does, and soon we're playing against her and her friend. While we're playing, I'm telling him that she was into him, and that he should chat her up, but he didn't believe me."

"Jack, come on," said Allie, shaking her curly black hair in exasperation. "No girl plays pool just to play pool."

"I didn't know," I said, a little defensively, "She played really well for a girl. I figured she liked to play pool."

"Sometimes, Jack, you are really oblivious about women." Rachel said, laughing.

"Anyway, Ritter and I won, and he finally realizes that he should offer to buy the girls some drinks. So, we go to the bar, and as we're waiting for drinks, he introduces himself, and she says that she and her friend are both named Robin. And so, Mr. Charming here says 'Wow, two Robins, and it's not even spring yet.'"

"You did not say that!" said Sophie, in disbelief.

"I did," I said, my cheeks were red with embarrassment, as everyone broke out into laughter. "I was trying to be witty." The girls laughed even more. "Alright, I knew it was lame as soon as it came out of my mouth. At least, I didn't make a Batman and Robin joke."

"You probably would have, if you could have thought of one fast enough," said Kyle, as the girls continued to laugh.

"So, how long did it take before she remembered she had somewhere else to be?" asked Allie, with a grin.

"Actually," I said, "she politely laughed, and we kept talking. In the end, she gave me her telephone number, and we ended up dating for a month, so I guess I must have been pretty charming." I looked at the empty glass before me. "I need a drink. Anyone else?"

Everyone told me their orders, and Kyle said he would come with me. As we walked to the bar, I took another look at the blonde. She was looking at me, but quickly turned away.

Justin Timberlake's *Senorita* started to play, when Kyle and I arrived at the bar. The bartender was busy with other customers, so Kyle took the opportunity to use the bathroom. When the bartender came over a minute later, I gave him our orders, and took my wallet out of the pocket in my jeans. As the bartender poured our drinks, I felt a light tap on my right shoulder. I turned around and looked into the eyes of the blonde with the gold blouse. Her eyes were dark blue, like the deep ocean on a sunny day. She was about 5'9", and along with her Van Dyne top, she wore a pair of dark blue jeans that hugged her hips and long legs nicely. I suddenly forgot that I had cancer.

"Sorry, but this fell out of your pocket," she said, holding a dollar bill in her left hand. I was happy to see that her ring finger was bare. She smiled, and two small dimples appeared near the corners of her mouth.

"Thanks," I said, with a little discomfort. As the Two Robins incident demonstrated, I am usually not very comfortable meeting women, or anyone, for that matter. Once I become more familiar with people, I would become somewhat charming and witty, but I usually do not do well with first meetings. As a result, I waited a beat or two too long before I spoke again. "Thanks. Um, can I get you a drink as a reward?"

"Sure," she said, still smiling. Apparently, my discomfort wasn't too evident. "I'll take a Ketel One and tonic. I'm Emma by the way."

"I'm Jack." The bartender came over with a couple of the drinks that I had ordered. I gave the bartender Emma's order and turned back to her. "So, Emma, do you live around here?"

"No, I live in Manhattan on the Upper East Side."

"Really? So do I, on 90th and First. Well, really between First and York."

"You're kidding!" She said, putting her right hand on my left hand. "I live on First between 88th and 89th."

The bartender came over with Emma's drink, and told me what I owed him. I gave him the amount in cash plus a healthy tip.

"So, we live two blocks from each other and we have to go to another state to meet," I said to Emma. The fact that I lived close to Emma made me more comfortable to talk to her. "So are you ..."

"Hey, what's up?" Kyle interrupted, coming back from the bathroom. I introduced him to Emma, and, after saying "hi" to her, he said, "Why don't I take those drinks to the girls."

"Can you carry them all?" I asked.

"Yeah, I think so." I helped Kyle pick up the four drinks, and as he walked away, he said, "Nice to meet you, Emma."

"You too." She said.

After Kyle had left, I turned back to Emma. "So, how long have you lived up on First?"

"For a couple of years now." She brushed some of her hair behind her left ear, and sipped some of her drink.

"Cool," I said. My mind scrambled to find the next thing to say. I suddenly remembered my favorite restaurant in my neighborhood. "So you have you ever been to Pinocchio's?"

"Pinocchio's?" She asked, with a weird look on her face, that I took to be puzzlement. I assumed that she had never heard of the place, which was not a surprise. It wasn't very well known.

"Yeah, it's a restaurant on First between 90th and 91st. It's small, but it has incredible Italian food."

For a brief second, her face held the weird look, but then she smiled. "Well, maybe you can take me there some time."

"I think I could arrange that," I said, returning the smile. I suddenly felt my discomfort melt away. So where are you originally from, Emma?"

Over the next twenty minutes or so, I learned a lot about Emma. The most important things I learned were that she was funny and interesting. Her last name was Murphy, she was 28, and, she grew up on Long Island. She had moved to Manhattan after graduating from UMass. After college, she had worked for a couple of banks, and currently worked for Bank of America on their high yield bond desk. She spent several minutes trying (unsuccessfully) to explain what high yield bonds were, and why some people made a lot of money off of them. The problem was not her description, but rather my comprehension skills. I knew very little about banking and securities.

Emma had never been to the Jersey Shore before that weekend. She usually spent her summer on Jones Beach on Long Island. A couple of her college friends had rented a house nearby, though, and had invited her to spend the weekend with them.

She turned then to look at her friends. "Looks like my friends want me to come back. Can you believe it?" She said with a smile. "I haven't seen them in two years, and they expect me to actually spend time with them?"

I laughed. "That's selfish, that's what that is," I said, as I realized that I felt a connection with her, something I had not felt with any girl I had met in a long time. "Um, could I get your number? Maybe, we could try Pinocchio's some time."

"I'd like that," she said, smiling. I obtained a pen from the bartender, and Emma wrote her name and number on a cocktail napkin. As she handed me the napkin, her fingers grazed against mine and I felt an electric current pass between us. Her smile grew bigger, and her eyes had this look, as if they held a special message for me. It was not a desperate, "please call me because I am 28 years old and not married" look. Nor was it a lascivious "call me because I know Cosmopolitan's six ways to drive a man crazy in bed" look. Instead, it was a look that said "I like you, and if you call me, maybe, just maybe, this could be something special." It was a look that could make a man change his plans for the future.

And then I went and fucked it up.

Suddenly, I remembered what my future was. I had cancer, and in five days, I would lose my right nut. With the surgery and recovery, it would probably be two weeks before I could call Emma. That was the best case scenario, if the cancer had not spread, and I was comfortable dating someone after the surgery. I did not want to think about the worst case scenario.

"Um, Emma, I ..., uh, there's something that's going on right now, with me, and it may be a little while before I'm able to call."

Her smile faded into a puzzled, disappointed look. I hated myself for erasing that smile from her face. "Oh. Is ..., do you have a girlfriend?"

"No, there's no one else." I desperately wanted to see that smile again. "Work has been so busy for me the last few months that I haven't dated anyone for a while now. And actually, work is still pretty busy, and there's this other thing that I'm dealing with. I want to call you, but it may be a couple of weeks before I can."

It was clear from her face that she was still puzzled and disappointed, but I thought that I had repaired the situation a little. "Okay, well, I hope you will call when you can." She gave me a smile that was a shadow of the previous one. "Have a good night."

"You too."

I walked back to my friends, with my almost depleted drink, swearing at myself and my traitorous testicle the entire way. I sat down and looked at Kyle and the women.

"Well, how did it go?" Kyle asked, after I didn't say anything.

"It must have gone well," said Rachel. Sophie and Allie nodded their heads in agreement. "She was really into you."

"Now, how could you tell that from over here?" I asked.

"Please. It was obvious from the way she looked at you," said Allie.

Sophie chimed in. "And the way she tucked her hair behind her ear, and then brushed your hand when she gave you her number."

"Were you guys watching us the entire time?"

"Yes," they said in unison, each wearing the same grin.

"We were waiting to see if you made some sort of robin/spring type of line," said Kyle, to the laughter of the girls. "Now tell us about her."

"Well, her name is Emma and she lives in Manhattan a couple blocks from where I live."

"Excellent," Kyle said.

"Yeah, and she seems really, really great."

"So why do you look like your dog died?" asked Rachel.

"Well, I got her number, but I think I screwed up." I finished the dregs of my drink.

"Tell me that you didn't try some witty line again," said Kyle.

"No, it wasn't like that. When I got her number, I realized …." I looked at Sophie and Allie. I still wasn't ready to tell them about my condition. "Just with everything going on right now, I realized that I won't be able to call her for at least a week or probably more. I mean, I do want to see her again …" I glanced back over my shoulder at Emma and her friends, and then turned back to the table. "I really want to see her again, and I don't want her waiting at her phone wondering when I was going to call. And then later, when I do, she doesn't talk to me because I didn't call her soon enough."

"What did you say?" asked Rachel.

I described what I said and how I said it. "Yeah, you may have screwed that up," said Kyle.

"I know," I said. "What do you think she's thinking?"

"If I was her, I would think that you weren't going to call," offered Allie.

"Girls," Rachel said, "it looks like we need another round. Why don't we let the boys talk it over?" The girls agreed, stood up, and walked to the bar.

I pushed my hands through my hair and sat back in my chair. "What should I have done?" I asked Kyle.

Kyle thought for a second before responding. "I don't know, dude. You probably made the right call. The only thing you could have done was tell her about the cancer, and that could have scared her off. That's too serious, too fast."

"That's what I was thinking. I mean, that's why I didn't want to hit on any girls anyway tonight. But then she came over, and we started talking …"

"Dude, you were screwed before the conversation ever started," Kyle said. "It's just bad timing. But hopefully, you'll call her in a week or so, and everything will be okay."

"Yeah," I said, unconvinced. "Maybe."

We sat there for a while in silence. When the girls came back, they sensed my reticence, and just talked amongst themselves. We drank for a while, and I stayed drunk, but the fun buzz I had was gone. All I could do was think about what the cancer had already cost me, and what more it could take before it was gone.

After a half hour, we decided to leave. I looked over at the table where Emma had sat, and noticed that she and her friends were gone. I hadn't seen them leave. Kyle was right. My timing sucked.

CHAPTER SIX

When Dr. Ross called me at work on Monday afternoon, I was working on the National Mutual brief. In fact, I had been working on the brief virtually every waking moment since I had arrived at my apartment Sunday afternoon from the Jersey Shore.

The weekend had been fun, and although I was still bothered by the outcome of my conversation with Emma, I had been able to keep my thoughts about the tumor under control. Once I was standing in my small apartment alone, though, that control was harder to maintain. To keep my mind off of my problems, I went back to work on the brief. I worked until midnight, and started again as soon as I arrived at work the next morning. I stopped only to eat lunch, respond to emails and to schedule a meeting with Mike Goldman, the partner on the National Mutual case, for 4:15.

As I worked, my concentration was focused solely on the brief. As a result, my writing ended up being really quite good. In fact, it was better than anything that I had written before. The words and the flow of the arguments came much easier to me than they had on the previous Thursday night, when writing had been like squeezing water from a rock. Not only was I able to show my work, but I was also being persuasive.

My focus on the brief was so intense that when Dr. Cross called at 3:45 p.m., I had forgotten that he was calling me with the test results. I pressed pause on my iPod, which was playing *Carry on My Wayward Son* by Kansas, and answered the phone.

"Jack Ritter," I said.

"Hi, Jack. This is Dr. Cross. I have your test results. Is now a good time to talk?"

I took a deep breath. "Yes, it is." I answered. I stood up, closed my door, and started to pace nervously in the small space around my office.

"Okay, it's the news we expected. The test results demonstrate protein levels that are indicative of cancer. I'm sorry, Jack."

After I had heard the original diagnosis on Friday, I had, for the most part, accepted that I had cancer. Yet, down deep inside of me, the spark of hope that I had felt in Dr. Cross's office had remained. That spark quickly died and tears came to my eyes.

I took another deep breath, and pushed down the sadness. People had been through a lot worse than what I would go through. "Okay. So, we'll be doing the surgery on Thursday then," I said.

"Yes; let me look at my notes, and I can give you the specific details." He paused for a second, and I heard some paper move in the background. "The surgery will be at 7:30 in the morning on Thursday at the NYU Medical Center. You'll need to be at the hospital at 6:30 AM. You shouldn't eat or drink anything for twelve hours before the procedure. Once the procedure is done, you'll be staying over at the hospital Thursday night."

Over the weekend, I realized that I had other questions that I should have asked on Friday. I now had the chance to ask them. "How will we know if the cancer has spread?" I asked.

"Well, we'll do a CAT scan on Friday. Do you know what that is?"

"Yes," I said. A CAT or "computer assisted tomography" scan was a procedure that took computerized images of internal areas of the body. When I was young, I suffered chronic migraines, and had a CAT scan conducted on my head.

"Okay. A week or two after the scan, we'll have the results, and we'll know if the cancer has spread. On Thursday, you'll also meet with an oncologist, who will schedule an appointment for you where you'll discuss the results of the tests."

"What will my recovery be like?" I asked. "Will I be able to go back to work next week?" Like attorneys at probably every law firm, I was concerned about the "Face Time" I spent in the office. Just as in many other aspects of life, perception was critical at a law firm. An attorney, whether an associate or a partner, who was seen in the office early, late, and on weekends was perceived to be a hard-working, dedicated attorney. Conversely, a lawyer who billed the same amount of hours as the first lawyer, or even more, but who was not seen in the office as often (because the second attorney did not procrastinate while at work or because he worked at home and on weekends) was not considered as hard a worker. As a result, Face Time was important, but especially for an associate, like me, who wanted to become partner. It was imperative, then, that my office was not seen as empty too long or too often.

Obviously, if I publicized my condition and the need for surgery, my time away from the office would be fine. The problem was that I only wanted a couple of people to know about my condition, so I needed to keep the amount of time out of the office to a minimum. At that point, I had lost Friday, and would lose Thursday and Friday. I was hoping that would be it.

"You will need to take it easy over the weekend," said Dr. Cross, "but you should be able to work on Monday."

"Great."

"Do you have any more questions?"

I thought for a couple of seconds, before answering. "I can't think of any right now."

"Well, you can call my office if you have any more questions. Otherwise, I will see you Thursday morning."

We hung up, and I stopped pacing around the office. It was 4:00 p.m., and I had fifteen minutes before my meeting with Mike. I sat back down and spent the next fifteen minutes spinning my wheels, trying to get back into the flow of the brief. All I could do, though, was to think about the surgery and losing my testicle.

━━◁┼▷━━

At exactly 4:15, I knocked on Mike Goldman's open office door. His office, like those of many other partners at the firm, had a window view of Central Park. Mike's office also was larger than the associates' offices and did not have furniture. Instead, Mike had an expensive modern desk and bookshelf set made of black steel and glass. The bookshelf was filled with pictures and awards that Mike had won over the years. Mike was sitting behind his desk when I walked in.

"Hey Jack," Mike said. Mike was in his early fifties, but retained a thick head of salt and pepper hair that I would have killed to have at 29. Mike was shorter than me, about 5'9" with a tennis player's build. He had a dark tan from a recent trip to the Caribbean, and was wearing a light blue, tailored work shirt and a red power tie. In terms of Face Time, Mike was the king. He was usually in the office by 8 a.m., did not leave until at least 7:00 p.m., and often sent out e-mails to associates and others late at night. I often wondered how much time he spent he had left to spend with his wife and kids. "Come on in, and close the door."

I walked into the office, and sat down in one of the empty chairs across from Mike's desk.

"So, Jack," Mike said. "Your email said that you wanted to talk about a medical issue that came up on Friday. What's going on?"

"Okay," I said. "On Thursday night, I found a lump ...," I paused, while I thought about how much information to give. I decided not to tell him too much. "And I knew it was serious. So I saw a doctor on Friday. He told me that he thought it was a tumor, and probably cancerous. He ran some tests, and about a half hour ago, he called to tell me that I have cancer."

Mike looked shocked. "Jack, that's terrible," he said. I nodded my head glumly, and looked past Mike at his Columbia Law school diploma. I was getting choked up, and could not look him in the eye. "Does he know how far along the cancer is?"

"He doesn't right now, but he thinks we caught it early. He did a physical examination and didn't find anything else. And apparently, with this cancer, the survival rates are, like, 95% if it's caught early."

"That's good," said Mike. "What are the next steps?"

"I'm going to have surgery on Thursday to remove the ..., uh, tumor." I almost said "testicle." "I'll be in the hospital overnight, and then on Friday, I'll go through some additional tests to find out if it has spread. Based on what the doctor says, I think I'll be out of the office two more days this week for the surgery. I'm not sure what will happen if the cancer has spread."

Mike nodded his head, as if he was agreeing with the plan. "Do you think the doctor knows what he is doing? I'm sure I can get recommendations from other partners if you want a second opinion."

"I think he knows. Kyle's uncle recommended him. He said that he's doing all the right things."

"Okay." Mike stood up suddenly, and turned around his bookshelf. The bottom of the unit had three black cabinet doors. He opened up the left door, which contained a small black refrigerator. He pulled two bottles of Red Stripe beer out of the refrigerator, opened both and offered one to me.

"I shouldn't," I said. "I want to work on the brief some more tonight so it's done by Wednesday."

"You're not working any more tonight, Jack," Mike instructed. "You just found out that you have cancer. That gets you an automatic "Get Out of Work Free" card. If the draft isn't finished by Wednesday, it's not a big deal. With the extension, we have plenty of time to finish it."

"Okay." I grabbed the beer and took a big drink. It had a light flavor, a little sweet, and not too bitter. It tasted great.

Mike sat down in the chair next to me. "When I was in Jamaica, I picked up a taste for Red Stripe. Every now and then, I'll drink them here and pretend that I am still on the beach. It's not too hard on a day like today." He gestured to the Central Park view, and then he took a look at me. "Jack, can I ask you a question? If it's too personal, you don't have to answer."

"Sure," I said, unsure of what he was going to say.

"Your cancer, is it testicular cancer?" Mike asked.

I was shocked. "How did …," I said, unable to finish the question. Kyle was the only one at the firm who knew and I knew that he wouldn't tell anyone.

Mike nodded. "When I was in law school, in the late seventies, one of my friends was diagnosed with testicular cancer. I learned a lot about the disease then, and have stayed informed since. I know that it hits young men, like you, and that the current survival rate is high. Knowing that, and seeing that you were reluctant to mention the type of cancer, I guessed that's what you had."

"Oh," I said. His logic made sense. "What happened to your friend?"

"Unfortunately, back then, the disease was fatal. He died three months after he was diagnosed."

"I'm sorry about that," I said, a little awkwardly.

"So am I," Mike said, and took a drink of his beer. We sat there in silence for a few seconds before Mike resumed the conversation.

"Anyway, that's not going to happen to you, and hopefully, you won't need any further treatment after surgery. But if you do, you should know some things."

"What's that?" I said.

"Whatever happens next, everyone at the firm will do whatever we can to help you. You're one of us, and we take care of our own. The fact is that you're not the first Garrick employee to have cancer. Some of those people took a leave of absence, and if you want to do that, we can make it work. Other people have continued to work, under a flexible schedule. If you want to do that, we'll figure out the best way to do that too. We'll move deadlines when we can or you can do document review or write law journal articles, if necessary. And I don't want you worrying about the brief. We have the extra ten days, so we have plenty of time to get it done."

"I appreciate that," I said, "but writing the draft is actually helping me keep my mind off things. And I'm doing well with it, so I'm pretty sure that I can finish it by Wednesday."

"Okay, but if there comes a time when work is hurting you, and not helping you, just know that you have options."

"Thanks." I took a drink from my almost empty bottle.

"One of the other things I wanted to discuss is how quiet you want to keep this," Mike said. "I'll have to let some other partners know, especially the partners you work with, and other people will need to know if you have any more absences. But we don't have to provide any specifics. We don't have to tell people you have cancer, and even if we do, we don't have to tell people the type."

"Um, I think, for now, I'd like to keep the circle of people who know pretty small. Kyle knows, but other than you, no one else at the firm does. If I find out the cancer has spread, well, I'm not sure what I'll do."

"That's understandable," Mike said. "I hope it hasn't spread, but if it has, do you mind if I give you a suggestion?"

"Okay," I said, with a little curiousity.

"Let's get another round, first." Mike stood up, went back to the cabinet, and pulled out two more bottles. He opened them, and handed me one. "When my friend found out, he said that he had no idea that he was in the age range for this disease, and none of us knew anyone who had suffered from the disease."

"It was the same with me," I said. "I had absolutely no clue about those things either."

"See," Mike said, holding up a finger. "And I think one of the reasons it's that way is because few patients want to talk about it. And I understand that. Our balls are part of what makes us men. Losing one has to be tough to handle. It's probably what a woman with breast cancer feels like when she has a mastectomy. So, I understand why anyone would want to keep the information quiet, but I don't think they should."

"Why is that?" I asked.

"Well, first, if you are open about it, you will increase awareness, and more men will know they need to check themselves. Who knows, you may even be able to save someone."

"That makes sense," I said.

"The other thing," Mike said, "is that I don't think it's good for people to keep secrets. When you hide something about yourself, you're essentially agreeing that the information is so bad that it should be hidden. Losing one of your balls to cancer is nothing that you should be ashamed of. If you tell people that you have testicular, you're showing that you're not ashamed, and that you're still a man. In the long run, I think that's better for you mentally than believing that it's something that you need to hide."

I thought about what Mike was saying. There was a definite logic to it. I also thought it was easier for Mike to say that since he wasn't the one actually faced with the choice.

"I'll think about it, Mike." I said.

"Good. In the end, whatever you decide, I support your decision. If you want to keep it quiet, I won't think any less of you."

We sat there for a little longer, finishing our bottles of beer. When I was done, I looked at Mike. "Thanks, Mike. I appreciate the talk." We both stood up, and shook hands.

"My door is always open if you want to talk more," Mike said. "Now, why don't you call it a day, and go out to a bar or something with some friends."

"Thanks." I left Mike's office and a minute later, I was in my office. I was a little buzzed from drinking the beer on an empty stomach. I thought about Mike's advice and wondered who I should call. I briefly thought about calling Emma. Mike's words about being honest with people were appealing, and I did want to see her again. But, I thought that telling someone you had cancer before a first date likely would quash any chance at that date.

I also could call up one of my law school friends, but none of them would be out of work at 6:00 p.m. on a Monday evening. For similar reasons, the Robinsons were out, and I had taken up too much of Kyle and Rachel's time already. That left Sarah, and the more I thought about it, she was the perfect choice. *Maybe*, I thought, *I could even get a repeat of Thursday night. Well, at least of those parts that didn't involve discovering cancerous tumors.*

"Sarah Danvers," she answered, when I called her at work.

"Hey Sarah, it's Jack."

"Hey, did you get the results from the blood tests?"

"Yeah, it was what we expected. I have cancer."

"Damn. I was hoping that you'd catch a break. How are you doing?"

"I'm okay. Like I said, it's what I expected. Anyway, I told one of the partners the news. He was great about it, and told me that I needed take the night off. So I wondered if you would like to grab a burger and a drink or two with me at Rathbone's."

"Well," Sarah said, after a brief pause. "I'm almost done with work, and I have no plans for tonight. I think I can meet you out, but I can only do dinner and one drink. I've got an early meeting tomorrow, and I can't be tired or hungover."

Looks like no Thursday night repeat, I thought.

"That's fine," I said. "Can you be there in a half hour?"

"No problem. I'll see you there."

Rathbone's is a bar and grill on 2nd Avenue between 87th and 88th Streets. It's named after Basil Rathbone, the actor best known for his portrayal of Sherlock Holmes in numerous movies in the 1940's. Despite the name, Rathbone's is not an English bar, but is, instead, more of a dive bar, with sawdust lightly scattered across the wood floor, which had been colored by years of spilled beer and other alcoholic beverages. Prior to three months ago, when New York banned cigarette smoking in public places, the bar also would have been pretty smokey.

Rathbone's was one of my favorite places to eat in the City. The burgers are served on toasted English Muffins and are super juicy. I never knew whether the juiciness was due to the meat they used, the fact that they broiled the burgers, or a combination of the two. Whatever the reason, the burgers were delicious.

When Sarah walked in, I was sitting in a booth near the back of the seating area, drinking a Sam Adams beer and watching baseball highlights on the nearest television. She was wearing more clothes than the last time I saw her, specifically, a black and red business dress with a pair of New Balance sneakers she always wore when traveling to or from work. Her business shoes would be in the large handbag hanging from her right shoulder. I waved her over to the booth.

"Hey you," she said, as she approached.

"Hey," I said, as I stood up and gave her a hug and a peck on the cheek.

We sat down and, when the waitress came over, we ordered a Cosmopolitan, another Sam Adams, and some cheeseburgers and fries.

"How are you feeling?" Sarah asked, after the waitress left.

"I'm okay, but it's been up and down. There are moments where everything feels normal, and then I remember, I have cancer …," *cancer, fuck;* "and it throws me for a loop again."

"Well, it's only been three days. It's probably going to take a while to deal with it. How was your weekend?"

I told her about my trip to New Jersey and the night at the Parker House. When I told her about my conversation with Emma, Sarah expressed some disagreement as to how I handled it.

"Jack, you moron!" She said, vigorously. "You should have told her.

"Sarah, come on." I said, defensively. "You know what it's like when you first start dating someone. You want things to be light. You're wondering whether there will be kiss at the end of the night, or whether there is going to be another date or what the other person looks like naked. You don't want to be wondering whether your date will be able to have kids or if he's going to have chemo and lose his hair."

"You have a point," Sarah conceded. "Still, if I met the right guy, you know 'the One,' I think it would be different."

"That's if you knew he was 'the One' right away," I countered. "What if I am 'the One' for Emma, but she doesn't know it until the third or fourth date? If I told her before the first date, and scare her off, she'd never know I was 'the One.'"

"This is why I hate debating with lawyers," Sarah said. "You're always using logic." She took a sip from her drink. When she put it down, she looked me in the eye seriously. "Jack, in normal situations, I would agree that the first dates should be light. But you're not in a normal situation, and Emma could help you get through all of this. Besides, you're not even sure that you're going to need chemo."

"Oh, I'm hoping it never happens. If I find out that it hasn't spread, I'm going to call her right away. Then we can go on a number of dates, and if it goes well, I'll tell her about my surgery, when the time is right.

Just then, the waitress brought our food to the table. I took a bite out of my bacon cheeseburger, savoring the taste. When I noticed that Sarah had taken a bite out of her burger, I used the opportunity to steer the conversation away from Emma.

"So tell me about your weekend."

She quickly swallowed the food and took a drink from her Cosmo. "Oh my God, speaking of meeting 'the One.' So, I'm not sure if you remember, but the other night, before we found the lump, I was talking about a blind date that I have this Friday."

"Um, yeah, I guess I remember you saying something about it." I took another bite from the burger, and used my napkin to wipe the juice from my hands and mouth.

"Well, my friend, Kathy, is the person that set me up on the date. So, Friday night, Kathy and I went to a party at a friend of a friend's apartment in Tribeca. Anyway, my blind date happened to be there, and Kathy introduced us. His name is Dan Harper, and he is hot. We hit it off right away, and talked for hours."

"Yeah? Did you hook up with him?"

"No," She said, giving me a dirty look. She held up her right hand and started counting her fingers. "First, I try to not hook up with a guy the same night I meet them. Second, I hooked up with you the night before, and I'm not the kind of girl who hooks up with two guys in less than 24 hours."

"But you did want to hook up with him."

"Well, yeah. He was hot, and I liked him, but a girl has to live by her principles."

As we ate, Sarah told me more about Dan. He was her age, worked at a hedge fund in Midtown, and, apparently, walked on the ground that Sarah worshipped. Listening to her, I started to feel some jealousy. Some of it was for Dan, who, unlike me, likely would see Sarah naked sometime in the next few weeks. Most of my jealousy, though, was for Sarah. Over the weekend, both of us had met someone we liked, but Sarah was getting the chance to act on that opportunity. While I still had a chance with Emma, it was small.

After Sarah finished talking about Dan, the waitress brought us the bill. We debated over the bill for awhile. Sarah wanted to pay for her meal, but I insisted that it was my treat, as I was the one who invited her out.

After I paid the bill, Sarah asked, "Are your parents flying in for the surgery?"

"Yeah, on Wednesday. They should be at my apartment by five or so. They'll be staying at my place until they leave on Saturday."

"They're staying at your place? They're not sleeping on your futon, are they?

"Of course not," I said, feeling a little offended. "They'll be staying in my room. I'll stay on the futon on Wednesday and Friday."

"That's good. Well, I'm going to visit you after your surgery, so I guess I'll get to meet them."

"Well, that should be interesting. Do you think I should introduce you as the girl who discovered my tumor?" I said, grinning.

"You don't think your parents would be incredibly grateful for my help?" She teased, with her own smile.

"Ha!," I exclaimed. "I'm tempted to tell them just to see the look on their faces."

We both stood up, and walked out of the restaurant.

"Well, have a good night," she said as she hugged me. "I'll call you before the surgery, okay?"

"Sure. Have a good night." We went our separate ways, and I walked north towards my apartment, and she went south toward hers. When I arrived home, I cleaned up my apartment and did some other work to keep busy, and to keep my mind off of Thursday.

At 10:30 p.m., my apartment was clean, and I had run out of things to keep me busy, so I went to bed, and watched the WB11 10:00 pm news. The sportscaster, Sean Kimerling, was talking about the New Jersey Devils' win in the Stanley Cup finale earlier that night. Hearing about the game made me think of Game 5, the Parker House and Emma. I wondered for the hundredth time whether I should have handled the meeting differently. Unsure, I soon fell asleep thinking about Emma's ocean blue eyes.

CHAPTER SEVEN

At 7:00 AM on Thursday morning, I was lying on a portable bed in a pre-op room at the NYU Medical Center. I had the room to myself and had just changed from my street clothes into the standard, ass-revealing hospital gown. A bed sheet covered the lower half of my body as I waited for a nurse to come in and "prepare" me for the surgery. I was unsure what the preparation would be, but I would find out soon enough.

My parents were waiting outside of the room, having exited so that I could change in private. They had flown into LaGuardia Airport the afternoon before, and arrived via taxi at my apartment about an hour later. I was there when they arrived, having finished the National Mutual draft an hour before. I had continued to write effectively, and thought that the draft may have been the best thing that I had ever written.

When I met my parents, they were happy to see me, although they both were clearly feeling sad for me. Mom gave me a long hug, and I received a handshake from Dad, as well as a hug, which he and I rarely shared. When they entered my apartment, Dad expressed his surprise at how small the apartment was. I explained that *Seinfeld* and *Friends* did not provide accurate representations of most New York City apartments, or even those of people making six figures for that matter. Given the size of the place, they did not fight me when I told them they would be sleeping on my bed, and I would be sleeping on the futon in the living room.

We went out for an early dinner at Pinocchio's shortly after they arrived, ensuring that I was finished eating twelve hours before the surgery. When we arrived at Pinnochio's, Mom asked me whether the food was as good as the Olive Garden's. I did a mental shaking of my head, and assured her that Pinocchio's was even better than the Olive Garden. I don't think she believed me. When she finished the meal, though, she said "That wasn't so bad," which meant she loved it.

While we ate, we talked. First, we compared the weather in Minnesota and New York. Then, Mom and Dad described their trip to New York. Neither of them had flown since 9/11 so they were surprised by all of the security changes at the Minneapolis and LaGuardia airports, especially at the presence of police carrying automatic rifles. Mom also provided the latest gossip from Oak Lake and our extended family. According to Mom, my uncle Al was refusing to speak with my aunt Joan, over some misunderstanding or another. I talked about work a little, including my work on the National Mutual case.

We went to bed early that night, but I didn't sleep well. I kept thinking about the surgery, and how it would change me. When I woke up at 5:00 a.m. the next morning, I felt tired and very anxious.

My mind was still troubled in the pre-op room. Lying in my bed, I realized that I had no idea how Dr. Cross would remove my testicle. I assumed that he would be cutting into my scrotum, but he had never given me the specifics, and I had failed to ask him. I realized while lying in bed that I hadn't asked him because I was trying to avoid thinking about the surgery.

Suddenly, I remembered a visit to my grandfather's farm one spring weekend when I was fourteen. My grandfather and my uncle Chris were castrating the two week old male piglets, and I had agreed to help them. I had helped out on the farm for years, feeding the cows and chickens, shoveling manure, and doing other chores, but that day was my first, and only, time that I helped castrate any animals.

When we entered the pig shed that day, I started to feel very claustrophobic and nervous. The shed was very narrow with an aisle separating the pig pens on the left and right. The shed was a little dark, lit only by two small light bulbs on the ceiling and four dirty windows, through which poked scattered rays of light that highlighted dust motes in the air. The shed was hot and the smell of pig shit was overpowering. I had helped butcher chickens on the farm every year, and had hunted some deer and pheasant with my grandfather and uncles in the fall, so I was not usually squeamish about the work we did on the farm. However, castration was different, because I kept imagining the same thing happening to me. By that time, I knew about the importance of my balls for sex, which was something that I couldn't wait to have. I also had read enough fantasy and mythological stories that referenced eunuchs to know how important a man's genitals were to his identity. They were not something like tonsils that could be removed without any consequences.

But I was in that shed that day because my grandfather had asked me to help, and I knew that my uncle Chris, who is about ten years older than I am, would call me a "wimp" or a "wuss" for a very long time afterward if I refused. In the end, to stop my uncle from busting my balls, I helped cut off the pigs' balls.

The process was relatively simple. Uncle Chris would hand me a piglet from the pen. I would hold it by its hind legs, stomach up and ass forward with its body pinned between my legs. My grandfather, a man of average height in his mid-sixties, used a new razor blade for the castration. I had never seen a blade like that before. I was only familiar with Bic disposable razors. My grandfather took the blade from a small, white paper envelope; the blade's sharp edges reflected the light coming from one of the shed's windows.

With each piglet, my grandfather cut the scrotum, reached in, pulled out the pig's nuts, and cut the testicular cord. My grandfather would throw the testicles onto the floor, where the dogs would have them for lunch. My grandfather applied iodine to each wound and the piglet would then be passed from me to Chris, who placed the piglet on the bedroll in the pigpen.

The memory of that day flashed through my mind quickly. I didn't remember how many pigs we castrated that day, but I remembered their light pink skin, and the dark red blood that splashed on them and me. I also remembered the squeals the pigs made when they were cut, and the pile of testicles on the floor. I was not sick to my stomach, but with each pig, I wanted more and more to run out of the shed. Instead of pulling a Clarice Starling, though, I stayed there and did my part until each of the pigs was castrated. Afterwards, over a dinner of beef macaroni hotdish, and not pork chops, thank God, my grandfather and uncle told me that I did a good job. I remember sitting there with a small sense of pride, but knowing that I would never do that again.

In the fourteen years since that day, I had probably recalled the event once, maybe twice. The memory was not a traumatic one, but it also was not pleasant. It was even less pleasant to recall moments before undergoing a similar procedure myself.

To my relief, I didn't have to think about it for very long. The nurse, a stout black woman in her early thirties and green nurse scrubs, came in moments later.

"Hello, Mr. Ritter. My name is Abby, and I'm here to get you ready for the surgery," she said, in a kindly voice. She was wheeling a cart that was covered by a blue paper towel. "I'm going to shave your body where the doctor will be making his incision." She handed me the paper towel, revealing a kidney shaped metal bowl below it, with a wireless electric clipper, shaving gel, and a blue Bic disposable razor. If the Bic had been a double edged safety razor, I would have bolted the room. "Can you lift up your sheet and gown, and place this cover over your genitals?"

"Okay." She turned away as I followed her instructions. I said "Okay" again, and she turned around.

"Now, just to confirm, the doctor is removing your right testicle, correct?" I nodded. "I know that may sound funny to ask, but this is one of the ways we make sure that we're doing the right surgery. So, we'll shave you here on your right side," she said, pointing to a spot above my genitals.

"So, the doctor will be cutting there, and not on the …, scrotum?" I said, a little unsure.

She held the clipper in her right hand. "That's right."

Well, I thought, *at least, I'm not getting the piglet treatment.*

The nurse looked at my face. "Are you a little nervous, hon?" I nodded again. "Alright, well, why don't you lie back, and I'll take care of this for you."

I lay back on the bed and closed my eyes. As the sounds of the electric clipper began, I distracted myself from the sound by compiling a list of my top five favorite genre TV shows. When the nurse finished a few minutes later, I had selected *Babylon Five*, *Farscape*, *Buffy the Vampire Slayer*, *Firefly*, and but was debating between the original *Star Trek* and *The Next Generation*. The nurse placed my gown down, and the bed sheet back over my lower half. "There you go, Mr. Ritter. I'll send your parents back in. The doctor should be here to see you in five minutes. After that, we'll do the surgery."

"Thanks," I said, as she left.

After she left, I lifted the sheet and looked down at my crotch. My right side was as bare as it was before puberty transformed it. I still had *Star Trek* on the brain, because I suddenly recalled the classic Star Trek episode *Let This Be Your Last Battlefield* and started laughing. I was still chuckling when my father walked into the room.

"Your mom is getting a can of pop. She'll be here in a second." My father was wearing an orange polo shirt and jeans. He had short gray hair, and was about five inches shorter and about sixty pounds lighter than I. He looked at me, with a puzzled look behind his glasses. "What are you laughing at?" He sat down in a chair next to the bed.

"I was just looking at where they shaved me for the surgery. One side is bare, and the other side isn't. And it reminded me of an episode of the original Star Trek series."

"Which one?"

"Do you remember the episode with the aliens, where half the people were black on one side of their body, and white on the other? And there were other aliens who were white on the opposite side, and black on the other?"

My father looked up and thought for a second. "I think so. Wasn't the guy who played the Riddler on the old Batman series in that one?"

"Yeah, that was Frank Gorshin. Good memory."

"Well, I'm not senile yet." My father said with a smile.

"Well, in the episode, the two groups hated each other, because their colors were on opposite sides. So, I don't know if it's because I'm tired or what, but I thought that my crotch was sort of like the aliens, one half hairy, one half bare. And suddenly, I imagined if it was hair and not color that was the difference between the aliens. I imagined Kirk pointing out to the aliens that they were the same: hairy on one side and bare on the other, and I imagined Frank Gorshin's character saying "we're not the same. They are bare on the right side, and we have pubes!'"

Dad looked at me for a couple of seconds, and then said, "Huh."

"What?"

"I didn't realize they gave painkillers to patients before a surgery."

"They haven't given me any drugs yet." I said, defensively.

"You sure about that?" Dad replied with a straight face, but a glint in his eyes.

"Very funny, dad," I muttered, as Mom walked into the room, with a can of Diet Coke. Mom was fifty-six years old, and the same height as my father. She had short black hair, and wore glasses, a green blouse, and blue jeans.

She looked at both my dad and me. "What's going on with you too?"

"Nothing," Dad and I said at the same time.

"Okay," she said, confused. "Jack, are you feeling all right?"

"Yeah, I'm just tired. I didn't sleep well last night."

"You should close your eyes, you know, for a bit."

My eyes were closed for about ten seconds, when Dr. Cross, and another man walked into the room. The second man was short and dark, and holding a tray in his hands. Both men were in light blue operating scrubs, and stood at the end of the bed.

Dr. Cross walked over to my parents, who were standing on the right side of the bed, and introduced himself to them. He also introduced his colleague, "Jack, this is Dr. Gupta. He will be the anesthesiologist for the surgery."

Dr. Gupta came over to the left side of the bed and set his tray on the table next to me, and shook my hand.

"It's nice to meet you," he said.

After the introduction, Dr. Cross continued. "Well Jack, we're ready to do this if you are."

I looked at my parents, who stood there with sadness on their faces, although Dad was hiding his emotion better than Mom. "Yeah, let's get this over with," I said, hopefully with more confidence than I was feeling.

"I will be giving you a shot of the anesthesia," Dr. Gupta said, "which will put you under. Once you're out, I'll put an IV line into your arm. That will keep you unconscious until after the procedure." He pointed at an IV bag on a pole next to the bed, and looked at my parents. "Would you like to say anything before we begin?"

I looked at my parents.

"Good luck, Jack," said Dad.

"We'll be here when you wake up, Sweetie," said Mom.

I nodded my head at both of them, and then looked to Dr. Gupta. He took a hypodermic needle from the tray, and moved it toward the crook of my left arm. "You're going to feel a pinch and then a sting." I closed my eyes, and felt him insert the needle (the pinch) and then, the drug passing into my arm (the sting).

"Can you count down out loud from ten to 1?" asked Dr. Gupta.

I followed his instructions. "Ten, nine, eight, ..." I don't recall what the last number that I said was, but I remember my last thought. It was of my grandfather's pig shed, and red blood on pink skin.

I woke up several hours later, with a dull throb in my groin. Both of my parents were in the room. Mom was sitting in a chair to my right and reading *The Da Vinci Code* and Dad, on my left, was watching a Western on the television in the corner of the room. I tried to speak, but my throat was dry. The sound that came out of my mouth was barely audible.

My parents turned to me, and saw that I was awake. "Jack, how are you feeling?" Mom asked.

"Water," I croaked.

Dad was already reaching for the water pitcher and plastic cups, when Mom said, "Ed, pour Jack some water."

"I'm already on it, Addy," He said gently to her, as he poured the water into a cup. He handed it to me and asked, "How's the pain?"

I sipped from the cup, and felt the cool water pass down my throat, easing the dryness. "Thanks," I said, between sips. After a couple of sips, I passed the cup back to him and said, "I'm hurting a little bit."

"Dr. Cross said that would happen," Mom symptathized. "He told us to ring a nurse for painkillers when you woke up." She reached to my side and pressed the nurse call button.

"Did he say how the surgery went?" I asked, my voice still a little hoarse.

"He said it went fine," Mom said. While we waited for the nurse, I thought about lifting up my sheet and gown to look at the wound. Instead, I turned my awareness to the area. It felt a little numb, presumably because of the anesthesia. Despite the numbness, I could feel my left testicle, and to no surprise, not the right one. I did, however, feel where it should have been.

When the nurse came in, Mom told her about the pain. The nurse said she would be back with some painkillers and she left. Two minutes later, she came back with two pills that I swallowed with some more water. She also told us that Dr. Cross would be back in a couple of hours to check in on me.

I was still feeling a little bit drowsy from the drugs, so I told my parents that I was going to close my eyes again, and sleep.

"Okay, Jack," Mom said softly.

I fell asleep soon after. I woke up a little bit later, and not much had changed. Mom was still reading *The Da Vinci Code*, and Dad was watching television, although a Dirty Harry movie had replaced the Western. My parents had moved the table with the water pitcher closer to the bed, and I was able to pour myself a cup of water.

"Are you feeling any better?" Dad asked.

"Yeah, the pain's less.» The dull throb in my groin had gone down to an ache.

"Good," Dad said, and turned back to the television.

"Do you need anything, Jack?" Mom said. I asked her to get a book out of the bag that I had packed for the stay. She pulled out *Harry Potter and the Goblet of Fire* from the bag and handed it to me. I had already read the book once, but the next book in the series, *Harry Potter and the Order of the Phoenix,* was coming out in less than two weeks, and I wanted to refresh my memory of the series before I read it.

I finished the first chapter as Dr. Cross walked into the room with another man. Cross had changed out of his operating scrubs, and was wearing a suit and tie, as was the other man, who appeared to be in his mid-fifties. There was a slight difference though between the doctors' attire. They both looked professional, but Dr. Cross's clothes were a little more stylish. For instance, Dr. Cross's tie was a red silk power tie worn to impress. The second man's tie was a conservative red and blue tie that looked like a gift a father would receive from his kids or grandkids on Father's Day.

The second doctor was of average height with dark, bushy hair and a beard. The beard was a mixture of black and gray, and while it appeared that the two colors had been fighting for dominance for some time, the gray was winning.

"Jack, how are you feeling?" asked Dr. Cross. He walked over to me and shook my hand.

"I'm okay. I was in a little bit of pain, but the pills helped."

"Good. This is Dr. Eli Schnee." Dr. Schnee walked over and shook my hand. "Nice to meet you."

"Dr. Schnee will be your oncologist, if we find out that the cancer has spread." Dr. Cross said, and then looked at my parents. "I'm going to need to check Jack's incision and his bandages, if you could step outside for a second."

"Sure," Dad said, and he and Mom stood up. They both gave me a look of reassurance and walked out.

"I spoke to your parents after the surgery. They seem like good people." Dr. Cross said as he lifted up the bed sheet and my hospital gown. There was a large bandage on my right side, where the nurse had shaved. He gently lifted the bandage, and looked at the incision. It was about three inches long, pointing from above my genitals to my right hip. "It looks good, Jack. The good news is that the surgery went fine, and I checked your left testicle during the procedure and it looked perfectly normal. We'll do a follow-up appointment in three weeks to make sure everything healed properly."

"Tomorrow," he continued, "the nurse will give you some directions on how to replace the bandages and keep the wound clean, but you will need to take it easy over the weekend, and no sexual activity with anyone for at least three weeks." I knew that last part would be easy. "Do you have any questions?"

"Would it be okay to use the bathroom?"

"Sure, if you feel up to it. Just be careful."

"Thanks," I said, and then thought for a couple of seconds. "Could you tell from the surgery whether the cancer had spread beyond the testicle?"

"I couldn't tell, Jack. The tumor on your testicle looked cancerous to me, but the pathology exams will tell us for certain. Tomorrow, we'll do the CAT scan that we discussed, and we'll know from that scan."

"We should have the results next week," Dr. Schnee said, "so I would like to set up an appointment with you for next Friday to discuss them, if that works for you."

"Sure, can I call your office tomorrow to set up a time?"

"That would be fine.

"Alright," said Dr. Cross, "if you need anything, please let the nurses know."

Both men left the room, and after a couple of moments, my parents came back in. After I described the conversation to them, we went back to reading books and watching television. The rest of the day passed that way with little variation. From time to time, we would talk about this thing or that. My mom would talk about *The Da Vinci Code* or my father would talk about the actors in the movies we watched. Sometimes, my mom would ask a question about my classmates. It was during one of those conversations that she asked me if I would fly home for my high school reunion.

"I don't know Mom. It's on August 1ˢᵗ, and I bought a ticket, but it all depends upon what the doctors find out. If the cancer has spread, and I have to have chemo, I'm not going. I don't want the reunion to turn into some pity party."

"Okay, but what about your ticket?" Mom asked. She looked at me in a way that suggested that she thought that I was making the wrong decision. Dad's look suggested that he understood. Of course, I was on painkillers, so he could have just had gas.

"It's a nonrefundable ticket, but I think I can reschedule the dates and use it to fly to Minnesota sometime later in the year. I'll probably use it at Christmas time."

Mom said that made sense, and went back to reading her book. I decided that it was time to use the bathroom. Despite the offer from Dad to help me, I was able to walk slowly to the bathroom by myself. After closing the door, I pulled up my gown to look at my scrotum. It looked like I thought it would. There was no loose area where the right ball had been. Instead the skin had tightened around the left one. Other than the scar above that would always be visible, even when my pubic hair eventually grew back, there was no evidence that I had ever had two balls.

"Hopefully," I said to myself in the mirror, "that will be the last of it." I used the toilet, and went back to my bed, my parents, and my book.

Several hours later, Sarah visited me. My parents had never met her, but I had told them a lot about her when we had dated. The night before, I told them that she and I remained friends. They did not find that odd, because I had remained friends with my high school girlfriend Kara Kane. I also told them that Sarah had helped me in the last week. I did not tell them how attractive she was, how close we were, or that she was the one who found the tumor.

When my parents met Sarah, they thanked her for helping me, and then, told me that they were going to buy some pop. After they left, Sarah and I talked for a little while about how I was feeling and her upcoming date with Dan. I was still tired and a little loopy from the painkillers, so she kept the visit short. Before she left, I wished her luck on her date, and she gave me a kiss on my forehead. When my parents returned after Sarah left, Mom had a weird look on her face, and said, "So, you're just friends with Sarah?" I wondered if she had been watching through the door somehow.

"Yes, we're just friends. Just like I'm still friends with Kara."

"Just friends, nothing more?"

"Ah, Mom. She's dating this other guy." That was the truth, if you considered their first meeting the previous Saturday to be a date. "There's nothing going on between us."

Mom gave me a look that said "bullshit," sat down and went back to her book. "Okay, if that's what you say."

I looked to Dad for assistance, but he just shrugged his shoulders and turned back to the television. He was smart enough stay out of the discussion.

I went back to my book and read for a while. At some point, an orderly brought me dinner, which contained food-like substances in the shape of a chicken breast, rice and green beans. I picked a little bit at the food, mostly because I was not very hungry. There was also some chocolate pudding that actually tasted like pudding.

I did eat most of that. For a moment, I thought Mom would give me a lecture on eating only the dessert, but she either decided that I was a grown man who could make his own decisions, or she took pity on me due to the events of the day. My money was on the latter.

Just before visiting hours ended, Kyle and Rachel stopped by my room. Their visit was short as well. My parents thanked them, as they had Sarah, but they did not leave the room. Kyle and I talked about work briefly, and he promised to check in on me the next day. Rachel brought a bound copy of the graphic novel *Sandman* as a gift. After they left, I turned to Mom and said, "Mom, before you ask, Kyle and I are just friends too."

Dad laughed, as Mom said, "Ha, ha, very funny."

After Dad stopped laughing, he said, "We should get going, Jack. Are you going to be okay?"

"I'll be fine. Are you guys going to be okay out in the City by yourself?" I recalled a telephone conversation that Mom and I had on a Saturday morning during my first year of law school. I had told her that I was going to rollerblade in Central Park that afternoon. She had asked me whether it was safe, and she was not talking about the dangers of rollerblading.

"We'll be fine Jack," Dad said. "We may be small town people, but we can handle ourselves."

"Okay," I said. "I'll see you tomorrow." They said their good-byes, and left. After a little while, I lifted my gown to take another look at my new reality. The sight depressed me, and I put the gown down and went back to reading.

CHAPTER EIGHT

Monday morning soon arrived, and I was eager to get back to work. Since leaving the hospital Friday afternoon, I had been cooped up in my apartment recuperating from the surgery. Friday night was fine. My parents and I stayed in the apartment eating pizza delivered from my favorite pizzeria and remembering the past. My parents told stories about my childhood, including some of the more memorable fights that I had had with my sister. I had a good time with my parents. My apartment was never meant for three people to stay there for hours on end, but for that night, I had no complaints.

My parents and the pain from the surgery both left on Saturday. I was happy with the pain's departure, but was sad to see my parents leave. Ever since I had moved to New York, I always felt some sadness whenever my visits with family ended. This time, though, the sadness was deeper. I loved the company and comfort that my parents had provided me during their visit. Normally, I felt comfort from the solitude of my apartment, but after my parents left, it made me sad.

Due to the doctor's orders, I spent my time that weekend with my ass firmly planted in my bed or on the futon. Despite some calls from a couple of friends, and a short visit from Kyle, I was alone with my thoughts. I tried to avoid them by reading Harry Potter, watching movies and football and playing video games on my Xbox. Those activities, though, only helped a little. When Monday morning came along, I couldn't wait to work, thinking that work would provide the mental diversion I needed.

Under orders from Mike Goldman, I had not checked my e-mails or voicemail all weekend. When I arrived in my office, I expected to find a slew of messages from people. To my surprise, no one had left any voicemails, and only a few people had sent any emails during my absence. I decided that Goldman and the other partners must have told people to leave me alone. One of the few emails I did receive was from another partner, Lauren Kaspar, with whom I had been working on a breach of contract case. We had filed a motion to dismiss the case a year earlier, and, according to Lauren's email, on the past Friday, the judge had denied our motion to dismiss and ordered our client, King Industries, to file an answer responding to the allegations contained in the plaintiff's complaint. Lauren wanted to have a meeting at 3 p.m. to discuss the answer that we had drafted months before, as well as drafting discovery requests.

After four straight days spent doing virtually nothing, I felt the need to do some heavy mental lifting. I pressed play on my iPod, and Warren Zevon's *Lawyers, Guns and Money* started to play. I pulled out my files on the King Industries case, and began re-familiarizing myself with their contents.

I spent about forty-five minutes reviewing the files and taking notes on avenues for discovery, when I heard a knock at my door. I looked up to see Elizabeth Jennings standing at my open door with a manila folder in her hand. "Hey, Jack, do you have a couple of minutes?"

"Sure, come on in."

Elizabeth walked in and sat down in one of my chairs. "How are you feeling?"

"Okay; just a little sore from the surgery, but otherwise I'm good." Mike Goldman had told Elizabeth that I had cancer and had a tumor removed but nothing more.

"Do they know if they removed the entire tumor?"

"Yeah, they got all of it. *And then some.* "But there is the chance that the cancer has spread. They did some tests, and I have an appointment on Friday afternoon to find out the results."

"Well, I hope the results are good."

"Thanks. What did you think about the brief?" I imagined that my draft, with her comments, were in the folder in her hand.

"It was great. You did an incredible job. I only had a few minor changes, and I put those in myself last Thursday, along with the introduction. Here are my comments so that you can see what I did." She handed me the folder. I took a quick look and saw only a couple of red marks. I felt a warm feeling of satisfaction and pride spread through me. *Awesome.*

"It really was quite good, Jack," Elizabeth continued. "Just so you know, when I gave it to Mike, I let him know that everything but the introduction was your work. He thought you did a great job, too. He sent the draft to the client on Friday, so hopefully, we should hear back at some point in the next couple of days. Maybe, we'll even be able to file the brief early."

"Really? Have you ever heard of anyone filing a brief early?"

Elizabeth smiled. "Never. I bet that we'll get the draft back on the 29th, and we'll still have to scramble to file this on the 30th."

"I won't take that bet," I said.

"Smart move," Elizabeth said, and stood up. "Well, I'll let you get back to work. I'll let you know when we hear back from the client." Elizabeth stood up and walked over to the door. Before she left she turned back to me. "Jack, I know you've got a lot of stuff going on, but you should be proud of what you did with the brief. You really did an incredible job with it."

"Thanks, Elizabeth." I said, as the first true smile that I had in over a week appeared on my face. When she left, I stood up, walked over to my door, and closed it. I lifted my arms in the air, and then pumped my right fist twice. "Awesome."

⚔ ⚔

Riding on the wave of that good feeling, I barely noticed as the week flew by. I was busy, but not work-until-one-in-the-morning busy. I spent most of the week drafting the discovery requests in the King Industries case. Each night, I found myself at home by 8:00 p.m., and was able to catch up on some DVDs I had bought, but had not had time to watch.

When Friday morning arrived, though, the euphoria had worn off, and a nervous fear had replaced it. It was the same nervous fear that I had felt two weeks ago in Dr. Cross's office. I was afraid to hear the results of the CAT scan I had taken a week earlier when I was in the hospital after my surgery.

The scan had not been pleasant for a number of reasons. For one thing, I went through the scan less than 24 hours after I had my testicle removed and I was still sore. When I arrived at the CAT scan room, I was told to drink a large bottle of barium contrast that had the consistency of milk of magnesia and the taste of chalk. When I finally swallowed the awful cocktail, I lay down on the CAT scan platform and a technician placed an IV into my left arm. The IV was connected to a mechanical, syringe-like device the size of a two liter soda bottle. The technician, a bespectacled black man in his thirties, advised me that the device, when activated, would inject an iodinated contrast into my veins that would help highlight my insides on the scan. He told me that as the contrast flowed into my veins, I would feel a "warmth" spreading throughout my body and a metallic taste would appear in my mouth.

He was right. As the contrast started pumping into my veins, I felt heat slowly spread from the inside of my left elbow down to my fingertips and up to my shoulder. The heat then spread to my upper chest and right arm. Suddenly, as the heat moved both up into my head and lower into my torso, my mouth tasted like I was sucking on a penny. The heat continued to spread down into my groin, and I felt it enter my scrotum and my left testicle. The absence of heat on my right side reminded me of the part of me that had been cut out a day before. The heat then moved down my legs and to the tips of my toes.

I hated the feeling of that heat in every inch of my body. The heat remained with me as the platform moved into the tube containing the scanners. Over the next several minutes and at various intervals, the voice of the technician, who was in the room next door, came through a speaker, advising me to remain still as the machine scanned my abdomen and groin. I am not usually a claustrophobic person, but at that moment, under those conditions, I was. I couldn't wait to get out of that tube, but every second I lay there felt like ten seconds. Finally, the scan was finished and the platform withdrew from the tube. While I was done with the scan that day, I knew that, regardless of the results, I would have to undergo scans again in the future to ensure I was cancer-free. I was not looking forward to those repeat performances.

Recalling the scan as I sat in Dr. Schnee's waiting room, I shuddered, and my fear of the scan results increased. I struggled to put down that fear. I kept telling myself that I had caught the cancer early, and that there was none left in my body. The problem was the pesky voice in my head that would say, *"Yeah, that's great, but what if …."* I would never let the voice finish its sentence, but it is probably easier to quiet a sick, crying baby than it is to silence that voice.

There were no crying infants in Dr. Schnee's waiting room when I arrived there Friday afternoon. In fact, it had been at least a half a century since the two men and three women in the waiting room had been infants. The two men and two of the women were obviously in various stages of cancer treatment. They had that "chemotherapy look" that was immediately recognizable. Each of them was bald, although the women wore scarves over their heads. They had no eyebrows and their skin was pale. Their clothes were also baggy due to the weight loss their cancer treatments had caused.

Looking at these people, I felt fear again. I had never liked hospitals, had never liked looking at sick people. I looked away from them, and immediately called myself a coward. These people were ill and fighting a deadly disease. They did not need the averted glance of some young jackass to remind them of how they looked. In an effort to ignore the shame, I started reading a Robert Jordan *Wheel of Time* book that I had brought with me. *At least there are no sick kids here.* I did not think I could handle looking at a child who had the chemotherapy look.

Fifteen minutes later, a matronly Hispanic nurse called my name. I followed her into an examination room, where she did the usual examination routine checking my height, weight, blood pressure, and other things. After she finished, she led me to Dr. Schnee's office, which was empty. She informed me that Dr. Schnee would be with me momentarily and left the room.

Superficially, Dr. Schnee's office was similar to Dr. Cross's office. He had a stout wood desk and bookshelf with diplomas and pictures. However, just as there were differences in the way they dressed, there were also differences in their offices. Whereas Dr. Cross had awards and pictures of Dr. Cross with politicians and celebrities throughout his office, Dr. Schnee only had pictures of his family, along with some simple watercolor paintings hanging on the walls. I had the sense that Dr. Cross's office was meant to impress his patients, whereas Dr. Schnee's office was meant to be comforting and soothing to his patients.

"Hi Jack, how was your recovery from the surgery?" Dr. Schnee asked, as he walked to the leather seat behind his desk.

"It was fine," I said. "I'm back to normal."

"That's good," Dr. Schnee said as he sat in his chair. "Jack, I'll get to the point. I reviewed the CAT scan results, as well as the report from the radiologist. The CAT scan showed swelling on the lymph nodes on the right side of your pelvic wall, and in your abdomen. Everything else is normal. In simple English, that means the cancer has spread."

I was rocked to my core, even more than when I originally found out that I had cancer. Only one thing was the same, and that was the one thought in my head: *cancer; fuck.*

Dr. Schnee continued to describe how the cancer had spread, and my treatment. My mind was lost in a fog, trying to cope with the news, so I registered only a little of what he said. The cancer was still treatable, but I would need to have four chemotherapy sessions. The first session would start in three weeks. These facts made their way to my brain briefly, and then the fog would roll in again, and I was lost.

Dr. Schnee then said something that I wanted to hear again. "I'm sorry, what was the last part, again?" I asked.

"The chemotherapy could impair your ability to have kids. It's not as likely as it would be if you had radiation treatments. But since it's a possibility, we recommend that patients bank some sperm before treatment. That way, you'll still be able to have your own children someday. I'll have my receptionist call the clinic to set up an appointment for you early next week. She'll call you with a time on Monday."

"Okay." My mind returned to the fog, and Dr. Schnee continued to talk. At some point, I said, "Uh, Dr. Schnee, would it be possible to go over this information again later? I'm having some trouble concentrating."

"That's fine. We can discuss it when you return for the blood tests two weeks from today." His blue eyes peered out at me from below his bushy eyebrows. He spoke softly, with obvious sympathy and understanding. "Jack, I want to reassure you that your chances of survival remain around 95%. The cancer has not spread too far, and the chemotherapy sessions should be more than enough to take care of it. I'm not saying that the treatments will be easy, but you're young and in good shape. You're going to be fine."

"Okay." I didn't know what else to say.

"Do you have anyone here with you to take you home?"

"No, I'm here by myself, but I'll be fine. I just need some time to think."

Dr. Schnee shook his head. "Jack, you need more than that. I've been treating people with cancer for over twenty years, and after all that time, I know that the most important thing to any cancer patient's treatment is to have a strong support system. Chemotherapy is going to be tough. You're going to need a solid group of people to help you get through it. Now, maybe you're not someone who is used to relying on people. If so, you'll need to change that. You might as well start today. Do you understand?"

"Yes." Deep down, though, I did not want anyone around me. I was taking this news much harder than the original news that I had cancer. I was faltering emotionally, and I knew that, soon, I would completely fall apart. I did not want anyone to see when I did. Yet, I knew that Dr. Schnee was right. Being with Kyle and Rachel had helped me deal with the original diagnosis. Someone could help me now.

"Do you have anyone, like a family member or a friend, who can spend time with you this afternoon or evening?" Concern had crept into Dr. Schnee's voice and into his eyes.

"My parents and sister live in Minnesota, but I have some friends that I could call."

"Good. Then my first instruction to you as your doctor is to tell you to call your friends," he said sternly, while his eyes retained their concern. "Do you have a cellphone?"

"Yes," I said, as I stood up from my chair.

"Do you promise that you will call someone when you leave the office?"

"Yes."

"Good." Dr. Schnee reached out his hand to me, and I shook it. "This is not going to be easy Jack, but I promise you, we're going to get you through it. Okay?"

"Alright," I said, softly. I didn't feel it then, but over the next few months, I came to like Dr. Schnee a lot. There's a Yiddish word I've learned that describes him perfectly. He was a *mensch*. He was a great doctor, but more importantly, he was a good man.

As I left his office, I decided that I would call Sarah. Kyle and Rachel had plans to stay at Rachel's parents in New Jersey, and I did not want to ruin another Friday night for them. As for Sarah, it was a Friday, and she likely had plans with Dan. Still, I had promised Dr. Schnee, so when I stepped out of the office building onto the sidewalk, I called Sarah at work. Unfortunately, her voicemail answered.

"Sarah, it's Jack," I said, after the beep. "Listen, I was wondering if you were around tonight. I saw my oncologist, and he …," I faltered, and felt the tears preparing to burst from my eyes. "He said that the cancer …" *Cancer; fuck.* "The cancer has spread and that I'm going to have to go through chemotherapy. I need …, Dr. Schnee said I need to have some people around me. It's almost 4, so can you call me when you get this message? I'm headed home now. Bye."

With that, I had fulfilled my promise to Dr. Schnee. I told myself that I should be happy that Sarah had not answered the phone. I practically broke down speaking to a machine. I knew I would have lost my composure if I had actually spoken with her. Still, I felt a little disappointment when I hung up.

I have little memory of the next two hours. It was like the one part of my brain, the part that separates men from animals and says "I think, therefore, I am," decided to shut down. The rest of my brain kept my body moving as I meandered through the City on my way home. At some point, somewhere along the East River Promenade, my cellphone rang.

"Hello?"

"Jack, it's Sarah." Her voice was thick with sympathy. "I'm so sorry. I've been in meetings all afternoon and I just heard your voicemail. How are you doing?"

"Um, not good." I figured the shorter my responses, the less likely I would break down.

"Well, don't worry. If you want my company tonight, you have it."

I felt relief and discomfort at the same time. "Thanks."

"Where are you now?"

"Um." I looked around for a landmark to get my bearings. From the buildings located to the west, I figured out that I was somewhere in the 80s. "I ..., I'm on the walkway by the East River. I guess I'm about fifteen minutes from home."

"Well, I'm leaving work now, so I should be at your apartment in about twenty minutes or so."

"Thanks Sarah."

"Don't mention it. I'll see you soon."

About twenty minutes later, I walked into my apartment. Tears formed in my eyes, but I refused to give them release. I told myself that I needed to be strong during the next four months, and I couldn't cry like a little kid every time things became tough.

I went into my bedroom and changed into some dark brown cargo shorts and a Superman t-shirt. When I finished, the intercom went off, and I buzzed Sarah into the building. While I waited, I poured myself some Maker's Mark, and downed it. *Cancer. Fuck.*

I heard a knock at my door and walked over to open it. Sarah was there, dressed in a pink business blouse and white skirt. Her face wore the sadness and concern that had been in her voice. "Oh, Jack. I'm so sorry." She came in and gave me a tight hug.

"Thanks Sarah." Her touch and sympathy brought the tears back to the surface again. I gently disengaged from the hug and led her into the living room. "Would you like a drink?"

"Not right now." Sarah went to the futon and sat down. "Come sit next to me."

"Okay," I said, and followed her instructions.

"How are you doing?" She asked.

"It's tough. I'm trying to hold it together." The words started to pour out in a rush. "I have to be strong through this, and ..."

Sarah interrupted me. "How long have you been 'holding it together?'"

"What?" I asked, frowning in confusion.

"Have you cried once since we found the tumor?"

"No, not really."

"Jack, you need to let it out." She said gently but firmly, as she looked me in my eyes, where the tears started to spill.

"I can't, I ..."

Sarah reached out and grabbed my right hand. "Jack, you've been told that you have cancer. You've lost a testicle, and now you know that you need chemotherapy. You have the right to be sad, and you need to stop holding it together."

I tried to protest further, but could not summon the effort.

"Just let it out."

So I did.

⊰⊱

Like most men, I stopped crying sometime before elementary school. Around that age, boys learn that we cannot "cry like a girl" whenever something goes wrong. Boys cannot be weak, and there is nothing as weak as a girl, or so we tell each other. Sure, we may get "something in our eyes" when we watch *Brian's Story* or *Field of Dreams,* when we hear Kevin Costner ask his father's ghost, "you wanna have a catch?" (Of course, we also bitch that he says "have a catch" instead of "play catch.") Rarely, though, do we ever just break down and sob.

Because I hadn't given myself that luxury in years, I had forgotten what happens when I cried. When you cry, when you really sob, the pain that you have been holding inside comes out. Without the pain, there is emptiness inside you. It's not a complete emptiness. Some grief and fear remain, but those emotions are much more manageable.

In Sarah's arms, I remembered what I had forgotten. Two weeks of pent-up sorrow, pain and fear poured out of me. I had held those emotions in, putting up a dam to stop them from overwhelming me. I had done a good job, but the dam was simply not enough to keep the emotions from overflowing. So I wept. I wept at having cancer, and I wept for the loss of my testicle. Mainly, I wept out of the fear of the treatments and months to come.

When I was finished, on that June night, I learned that sometimes it's good to cry like a little girl. Before the end of the year, I would learn a lot more, including how strong a little girl could be.

I don't remember how long I wept in Sarah's arms, but at some point, I sat up, and looked at her.

"Thank you," I said, wiping my eyes.

"You're welcome," she said. "How do you feel?"

"I feel …, well, I feel like I need a drink," I stood up. "Can I get you one?"

"Sure. What do you have here besides Maker's Mark and Diet Coke?"

I walked over to the kitchen and she followed me. "My dad was drinking gin and tonics when he was here. I have some left. Does that work?"

"Sure," Sarah said, and I grabbed the gin and tonic bottles from my cabinet. "So really, how do you feel?"

I looked at her, and shrugged. "Not good, but better than I was feeling before." I felt the familiar need to hide my feelings, but after having shown so much already, I decided to keep going. "I'm scared, you know?"

"What are you scared of?" She asked. I frowned at the question, thinking the answer was obvious, but then I remembered that her father was a psychologist. Sarah obviously had learned some things from her dad, and was trying to coax more out of me.

"Right now, I feel like I'm scared of everything." The words came out in a rush. Like my tears, once I gave the words a little release, I could not stop them from fully coming out. "I'm scared about going through chemo, and everything that comes with chemo. Losing my hair. Feeling like shit. Throwing up. I'm scared that I won't be able to have kids after this, and I'm scared …, I mean this is cancer."

She came over to me and hugged me again, and we stood in silence for a while. "Jack, if I was in your position, I'd feel the same way. It's okay to be scared." She stepped away, and I continued to make the drinks. "Is there anything else you're afraid of?"

"Yeah," I said, nodding my head slowly. "I'm afraid of what people will think about me, when they find out I have testicular cancer. I'm scared that people will see me as a one-nut freak, a half of a man."

"Jack, you are no less of a man now than you were before we found the tumor."

"I know. That's what Rachel said as well, but still, I can't shake the idea. Here's your drink." She took her glass and took a swallow from my own. "It's like, I have this image of myself in my head, this image that I want to project. I'm this guy who is strong and in charge of his life; not a victim with one testicle." I looked down at my t-shirt, and then thought about my posters at work and what Hal had said months ago. "It's like, I want to be Superman, the Man of Steel. Having cancer, going through chemo, though, I'm more like …, I don't know, Cancerboy, the Clipped Crusader. I know I shouldn't care what anyone else thinks, but still, I …"

"So don't tell people that you have testicular cancer," she said matter-of-factly. "Tell them you have cancer, and leave it at that. If people ask, just tell them it's personal."

The idea was appealing, and I admit that I considered the idea. However, I remembered my conversation with Mike Goldman, and what he had said about not hiding my disease. He was right. "No, I can't. I had no idea that I was in the age range for testicular cancer, and that I was supposed to check myself once a month. I'm not the only guy out there that doesn't know. If I talk about it, maybe someone who hears me will start checking himself, and be able to find his lump early too."

"So you're willing to have people think differently about you, perhaps even say things behind your back, just because it *may* help someone else?" She asked.

"Yes, I guess I am."

Sarah smiled. "Jack, if you talk like that with people, no one with more than half a brain will ever think you're less than a man."

"Are you sure?"

She was silent for a second, apparently gathering her thoughts. "Do you remember the first night I ever spent in your apartment in the Village when we were dating? We were lying in your bed after we had sex, and I commented on the Superman poster in your bedroom?

"Yeah, I do." We had been out together earlier in the evening at a party hosted by one of her friends. We had come back to my place. We rarely did that, but did that night, because my apartment was close to the party. I remembered having a particularly fun time with her in my bed that night. "You joked that you never realized how much looking at a man in tights during sex could turn you on."

"Yeah, that was a nervous joke," Sarah said. "I mean, I knew that you liked sci-fi and comic books, but I didn't realize that you were that big of a fan. Suddenly, I was worried that I was dating this man-child who was going to start talking about how Superman used his eye lasers to beat Lex Luthor in issue 142, or his super-speed on Doctor Doom in issue 244."

I wanted to tell Sarah that Superman had heat vision, not eye lasers, and that Dr. Doom was a Marvel villain and couldn't fight Superman, but I sensed that would contradict her point.

"But," Sarah continued, "that's not what you did. You talked about why you loved comic books, and how the best of them told incredible stories of hope and redemption. You even told me about that one story, you know the time travel love story. What was it?"

"Astro City, The Nearness of You," I said.

"Yeah, that one," she said, nodding her head. "It was beautiful. And you spoke so passionately and confidently. It was attractive. I thought you were a man before you took me to bed, and what you told me didn't make you less in my eyes. If anything, I liked you even more."

"So what you're saying is …?"

"People won't doubt that you're a man, because you'll show them you are one," Sarah said. "When you tell people that you have testicular cancer, you'll talk confidently, like it's no big deal, just like with comic books. If you do that, no one will question your masculinity." She paused. "And if they do, well, fuck them."

I sat for several seconds thinking, amazed by what she had told me and the feeling behind her words.

"Well, what are you thinking?" Sarah asked.

I looked at her and smiled. "I think that I'm glad that you could be here with me."

"You're welcome," she said. "I'm hungry. Are you hungry?"

"Yeah, I'm hungry. Can we stay in though? I have to tell my family, and Kyle, and I'd like to do it from here."

"Sure. I'm here as long as you need me."

"Are you sure? You don't have any plans with Dan?"

"Not tonight. I'm going to see him tomorrow."

"What date is that, the second?"

No, it's the third." She blushed a little, and stood up with our empty glasses.

From her blush, I knew that their date would likely end with the usual third date activities. I wondered if Dan would talk about comic books afterwards too. "That's great. I'm glad it's going well."

"Thanks. I'm going to refill our drinks and order some pizza. You can make some calls and we'll get a little drunk tonight."

"Works for me."

We spent the evening that way. I called my parents, Jesse, and Kyle, and between calls, Sarah and I ate and drank. During the calls, Sarah sat next to me, and offered me comfort when I needed it. At times, she held my hand, and at others, she offered a smile. She would re-fill my drink glass when it was empty, and offered me some tissues. I cried a little, especially when I talked to my parents, and later Jesse, but only a little. I had shed most of my tears with Sarah.

Everyone handled the information as well as they could. I think they had prepared themselves for the news better than I did. They all offered to help me in any way that they could, and my parents and Jesse offered to fly out if I needed it. When Dad asked if they could share the news that I had testicular cancer with others, I gave him my permission.

Somewhere around 9:00 PM, after I spoke to Kyle, I hung up the phone. Sarah and I had finished the pizza. Of course, I had eaten most of it. She didn't eat much more than a slice. We were both a little tipsy from the alcohol. The night had been tough, and I was exhausted, both emotionally and physically.

"God, I'm tired." I said to Sarah. "How are you?"

"Yeah, I'm wiped too. I probably should be going. Do you think you'll be okay?"

"Yeah, the hardest part is over. I'll probably go to sleep after you leave." We both stood up from the futon, and started walking toward the door. Before we got there, I turned to her. "Sarah, I said it before, but I'm glad that you were here. You've really helped me tonight. More than I expected."

"We've been through a lot of things since we met, Jack, but I will always be your friend. I'm here whenever you need it."

"Thanks." She reached out, and we hugged each other. I held her close, her soft, warm body against mine. Without letting go, we looked at each other. Suddenly, before I knew what we were doing, we were sharing a soft, gentle kiss. After a long moment, Sarah broke it off, although she did not let go.

"I can't, Jack."

We released each other at the same time. "I'm sorry," I said. "I shouldn't have done that. You were just being a good friend, and …"

Sarah shook her head. "I was kissing you too. I want to, but I can't. I really like Dan, and I think there may be something there, you know?"

"I understand." I didn't want to, but I did. She was right. I was attracted to her, and I cared for her, but I wasn't in love with her. She deserved someone who could be. "Besides, with my surgery, I'm not supposed to do anything physical for three more weeks."

Sarah reached out and held my right hand. "I'm still here to help you; just not like that."

"I know. Thank you." I leaned down, keeping my body separate from hers and kissed her on the cheek. "Good night, Sarah," I said, and opened the door.

"Good night, Jack, and take care of yourself."

I closed the door, and leaned my head to it. "Dan Harper, you are a lucky man," I whispered. I walked back into the living room and looked around. For the second time in eight days, I had enjoyed company in my apartment, and, for the second time, I felt loneliness in its absence.

Later, I lay in my bed, still alone. The WB11 10 o'clock news was on, and Sean Kimerling was talking about New York baseball. I paid little attention, as I felt sleep's soft caress on my mind. I knew that I would not be watching Seinfeld that night.

Before I fell asleep, I thought about the day, and the days ahead. What Sarah had said was on a loop in my mind. *No one will doubt that you're a man, because you will show them you are one.* I had some decisions to make, decisions about how I faced what lay ahead and how I would beat it. I had made one decision already that day, when I decided that I would no longer keep my condition a secret. I would make more decisions about my treatments and work in the days to come, but that night I decided how I was going to handle my treatment. I would do exactly what Sarah had said I should do. I was going to show people, prove to them, that I was still a man. My life would change in the next four months, but I wouldn't let it change any more than was necessary. I would take time off for chemo treatments, but other than that, my life wouldn't change in any way. I would show people that how strong I was.

For the previous two weeks, I had taken my lumps from cancer, both literally and figuratively. Cancer had made me depressed, kept me up at nights, and had taken a physical part of my manhood. *No more,* I thought. For the previous two weeks, "cancer, fuck" had been in my head like a mantra of disbelief. From that point on, I had a different mantra, a mantra of defiance and anger that could help me face what was coming.

Fuck cancer.

CHAPTER NINE

I woke up the next morning to a pain that felt like a vise squeezing my head. I opened my eyes, realizing that I had a hangover and a dry mouth that tasted like something had decomposed in it. I thought about the five drinks that I had last night with Sarah. Sarah, whom I had kissed, and who probably would be waking up tomorrow morning with another guy. "Shit," I said.

I looked over at the clock on the nightstand by my bed. It read 7:00 AM, which was about three hours earlier than my usual Saturday morning wake-up time. I needed some Advil and water, and maybe some more sleep. I arose from the bed and walked to the bathroom to use the toilet and grab the Advil.

My mind was foggy from the hangover and the sleep, but my emotions were under control. The fear and grief were still there, but they were like small drops left in a bathtub after the plug is pulled. There was not enough left to drown my mind.

I felt the anger, though. It was a small flame in the back of my head, ready to flare up with some fuel. *Fuck cancer.* It was the anger and the mantra that changed my mind about going back to sleep.

I needed to be proactive, and I needed to move. I decided that a run might help me. I could sweat out the booze, and it would give me the time to make some more decisions.

After swallowing some green Advil gelcaps with a glass of water, I went back to my bedroom and dug out pair of running shoes from the back corner of my closet. I found some running clothes and put them on. Holding a small water bottle in one hand and my iPod in the other, I walked out of my apartment.

Five minutes later, I was doing a slow jog down the East River Promenade. The sun was peeking out from behind some clouds, but it was warm. My iPod was playing the Red Hot Chili Pepper's *Can't Stop*. It was not an easy jog, as the months of inactivity and the boozing the night before took their toll. However, I ran at a slow pace, and with each step, I felt better. As my mind grew clearer, I started planning.

My first order of business would be to call some friends, both here in the City and back in Minnesota. My friends in Minnesota probably would not be able to do much for me in the future beyond phone calls, but I figured that could still help. More importantly, they deserved to find out directly from me rather than from the gossip mill coming out of Oak Lake. I would also call my law school friends, and, on Monday, tell people at work.

I ran for thirty minutes. When I was finished, I was winded, sweaty and tired, but I felt good. In fact, I felt good enough that I decided to continue running in the days and weeks to come. I figured that the chemo treatments could be easier on me if I was in better physical shape.

After a shower and a breakfast at the Blue Moon Cafe, I started calling my friends. My first call was to Jim O'Dare, a close friend from law school. I had met Jim in the first few weeks at NYU, and had become good friends with him. He had attended to Yale and had been on the varsity football team. He had played defensive tackle, so he was a big guy, both in size as well as spirit.

Jim and I had a great friendship, although it was competitive, especially from my end. Because he had gone to Yale, I continuously felt the need to prove myself against him. Whether it was grades, moot court results, the bar exam results, or picking up women when we were out, I consistently sought to equal or surpass Jim. For the most part, I had held my own.

After law school, Jim became an associate in the bankruptcy department at another large New York firm called Adam, Sage & Jagger. Because Jim worked as hard as I did, we didn't speak as often as we would have liked. The last time we spoke, about four months before, he had been getting ready to work on a trial that was set to last two months.

"Jim O'Dare."

"Jim, hey, it's Jack Ritter."

"Ritter, how are you doing?" Jim said. "Are you calling from the office?"

"Naw, I'm not working today."

"Not working? Wow, I didn't realize that life had gotten so soft at Garrick," he said with a laugh.

"No, it's the same. I'm not working due to some personal things, which is why I'm calling."

"What's going on?" Jim asked, his tone becoming serious.

"I have testicular cancer." My voice wavered a little as I said the words. I swallowed and steadied myself. *Fuck cancer.* With that, I felt stronger.

"Oh, shit."

"Yeah."

"How bad is it?"

"Well, I caught it early." My voice became stronger as I spoke more. "I had a tumor on my right nut, and I had surgery two weeks ago to remove it. But I found out yesterday that it's spread to some of my lymph nodes. I'm going to need to go through chemo."

"Fuck. What's the outlook?"

"The survival rate is 95%, so I'll be fine in the long run. I just have to go through chemo to make sure."

"At least that's good. What can I do to help?"

"I don't think anything right now. I go into the hospital for chemo on July 14th. I'm not completely sure of the details, but it looks like I'll be there for several days. And I'll have to go several times."

"Have you talked to any of the other guys yet?"

"Rich and Barry? Not yet. I was thinking about calling them next."

"Okay. So how are you taking everything?"

"I guess okay. It's been rough, you know? I know it's been three weeks, but it's been like a whirlwind, and I'm still in shock. When I think that I have cancer ...." *Fuck cancer.* "Well, it's unreal. But my parents flew out, and Sarah's been great."

"Sarah, the girl you dated our first year? Are you two back together?"

"Nah. We're just friends."

"Okay," Jim said, in the universal way that people use when they heard something that makes no sense. "Well, I'm here to help any way that I can. In fact, I know one thing we can do. I think you, me and the boys should have a night out before you go in for chemo. You know, eat, drink and be merry, like we did back at NYU. I'm thinking next Thursday makes sense. The next day is July 4th so everyone will have that day off. How does that sound?"

It had been over a year since I had been out with the law school gang. A night out with them was something I missed, something I needed. "That sounds good to me."

"Great. I'll get in touch with Rich and Barry and set the whole thing up."

"Thanks Jim."

"Like I said, anything I can do to help. It's been too long, Ritter. We need to stay in touch more."

"I agree, but you know how busy law firm life gets."

"I surely do. I'll let you make your calls, but I'll call you tomorrow okay?"

"Sounds good."

"Cool. Take care of yourself, Jack. Everything is going to be good, you know?"

"I hope so. I'll see you."

I hung up, with a sigh. The call was tiring, but, for the most part, I had remained composed. I still owed calls to Barry and Rich, as well as my friends back in Minnesota. *It's going to be a long day.*

⋈ ⋈

On Tuesday afternoon, I found myself waiting at the Midtown Reproductive Clinic. A receptionist from Dr. Schnee's office had called me on Monday informing me of the appointment. I had arrived early, filled out my forms and waited my turn. I had brought *the Wheel of Time* book that I had not yet finished, but I was having trouble paying attention to it.

To say that I was uncomfortable at that moment would be an understatement. After all, the situation was awkward and absurd. In the most basic terms, I was sitting in a public place waiting for a woman to lead me to a private room where I would masturbate, wank, jerk off, bust a nut, choke the chicken, stroke the one-eyed snake, yank the crank, enjoy the original selfie or whatever you prefer to call it.

I wasn't uncomfortable with the underlying activity itself. In fact, I was quite familiar with it, and had been since 8th grade. Still, it was an activity to be done in private without anyone's knowledge. It certainly was not something that I waited for someone to tell me when it was my turn to do it.

The fact that there were four other people in the waiting room, three men and one woman, made the situation more awkward.

Two of the men seemed comfortable, so I assumed they had done this before. The woman was thin, in her mid-thirties, and was with one of the other men, apparently her husband, who also was in his mid-thirties. From the look on his face, he was not comfortable with the situation either. I imagined that they were concerned about their ability to have children. I understood the concern. I felt the same way.

After fifteen minutes of waiting, a young, cute nurse entered the waiting room and called my name. I stood up and followed her out of the room. She walked me down the hall to another room, and opened the door. "Here you go. There's plenty of material in there, like videos and magazines, to help you." She handed me a specimen cup. The cup had a label with my name and a patient number. "Please ejaculate into this."

I looked at the cup and thought about the mechanics needed to accomplish the task. The cup really was not properly engineered for it.

"When you are done, please screw the lid back on. There is a sink and paper towels in the room. You can use them to clean up when you are finished. Do you have any questions?"

"No, I think I'm good. Thanks."

The nurse walked away. I took a big sigh, walked into the room and closed the door.

"Aw, the nurse didn't offer to give you a hand?" asked Barry Mason, with a huge smile. It was Thursday night, and Barry, Jim O'Dare, Rich Swift, and I were sitting at a table at Peter Luger Steakhouse in Brooklyn. Luger's, which resembled an old time German beer hall, had been a Brooklyn staple for over a hundred years, and was my favorite steakhouse in the City. They know steak, and while they offered other entrees, such as lamb and fish, the waiters, by their expressions, discouraged such choices.

All of us were dressed semi-formally in sports coats, button down shirts and slacks for the occasion, although Barry was dressed a little more garishly than the rest of us. While Rich, Jim and I wore blue or black blazers, Barry's coat was shamrock green and was paired with a white shirt, and light yellow slacks. On anyone else, his attire would have been clownish. On him, even with his red hair and short stature, it looked stylish.

We had just ordered our drinks when Rich had asked what I had been doing that week. I described my visit to the sperm bank and my discomfort before entering the room, when Barry interrupted me with his joke. Barry was the jokester of our group. He was often crass, but he probably was the smartest legal mind at the table. He graduated near the top of our class at law school, and afterwards, he had worked as a law clerk for a federal appellate court judge. At that time, he was working at Kord and Carter, another large firm in the City.

"No, Barry. Jack was at a clinic, not a porn set," said Rich, with a mock exasperated tone. Rich worked as an Assistant District Attorney at the Manhattan District Attorney's Office. Rich was my height with blonde hair and very fit. Rich was wearing a black sports coat with a crisply pressed white shirt and khaki slacks. Rich was a runner and in the middle of training for his third New York marathon that year. He was much more reserved and straight-laced than Barry or even Jim and I, but he still had a good sense of humor.

"True," I said, "but ironically, one of the porn videos in the room was called "Sperm Bank Nurses II.""

"You're shitting me," said Rich.

"Of course I am," I said, letting a smile creep out. Everyone laughed.

"Speaking of porn, what types of 'materials' did they have in the room?" Jim asked. Jim was 6'5" and still carried much of the weight from his football days. Only some of it had turned to fat. His brown, curly hair was receding a little more than mine, making him look about five years older than his age. He wore a blue sports coat and a light blue shirt.

"You know, the big magazines, *Playboy, Penthouse, Hustler,* plus some others I had never heard of. They had a handful of videos, including a weird Japanese one."

"I'm afraid to ask, but how was it weird?" asked Rich.

"Let me guess," said Jim. "They blurred the genitals," Jim said. Everyone gave him a weird look. "That's how they censor porn in Japan," he said, defensively.

"Jimmy boy, you dog," said Barry. "I didn't know you were so deviant. How did you know that?"

"I spent a couple of weeks in Japan on one of my cases," said Jim. "Why would the clinic have that video? I mean, what guy would choose a censored video over a regular one?"

"You know what they say," Barry said, with a grin. "Different folks, different strokes. Literally."

"Oh, that's a bad pun," I said, as everyone else laughed.

"Will you have to go again?" Rich asked.

"I'm not sure. They are going to run some tests to determine how many swimmers I have. They were supposed to call me today to let me know. The message is probably on my answering machine back home. But, since I'm working with half of my original equipment, I'll probably have to go again."

"About that," said Barry, "do you …" He stopped when the waiter came over with our drinks. After giving us our drinks, the waiter took our food order. We were splitting the porterhouse cut for four, and selected the creamed spinach, German fried potatoes, and onion rings for our sides. My mouth watered, and my arteries narrowed, from the thought of the meal.

When the waiter left, Jim raised his glass. "I'd like to make a toast. To our friend, Jack. You've been dealt a raw deal, but I know that you are going to come through it just fine. Anything you need, buddy, we're here to help."

Rich and Barry nodded their heads in agreement, and we all drank.

"Thanks guys. I really appreciate it." I said. I turned to Barry. "Were you going to ask something?"

"Yeah." Barry looked a little embarrassed. "Do you have any feeling from the testicle you lost, you know, like how they say amputees can still feel the body part they lost?"

"Barry, come on!" said Rich, shocked. Jim was shaking his head.

"No, it's alright," I said. I was a little shocked that he had asked the question, but it was a fair one. "I wondered the same thing before the surgery. I haven't really felt that. It doesn't feel like it's still there. It's more like I feel its absence, you know?"

"What do you mean?" asked Jim.

I thought for a second. "It's like the New York skyline. When I look at the south part of the island, I'm used to seeing the Towers there, but they're not there. It's like I can see the outline where they were, you know, the hole they left in the Skyline."

"Anyway," I continued, "that's what it's like with my nut. I can feel the hole where it should be. My mind knows that there should be something there. It knows every millimeter where it should be and feels that there's nothing there."

An uncomfortable silence followed my description. I felt the need to fill it.

"Of course, it probably wouldn't be so bad, if I didn't' have such big balls in the first place." Barry spit up some of his drink, Rich chuckled and Jim started laughing hard.

"Great," said Barry, "now, I'll have that image in my mind."

A little bit later, the food arrived. Each of us started putting heaping portions of the steak and sides on our plate. The steak was incredible. I firmly believe that only the most ardent of vegetarians could find the strength to abstain from such food, and even if they did, they could not do so without some small amount of envy.

"So, Jack," said Barry, after washing down some spinach with scotch, "what's the plan for the chemo treatments?"

"According to my doctor, I need to have four sessions, one week a month for four months. I'll be hooked up to an IV twenty-four hours a day, so I'll be there overnight. My first session starts July 14th, and I'll be there until the 19th."

"Will you be stuck in bed the entire time?" Jim asked.

"I'm not sure," I replied, after a bit of spinach. "I hope I'll be able to move around. My doctor said that NYU has this wing for patients who need to spend long periods of time in the hospital. I've been told that the rooms are more like hotel rooms, and that I'll have a room to myself."

"You said on the phone that the survival rate was 95%," Rich said. "So once the chemo treatments are done, you'll be cured? The cancer won't come back?"

I took a big bite of steak. The discussion was getting in the way of my eating. "My doctor said that there is a very small chance the cancer would return. I'll have to have regular checkups for several years. But in all likelihood, this would be it."

"Why is that?" asked Rich. "Why is testicular cancer curable?"

"Well, twenty years ago, it wasn't curable; it was fatal. Apparently, it's curable now because of drugs they have. The doctor said that it's more susceptible to the chemotherapy drugs because it's particularly fast growing. The chemo drugs work by killing fast growing cells. That's why chemo patients lose their hair. Hair cells are fast growing cells, and the chemo kills them. Other cancers move slower, so chemo isn't as effective on them."

"So, are you going to lose all of your hair?" asked Barry. "You've got a lot of hair on your body; you gonna lose all of that?"

"From what I have heard," I continued, "most likely, I will lose the hair on my head. I'm not sure about the rest."

"Are you going to shave your head before then?" Jim asked.

"I've been thinking about it, but I decided that I'm keeping my hair as long as I have it. If it starts falling out, then I'll have it all shaved off. But I'm not going to take that step unless I have to. I want my life to be as normal as possible for as long as possible."

The talking stopped for a while as we continued to eat. After a minute, I said, "Enough about me. What's going on with you guys?"

"Same old, same old for me," said Barry. "The wife is doing well, and work is still busy as usual."

"Well," Rich said, "it's funny that you mention the sperm bank, because I may have to be visiting one pretty soon."

"What's going on, Rich?" Jim asked.

"Ah, Hope and I have been trying to have a kid for a while now, and we're not having any luck. It's starting to wear on us, and we've reached the point where we've gone to see a specialist. She's recommending that we both get tested. At some point, I'll probably have to see how many swimmers I have."

"That's too bad, Rich," I said. I was a little shocked that Rich had shared the news. As long as I knew him, Rich was a very private person. At the start of our third year in law school, his sister was in a serious car accident, but none of us found out until graduation. In addition, Rich's information reminded me that I wasn't the only one with problems. "I hope everything is okay with you guys."

"Well, if you ever need any help getting Hope pregnant ...," Barry said, with a grin.

"Oh really?" Rich interrupted. "What type of help can you give?" His tone was serious, but his smile and eyes indicated that he was ready for Barry's joke.

"I know some good doctors that can help," Barry said, with a mock innocent look.

"Thanks, I'll keep that in mind," Rich said, wryly."

"How about you, Jim? Anything new?" I asked.

"Well, Barry knows already," Jim said. "Do you guys remember Donna Morse from school?"

"Yeah," Rich said. "Cute girl. Tall. She was dating that douche, Alex something, throughout school."

"She's dating a new douche now," said Barry, pointing at Jim.

"You?" I asked. Jim nodded. "Wait, didn't she take a job at Adam Sage, too?"

"Yep," replied Jim. "She's in the M&A department." 'M&A' stood for mergers and acquisitions. M&A partners advise corporations when they acquire new companies to ensure that such transactions meet all legal requirements and goals.

"How long have you guys been dating?" asked Rich.

"About six months now. We were hanging out at the Christmas party, drinking some holiday shots. We reminisced about school, and commiserated about firm life. Well, one shot led to five, and before we knew it, we were hooking up in a corner of a bar at the end of the night. We've been dating since."

"Is it serious?" I asked. Jim and I really had been out of touch, I thought, if I didn't know that he had a girlfriend for six months.

"Yep. We've met each other's families, and we're going on a vacation to California at the beginning of August."

"Wow," I said, hiding my surprise. As long as I had known Jim, he had never been in a serious relationship. Throughout law school, he had hooked up with a number of women, and he and I had often been each other's wingman in law school. In fact, I had learned the phrase "a kiss and a cuddle" from Jim. Barry and Rich had been in their relationships with their spouses, so when I looked for women to meet at night, Jim had usually been at my side.

"Your firm allows people to date at work?" asked Rich.

"It depends," Jim said. "A partner isn't supposed to hook up with an associate and people who work directly together aren't supposed to date," Jim said, as he used his fork to get some more steak slices from the platter. "But because we never work together, it's not that big of a deal. Plus it's not like we're doing it at the firm."

Jim looked at each of us and he placed a piece of steak on his fork. "Well, at least not often," he added, with a feces consuming grin, and stuck the steak in his mouth.

"That's my boy!" Barry said, and we all laughed.

"Anyway," Jim continued, "I think the firm realizes that everyone needs a social life. The way they work us, it's virtually impossible to date someone outside of work."

"It can't be that bad," said Barry. "I still have a social life with my wife. Not as much as I would like, but we still spend a night or two together every week."

"Yeah," Jim said, "but you don't need to spend as much time with someone you've been with a long time as you do when you start dating someone. When you first start dating someone, you have to spend a lot of time with them to get to know each other. It's really hard to do that if you're at the office six to seven days a week working a ninety hour week."

"I don't know …," said Barry.

"Barry," Jim said, "let me tell you about something I noticed recently. Every person who has made partner in my department since I was hired is married, and they all were either married before they started at the firm, or were in a relationship with the future spouse at that time. I think it's easier for someone with a spouse or significant other to bill the hours they need to make partner than someone who is dating."

"I had never thought about that," said Barry. Neither had I. Suddenly, I looked around the table and realized that I was the only guy at the table without a girlfriend or a wife. In fact, of all of my friends, in New York and in Minnesota, I was the only one that was not in a serious relationship. *Fuck*, I thought.

A different thought crossed my mind next. *Stop feeling sorry for yourself. You're not going to get through this feeling sorry for yourself.*

"Listen," said Jim. I'm not saying that it's impossible to meet and marry someone while working, and still make it to partner. But it is tough. The fact that Donna and I work at the same place makes it easier. During the week, we almost always have dinner together at the firm cafeteria, and we often leave work together to go back home."

"And apparently, you *schtup* at work too." I said, hoping some humor would lift my thoughts. The guys laughed.

"Yeah, so where'd you guys do it?" asked Barry. "The law library, right? Now that everyone does their research online, the library's always empty."

We spent the rest of the night that way: four guys busting each other's balls and telling inappropriate jokes; four friends enjoying good food and good alcohol. Every so often, my thoughts would go to my upcoming chemotherapy treatments or to what Jim had said, but, for the most part, I was able to have a great time with my friends. It was the last really great night I would have for months.

CHAPTER TEN

Three days into my first chemotherapy session, I recognized the side effects of the treatment. The chemotherapy drugs made me feel exactly like I felt during the worst hangovers I have ever had. It was not like the first part of a hangover, when I would wake up with a splitting headache. It was like later in the day, when I suffered from exhaustion, the lack of appetite, the nausea and other stomach issues.

Mostly, though, I recognized the mental sluggishness that comes with a hangover. During that first visit, I had brought two books, *American Gods* by Neil Gaiman, and *The Amazing Adventures of Kavalier and Clay* by Michael Chabon, to the hospital, figuring that I would have plenty of time to read while I was there. However, during the second day, a fog rolled into my mind, and I was unable to focus enough to read. When I had the chance, I asked Dr. Schnee whether such symptoms were normal. He told me that many chemo patients had complained of similar symptoms, calling it "chemo brain." He said that it could last during the treatment and, perhaps, for a couple of days after the treatment. After I received that information`, I stopped trying to read and spent most of the time zoning out, listening to music or watching TV.

My days in the hospital were, for the most part, the same day after day. I had my own room, which looked like a Holiday Inn hotel room that came with a hospital bed and a hospital bathroom. There was no free HBO or Cinemax. For each hour of the day, from Monday morning to Saturday morning, I was hooked up, via an IV needle in one of my arms, to a pump that monitored the IV drip of chemotherapy drugs into my arm. The pump also contained a countdown timer for the IV bag, which lasted eight hours. At the end of each eight hour period, the pump would sound an alarm. During the day, that didn't pose a problem but at night, at 2 a.m., a nurse would come to my room to change the IV bag. I woke up each time that happened.

Each morning, I would wake up, make an attempt at eating breakfast, and then take a shower, making sure to keep the arm with the IV needle away from the water. After the shower, I would put on a pair of athletic shorts or sweatpants, and one of my T-shirts. Next, I would take the elevator to the floor where the main chemotherapy room was located. There, a nurse would insert the IV needle into a different vein on my hand or in my arm. On my first day, the nurse told me that changing veins everyday was necessary because, over time, IV use would harden the veins and make them difficult to use. By switching up the veins, the nurses hoped to extend the use of the veins.

After the bag was changed, I would sit in the chemotherapy room for a while, often with a couple of other patients. I would listen to music, and stare at the East River and Queens. After an hour or so there, I would walk back to my room and zone out in front of the TV for the rest of the day. At some point, my parents or Jesse would call to check on me, and, from time to time, so did some of my friends.

Every night, a new visitor or two or three would arrive. Sarah visited three times that first week. Jim, Rich and Barry came by too, as did Mike Goldman, Elizabeth Jennings, and other work colleagues. Sometimes they came with gifts. Jim brought a collectible Daredevil statue, and Elizabeth gave me a Buffy the Vampire Slayer episode guide signed by Joss Whedon. By the time my visitors showed up, I was always exhausted and feeling sick. Still, the visits were my favorite part of the day.

During my first stay at the hospital, Kyle visited every night around six o'clock. None of the visits were very long, at most fifteen minutes. Kyle was busy at work, preparing for the Qualtech trial that would start the second week of August.

On the third night that he visited, I was lying in my bed, wearing a blue Star Wars t-shirt that said "Han Shot First" and a pair of gray and black Nike basketball shorts. One of the nurses had just left the room after replacing the empty IV bag with a new one. My *Monty Python and the Holy Grail* DVD was playing on the TV. Despite my chemo brain, I was able to pay attention to it much better than I could read a book. Of course, *The Holy Grail* didn't require a lot of focus.

That night, Kyle walked in wearing a blue pinstripe suit, with a white shirt and blue tie. "Ritter," Kyle said, "how are you feeling tonight?"

"I'm okay," I said. "I'm tired, and the nausea's worse, but I can handle it."

"Did you eat anything? I brought a couple of slices from the place across the street. It's pretty good." He put a pizza box on the hospital bed table, and sat down in the chair next to the bed. I could smell the bubbling grease and cheese inside the box, and suddenly, I felt my appetite growing, despite the nausea.

"Thanks. I haven't eaten much but I'll try it in a little bit."

"Anything new today?"

"Well, just before you got here, I was thinking of some silver linings to this whole thing. You know, something to keep positive about."

"Yeah? You come up with anything?"

"Several things actually," I said. "I was thinking that losing my hair may be a good thing."

"Oh, really?" Kyle said, doubtfully.

"Well, for one thing, when I'm bald, I'll be able to save some money. I won't need to go to the barber every month, and I won't need shampoo or hair gel."

Kyle smiled. "Well that's true."

"Plus, losing my hair will let me know what I look like when I'm bald. If I look good, I won't feel so bad about losing my hair when I grow older. If my bald head is a mess, when I'm older, I'll take the William Shatner route or get hair plugs."

Kyle smiled. "Did you figure out anything else?"

"The only other thing I thought of was that if I ever get kicked in the groin, or if I get blue balls, the pain will be only half as bad."

Kyle snickered, and shook his head. "Given your sex life, that *is* a good thing."

"Thanks a lot. How's the trial prep going?"

Kyle sighed, and suddenly looked tired. "Pretty much as you would expect. I was up until 2:00 AM last night putting exhibits together for the *in limine* motions. I've got to go back in a little bit, but tonight, we should be done a little earlier than we were last night."

"Do you think there's any chance the case will settle?"

Kyle shook his head. "Probably not before the trial. It's gotten pretty personal. The other side accused the client of fraud and perjury, and tried to have us sanctioned. The client is willing to settle for ten million, but during settlement negotiations, the other side wants four times that amount. The client says he will only pay them that much if he loses at trial."

"So you'll be spending a month in Boston?" I asked.

"Other than some weekend trips home here and there, that's what it looks like."

"You know you don't have to come by here every night. Especially, if work is that busy." The hospital was on First Avenue between 31st and 33rd Streets. With the travel to and from the hospital, it had to cost Kyle at least an hour and a half each day to visit me. I was grateful that he visited, but I knew it made his life tougher, especially with a wife and daughter at home.

"Hey, I'm just looking to keep my visit average up. I'm not going to be able to stop in during your next session, so I need to load up now."

"Well, thanks," I said. "It's good to have you stop by, and thanks for the pizza." I opened up the box and pulled out a slice. "You want one?"

"No thanks. I had one when I was down in the pizza place." I took a bite of the pizza. I have had better pizza, but even mediocre New York pizza was better than 95% of pizza elsewhere. The pizza Kyle brought was better than mediocre. As I ate the slice, Kyle and I watched the movie, as King Arthur dealt the Black Knight his "flesh wound."

As we sat there, my mind drifted to what Jim had said a week before at Peter Luger's. I decided to see what Kyle thought of the subject. "Kyle, most of the partners in the litigation department are married, right?"

"Yeah," he said, with a puzzled look on his face. "A couple of them, like Lauren Kaspar, are divorced, but the rest are married I think."

"Do you know if any of them met their spouses while they were working at the firm?"

"That's a weird question. Why do you ask?"

I described the dinner conversation that I had had with Jack, Barry and Rich. When I finished, I asked him, "So what do you think?"

"Well, I suppose that probably most of the people who have made partner fit that pattern." Kyle sat back in his chair. "The life isn't easy, no matter what position you're in. It's tough for Rachel and I. It bothers us that we don't spend more time together and with Megan."

"But," he continued, "it's probably easier for us because we met and got married before we started at our firms. We were able to grow together before we started the firm life. We knew what our lives would be like, and we love what we do. Now, I don't think that means that you can't start something with someone and make partner at Garrick. I think it's possible to do both. Tough but possible. Are you thinking you can't?"

"I don't know," I said, shaking my head. "All along, I've been thinking that I could, but, after what Jim said, I'm not sure."

"Don't worry about it now," Kyle advised. "You've got enough on your plate."

"Yeah, I guess you're right," I said, with more assurance than what I felt. I took another bite of the pizza.

"So, what time are you getting out on Saturday?" Kyle asked.

"Mmmf …," I muttered, with the pizza in my mouth. I quickly swallowed the bite. "Uh, probably around 10:30 in the morning. The last I.V. bag should be done by that time. Why?"

"Because I'm going to pick you up and take you home that day, and stick around for a while."

"As much as I appreciate it, Kyle, that's not necessary. I'll able to catch a cab home by myself."

"Maybe, maybe not. Either way, it's better for you have someone around to make sure you're okay. Plus, you're going to need help carrying home some of the gifts people brought you." He gestured toward the Daredevil statue, the *Buffy the Vampire Slayer* book and a plant that a female colleague from Garrick brought.

"What about trial prep?"

"The team has the weekend off."

"You should be spending that time with Rachel and Megan."

"I will. I'll spend about three or four hours with you, and they'll have me for the rest of the weekend. Now, enough debate; I'm helping you out. Alright?"

"Alright. Thanks Kyle."

"You're welcome." He looked down at his watch and sighed again. "Well, if I want to take the weekend off, I need to get back to work. I spoke to some others, like Wayne and Hal, and they'll be by in a little bit." Wayne Clark and Hal Allen were colleagues of ours in the Garrick litigation department. "Is there anything I can get you before I go?"

"Nah, I think I'm set." I looked down at the pizza box, and realized that I had eaten both slices. I was a little nauseous, but it did not feel like the pizza would come back up. "Thanks for the pizza, Kyle."

"No problem. I'll see you tomorrow."

"See you."

I watched as Kyle left and turned back to the TV to see Arthur and his knights receive their instructions to seek out the magical Holy Grail. Soon they would be traveling to a castle controlled by the French and another controlled by amorous female nurses and doctors. I smiled for a second thinking of those scenes. I closed my eyes hoping to get a little sleep before my next visitors arrived. Luckily, my chemo brain complied.

CHAPTER ELEVEN

"Crap," I said, as I stared at the three strands of hair lying in my right hand. I was in my office and had just finished reading the plaintiff's brief opposing our motion to dismiss in the National Mutual case. After putting the brief down, I had sat back in my chair, unconsciously running my hand through my hair. Almost immediately, I realized what I was doing, and pulled my hand slowly from my head; too late, though, to stop the damage.

It was Friday August 1st, two weeks after my first chemo session. I had noticed that morning, for the first time, strands of hair lying in the tub drain after my shower. Seeing the strands, I knew that my hair was finally falling out from the chemo, and that it was time to have my head shaved. I figured, though, that if I left my hair alone during the day, I would be safe until Saturday when I could have my barber shave it. The task was tougher than I expected. I had caught myself running my hands through my hair three times before 10:00 a.m.

Other than my falling follicles, I was feeling okay physically. It had taken me three days to recover from my first chemo session, but once those days passed, I felt no different than I had before my session. My life went back to its normal routine, including the long work hours. With the King Industries work, and other tasks, I was working until 11:00 PM on most nights. Unfortunately, with the late nights, I was often unable to wake up early in order to run before work.

Emotionally, I wasn't doing as well. Losing my hair certainly didn't help me, but there were other issues as well. My high school reunion was taking place that night, and as I had predicted to my mother, I had decided to stay in New York rather than to go home and take part in a pity party. Plus, with my planned absences for my chemo treatments, I had decided that I would not take the week off from work as originally planned. I thought that I had made the right decisions, but I was not happy about them.

I hoped that working on our reply to the plaintiffs' brief in the National Mutual case would keep my mind of my troubles. The reply was due on August 15th. Luckily, as Elizabeth told me earlier in the morning, the brief only had to be ten pages long. She also said that Mike wanted to see an outline for the brief by Monday morning, and a draft by the end of day the following Friday, the 8th. Based upon my calculations, that gave me enough time to do the brief. Still, I would only have a little bit of free time until the 15th, my last day of work before the next session.

I shook the hair from my hand. I was about to do a second, more thorough review of the brief when my phone rang. Sarah's number was on the caller ID.

"Jack Ritter," I answered.

"Hey, Jack, it's Sarah." For the first five or six days after I had left the hospital, Sarah, along with Kyle, my parents, and Jesse, had called me every day to find out how I was feeling. The calls had decreased afterwards. Sarah now only called me every other day.

"Hey, Sarah. How are you doing?"

"I'm good. Are you still feeling okay?"

"Yeah," I said. I considered whether to share my hair situation with Sarah. Despite that night in my apartment, I still was hesitant to share things with her, or anyone else for that matter. *Ah, what the hell.* "But I noticed this morning that my hair has started falling out."

"Well that sucks. How are you handling it?"

"Okay, I guess. I knew it was going to happen at some point."

"So what are you going to do?"

"I thought that I would go to my barber tomorrow morning and have him take it all off."

"You mean the Russian who has that barber-slash-shoeshine shop in the 86th street subway station?"

"Hey, don't call him a Russian," I warned. "He's Ukrainian and gets pissed if you call him Russian."

"Whatever," Sarah said, dismissively. "You know, I think I've got a better idea. I could get you an appointment tomorrow with my hairdresser, Jade. What do you think about that?"

I don't need a hairdresser; I'm not going to have any hair to dress. "Sarah …," I started.

"Hear me out," she interrupted. "I've gone to Jade for a long time, and she's great. Anyway, she told me before that she helps chemo patients shave their heads, so she knows how to handle the situation."

"Sarah, all anyone needs to know is how to use some clippers and a razor." I picked up a Nerf basketball from my desk, and threw it against the wall, catching it on the rebound. I threw it back again, and caught it.

"And what if it gets a little emotional? Do you think the Ukrainian is going to know how to handle it?"

She had a good point, but I was never good at conceding points. "Jeez, you cry in front of a girl once and she thinks that you'll cry at the drop of a hat." I said, sarcastically.

"I don't think you're going to break down," Sarah said. "But it's gotta be a tough situation, even for a guy. I think it will be easier with Jade."

"I'm not going to pay 100 bucks or whatever for a hairdresser to shave my head."

"It won't cost you anything. Jade told me that she's does this type of thing for free. All we have to do is give her a tip and that won't be any more than whatever you would pay the Ukrainian."

"I don't know …"

"Alright, I wasn't going to tell you this, but Jade's hot. Plus, she has some big boobs."

She convinced me, but I was not ready to let her know it. "Ah, but the Ukrainian's got a gentle touch and sparkling eyes."

"Jack, you are being annoying," she said, the exasperation clear in her voice. "Wait, does the barber shop have air conditioning? Because it's the middle of August and it's sweltering out there.

I forgot about that. The shop did have air conditioning, but it didn't always work. Even when it did, it didn't cool down the shop enough. "Okay, Sarah. I'll go."

"Great. Now on to the reason I called. Do you have plans for tomorrow night?"

"I was thinking of grabbing drinks with some guys, but there's nothing set in stone."

"Do you want to come to a party in SoHo? Dan and I are going to be there."

I wasn't inclined to go to a party on the first night I was bald, but I fought that feeling. *Fuck cancer.* My bald head was going to be seen sometime, so I might as well do it when alcohol was available. "Wow, so I get to meet the Great Dan." I thought for a second. "Wait, is this going to a third-wheel situation?"

Sarah laughed. "No. A bunch of my friends are going to be there, and it's the first time a lot of them are going to meet him. I'm hoping that you all get along."

I sensed something in Sarah's tone. "This is important to you, isn't it?"

"Yes, it is," Sarah said, seriously. "I really want my friends to like Dan."

"Well, then how can I say no? I'm in."

"That's great," Sarah said, happily. "Thanks so much, Jack."

"You're welcome."

"So, here's the …, uh." Sarah paused for a couple seconds. "Looks like I have a call on the other line. Can we talk this afternoon so we can plan out tomorrow?"

"That's fine. Give me a call when you can." I pulled the phone from my ear, and noticed a few strands of hair on it. I hoped that my hair would make it to the next day.

⇥⇤

Just after lunch on Saturday afternoon, I met Sarah at Bella Femme, her beauty salon, on Second Avenue and 79th street. The salon, like the rest of the City, was pretty empty. It was an August weekend, which meant that many people either were on vacation or were spending the weekend in the Hamptons or at the Jersey Shore. In fact, other than Sarah and I, there were only three customers in the salon. I was the only one with a Y chromosome.

My minority status in the salon increased the apprehension that I was already feeling about shaving my head. I had mixed feelings about my hair. For most of my life, I had not been happy with it. Before college, it had been too straight and thin. In college, it started to get curly, but six months afterwards, my hairline began to recede. Over the years, the receding had continued, albeit slowly. Yet, it was my hair, and even receding hair was better than no hair at all. Sarah had been right; the day was going to be tough.

As I sat with Sarah in the waiting area, I was very quiet, as I usually am when I am moody. Sarah knew me well enough to suffer through my silence, and spent her time reading one of the women's magazines the salon provided. From what I could see, the salon didn't have any men's magazines. After a few minutes, I broke the silence.

"Which one is Jade?" I asked Sarah.

"I don't see her," said Sarah. "Maybe she's finishing her lunch in back."

Just then, I heard the receptionist say my name. "Looks like it's my turn," I said to Sarah, and we stood up and walked to the receptionist desk. "I'm Jack Ritter."

The receptionist, who looked like she was barely out of high school, was a tanned brunette with blonde highlights, and a tight pink dress. "Marisol here will wash your hair for your appointment." She pointed to a middle-aged short Hispanic woman, standing about five feet away.

"Um, I think there may be a mistake," I said. "I'm just here to have my head shaved, and I washed my hair this morning." I had washed it very, *very* gently.

"Everyone, like, has to get their hair washed before a session," said the receptionist, in an attempt at a stern tone. "It's, like, a law, or something."

Cosmetic Law was not offered at NYU, so I could not challenge her claim. I turned to Sarah, who was looking around the room.

"I still don't see Jade," she said. "Looks like you will have to go with her. I'll stay over here for now."

"Alright." I followed Marisol to the back of salon where an empty row of reclining black seats and sinks stood. Marisol pointed to one seat. "Sit here, please," she said, in a heavy Spanish accent.

"Um, be careful when you wash my hair," I said. I wasn't sure how to warn the woman what could happen if she scrubbed too vigorously. While I was forthright about my cancer with the people I knew, I wasn't quite ready to discuss it with every stranger I met. "I'm, uh, having treatments done, so some hair may fall out."

Marisol nodded her head in apparent understanding. I sat down in the chair and she placed a waterproof cape on me, tying it around my neck. She then eased the seat back, lowering my head into the sink. As she turned on the water faucet above my head, I closed my eyes. After a few seconds, she worked her hands through my hair to ensure it was thoroughly drenched.

Suddenly, I felt Marisol yank her hands from my head. "Ayeeh! Mister, mister," said Marisol, pronouncing it "meester." "Your hair, your hair!"

I sat up quickly, causing water to pour down my face, neck and shoulders. I looked back at Marisol, who looked at me and, then, the sink with obvious concern. I looked at what worried her: a large amount of hair was sitting on the bottom of the sink. There was so much hair there, that I wondered how much hair was left on my head.

"Is everything okay?" said a voice from behind me. I turned to see an attractive woman in a hairdresser's smock with curly copper hair that hung to the top of her ample chest. Her eyes were the color of, well, jade. I assumed this was Jade, which meant that either her name was a nickname or her mother was an incredible fortuneteller.

"Yeah, I'm fine," I replied. "Are you Jade?"

"Yes, and you must be Jack." She handed me a towel to dry off my hair. "What happened?"

As I gently dried my hair, I described what had occurred.

"Marisol doesn't speak a lot of English," said Jade, when I finished. "I guess she didn't understand what you were saying." Jade turned to Marisol and spoke some Spanish. Having never studied

Spanish, I only recognized one word: cancer. When she finished, Marisol turned to me with a sympathetic smile, patted my arm, and said "I'm sorry, mister."

"That's okay. It's not your fault," I said, and Marisol left.

"I'm sorry about this," said Jade. "Before my break, I told the receptionist to send you straight to me, but the dumb girl must have forgotten. Are you sure you're okay?"

"Yes. I'm actually more worried about Marisol. She must be freaked out."

"She'll be fine," Jade assured me. "Are you still up for this?"

Given all the hair in the sink, I didn't have a choice. "Sure. I'm all yours."

"Is that a promise?" She said, with a sparkle in her eye and a devilish smile.

I was taken aback by her frankness, and unable to say anything. When I did not answer, she said, with her smile still on her face, "Follow me," and walked towards the hairdressers' stations. As she walked, Jade saw Sarah in the waiting area and motioned to her to join us. Along the way, I noticed one of the customers stealing glances at me, while the other people in the salon either did not notice my head, or had the tact to pretend to do so. When we arrived at Jade's station, she said, "Here's your seat."

When I sat down, I looked at the mirror to survey the damage. Given the amount of hair in the sink, I had expected to see large bald spots scattered across my head. Thankfully, it was not that bad. My hair retained much of the shape and look it had before; it was just much, much thinner. It didn't look good, though. In fact, I looked like a bald man wearing the world's worst toupee.

"Hi, Jade," said Sarah, when she arrived.

"Hey Sarah," replied Jade. She pointed to the hairdresser station next to us. "Go ahead and take the seat there. Crystal's not working today." Sarah put her handbag on the counter and sat down in the chair. You didn't tell me Jack was so good looking."

"I figured it would be a nice surprise," said Sarah, with a wink to me.

"Well, it is," said Jade, as she adjusted my seat to the right height for her. "So, Jack, Sarah's told me that you've been going through chemo. Are you feeling okay?"

"So far, it hasn't been that bad."

"Good." Jade walked back in front of me and leaned back against her work station, putting her cleavage directly in my line of sight. Like the gentleman I was, I only took a quick glance before looking Jade directly in her eyes. "Sarah's probably told you that I've done this before for people. I know how hard this experience can be, so I want you to be as relaxed as possible. And I've always found that nothing relaxes people better than alcohol. How does that sound?"

"It's a little early in the afternoon, but, sure," I said, making a conscious effort to look her in the eyes.

"Good. We keep some in the back for special occasions. What's your poison?"

"What do you have?"

"We have a lot of white wine, but I'm guessing that you are not a white wine kind of guy. I don't think we have any beer, but we have some vodka, gin, whiskey and some mixers."

"I'll take Maker's Mark or a bourbon if you have it. And Diet Coke with it."

"A bourbon guy; nice. I don't usually drink bourbon myself. When I do, I get pretty frisky," she said, her eyes sparkling.

I caught myself looking at her chest, and quickly looked back into her eyes. The smile on her face told me that she knew where my gaze had been. "Well, I guess we can't have that with all these people around," I said.

"I know, right?" she replied, with mock disappointment. "Sarah, how about you?"

"Not me. Usually, I get frisky after drinking tequila," replied Sarah, with her own mischievous smile.

Jade laughed. "I meant, would you like something to drink?"

"Sure; I'll take a Chardonnay."

"Great, I'll be right back." Jade left and I watched her walk towards the back of the salon. Because of the smock she was wearing, I was unable to tell whether her behind was as shapely as her front.

"Maybe you guys should get a private room," said Sarah, interrupting my thoughts. She was still wearing the same smile.

"What?" I said, confused. It took me a second to realize what she had said. "Oh, very funny."

"I told you she was attractive, didn't I?"

"Yes, much better looking than the Ukrainian. Although, I wouldn't have had a problem washing my hair with the Ukrainian."

"What are you talking about?" asked Sarah.

"You didn't see?" When she shook her head, I described the mayhem with Marisol.

"Jeez. Are you okay?"

"Yeah, like I told Jade, I think the hair washer was more freaked out than I was."

At that moment, Jade walked over carrying a glass of wine for Sarah, and a low ball cocktail glass that appeared to have far more whiskey than Diet Coke. She handed us the glasses. "Unfortunately, since I'll be handling some sharp tools, I can't join you with a drink. Here you go."

"Thanks," we said together.

"Jinx," whispered Sarah.

I took a drink from my glass. The stronger-than-usual burning feeling in my throat confirmed that Jade had poured only a small amount of Diet Coke into the drink. I felt some of the tension leave my body.

"Okay," said Jade. "Let's get to work. I'll use the clippers first, and then we'll go to the straight razor." She started by cutting a reverse Mohawk into my hair, and then continued on with the rest of my head. From time to time, she would stop so that my hair would not fall into my bourbon as I took a drink.

As I watched my hair fall onto my shoulders and onto the floor, sadness started to set in. I started breathing in and out slowly, and I felt moisture begin to gather in my eyes. I took another big swallow of the bourbon, hoping the alcohol would somehow cut off the flow of tears. It didn't work as well as I hoped. I tried another tactic, hoping some conversation would take my attention from my head.

"Jade," I said, "How did you get started doing this for cancer patients?"

"With my mom," Jade replied, as she continued to clip my hair. "About three years ago, she was diagnosed with Stage Two breast cancer. She's okay now, but she had to have a mastectomy, and some radiation and chemo treatments. When she was first diagnosed, I felt so useless, you know? Here's the woman who took care of me so many times, and I felt I couldn't care for her. But when her hair started falling out, I knew what I could do. Anyone with clippers and a razor could shave her head, but I knew that, as her daughter, I could make the process easier for her. And I did. Also, I helped her afterwards with her look with make-up and other things so that she felt less self-conscious.

"So that's why I do this for free," she said. "I know I can help, and I know how much people feel when I do. Often it's by shaving someone's head, or helping with a wig. Sometimes it's drawing in their eyebrows, or helping with make-up. Anything I can do, I do."

"Well, I'm glad your mom is okay, and I appreciate you doing this for me." I said, my eyes misty from Jade's story.

"You're welcome," Jade said, as she finished with the clippers. She gently touched my now stubble-covered head. "You're going to look good bald."

As I looked in the mirror, I had to agree. I certainly looked better with hair, but my skull did not have any large bumps or valleys in it. For the most part, it was a perfectly shaped head. I still would have preferred to have had my hair, but the outcome could have been a lot worse.

"Let's shave the stubble off your head and face and we'll be done," Jade said, as she pulled a straight edge razor from a drawer. She then applied a layer of shaving cream to my head. The shaving cream must have had some menthol in it, because I felt the familiar cool sensation on my head. When my head was covered in cream, Jade started shaving. Other than in the pre-op room before the surgery, I had never had a woman shave me, and that was a completely different experience that I barely noticed. I definitely noticed Jade shaving me, and I liked it.

When Jade was done with my head, she wiped off my skull with a towel. Then, she applied some shaving cream to my face. As per my usual weekend routine, I had not shaved that morning. When the blade touched my throat, my shoulders involuntarily tensed up, as I remembered a mobster movie where a wiseguy was killed in a barbershop with a straight blade. Jade probably sensed my tension, because her touch became gentler. At one point, as she was shaving the left side of my face, she tilted my head back to rest against her breasts. My shoulders relaxed, as I started concentrating more on her body's touch than I was the touch of the razor on my jugular. I did feel a different sort of tension, though, below my belt.

Once Jade had finished shaving, she used a towel to wipe off the remaining shaving cream from my face, neck and ears. Next, she applied an after shave gel to my face and head. "So what do you think?" she asked.

I look like Lex Luthor, I thought. I ran my right palm over my head, feeling my skull. It wasn't as smooth as I expected, although I probably should have known better. There was still some stubble on my head, just like the stubble on my face after a shave. "I don't think it's too bad.

"You look good, Jack," said Sarah. "I don't think people will know you're going through chemo when they see you."

At least not right now, I thought. *We'll see how long that lasts.* I looked at Jade. "Am I going to need to shave it again in a week or so?"

"Probably not. The hair you have is still going to fall out. It will probably all be gone in a week."

"Okay," I said. Jade reached down and untied the cape, and then she brushed the remaining hair off of my neck and body. When she was done, I stood up. "Thanks Jade," I said, as I handed her a generous tip. "I really appreciate this."

"No problem," she said. She grabbed a business card from the wall, wrote on the back of it and handed it to me. "Feel free to give me a call, if your hair does come back, and you need it cut. Or if you want to share some bourbon some time." She said the last part with her devilish grin."

"Thanks. I'll think about it."

"Be sure you do," Jade said. She then turned to Sarah. "Sarah, I'll see you in a month or so."

"Sounds good," said Sarah. Sarah and Jade hugged, and then Sarah and I walked out of the salon into the hot August afternoon. The bright sun felt hot on my head. I rubbed my head again, and realized that I would need to put sun block on my head or wear hats in the future.

Sarah put her arm in mine, as we walked north up Second Avenue. "How are you doing?"

"Okay. You were right. It was emotional, but everything in there …." I paused and motioned back towards the salon. "It helped. Thanks."

"Well, I'm sure Jade's attention was a big help," she teased. "In fact, she was helping so much that for a second I was worried you wouldn't be able to stand up after the shave." She glanced at my lower body to emphasize her point.

"Ha ha," I said. She was right, though. It had been a close call.

"So are you going to call her?"

"Nah," I said, shaking my head. "She was probably just doing some sympathy flirting or trying to take my mind off my hair." I rubbed my head again. "And even if she wasn't, it's just not a good time."

"Jack, it's been a tough day, so I'll only say this once, and let it go. Her flirting was real, and I think you're making a mistake. You should call her and go drink bourbon together and just have fun. She knows you have cancer and still wants to go out with you. You should do it."

She doesn't know the type of cancer though, does she? "Sarah .."

"I've said my piece, she said, as she raised her hands. "Are you still coming to the party tonight?"

"Do you think I'm going to miss the chance to meet the re-nowned Dan Harper?" I asked with a smile. "I need to find out if the legends are true."

"Ha ha. Do you promise to have fun?"

"I will do my best," I said, and I meant it.

"You better," Sarah said. She took a look around to see where we were. "I need to get a manicure at the Korean place on 82nd. I'll see you in SoHo around eight. You have the address, right?

"I do. And thanks again Sarah." We hugged briefly, and I gave her a brotherly peck on the cheek.

"You're welcome. See you later." She crossed the street going west, and I turned to walk east, feeling the stubble on my head as I went.

⚔︎

According to my alarm clock, I arrived home from the party at 12:45 a.m. I was a bit drunk, and fumbled a bit as I undressed in front of my dresser in my bedroom.

The night had been a little uncomfortable, but all in all, fun. One of Sarah's college friends threw the party in her apartment in SoHo. About twenty people had attended, and I knew almost half of them. I was more than a little self-conscious about my head. Of the people I knew, most of them knew I had cancer, and had been kind. A couple people had not known, including one of Sarah's girlfriends, Emily. Emily had asked me "why in the world, would you ever shave your head?" I told her that I was going through chemo, which made things even more awkward.

Meeting Dan was also a little awkward. He knew that Sarah and I had a history, but clearly not the full extent of it. Like a gentlemen, I didn't reveal that information. The awkwardness didn't last long, though, thanks in part to the copious amounts of alcohol we both drank, and the fact that Dan was a bit of a sci-fi geek, although not as big of one as me. We spent most of the night talking about *The X-Files, Star Trek, Firefly* and other shows. From time to time, he would turn to look at Sarah, and I could tell that he had fallen for her. *Good for her,* I thought, as I stripped off my clothes in my room, *he's a good guy.*

When I finished, I looked at Jade's business card, which lay on top of my dresser. I thought about her bright green eyes, and the way she felt when she touched me. Lying next to it was the bar napkin with Emma's phone number. *Emma, with the ocean blue eyes.* For probably the hundredth time in the two months since she had given me the number, I toyed with the idea of calling her in the morning. *Or should I call Jade?*

With a sigh, I fell into bed. I reached up to feel the stubble on my head. It had been a long day. I would be busy the next day as I worked on the National Mutual outline. I could call Emma or Jade, or both, but between work and my treatments, I simply did not have enough time to spend with either of them. But, as I lay there, I dreamt about what would happen if I did, blue and green eyes dancing in my mind.

CHAPTER TWELVE

I spat into the toilet, trying to rid my mouth of the bile in it. A minute earlier, I had been lying in my hospital bed, watching *Airplane* on the television, when I had felt the need to empty my stomach. I had hurried to the bathroom, pulling my IV pole with me, and had dropped to my knees in front of the toilet just before the retching began. Unfortunately, it was mostly a dry heave. Only a small amount of bile came up. On the positive side, though, the overwhelming urge to vomit had passed, at least temporarily. It was the third time I had rushed to the bathroom that day.

I stared into the toilet bowl, and at the yellowish brown gall floating in the water. I spat one more time. Once I was satisfied that all of the bile in my mouth was gone, I stood up and flushed the toilet. Grabbing my toothbrush and toothpaste, I started brushing the awful taste from my mouth.

It was the middle of the afternoon on Wednesday, August 21st. I had been in the hospital for my second chemo session since Monday morning, and I felt twice as bad as I had during my first treatment. The nausea had started the night before, and was much stronger than my first visit. In fact, all of my symptoms were stronger. I was completely exhausted, and just wanted to nap all day, but my chemo brain kept me from falling asleep. I also was suffering from constipation. The nurses had given me a couple of suppositories to use if the constipation became too much to bear. I did not look forward to inserting the suppositories, so I was hoping that the constipation would work itself out.

"Hello?" I heard a man's voice outside the door to the bathroom.

"Just give me a minute," I said, and rinsed the toothpaste out of my mouth with water. I quickly washed my hands, feeling the hardened veins on my left hand and arm. After I straightened out my blue Captain America t-shirt and black basketball shorts, I walked out of the bathroom.

Jim O'Dare was standing next to my bed, a rollaway litigation bag next to him. He was wearing a Navy blue suit, white business shirt with cufflinks and a light blue tie. He was smiling, but I saw the smile waver a bit when he saw me. "Dude," he said. "You look like you've been hit by a bus. You okay?"

"Yeah," I replied with a small smile, "it was only a small bus." Not too long after I started telling people that I had cancer, I had realized that people interpreted my humor as a sign that I was handling everything well. After that, I made an effort to be humorous around people, regardless of how I was feeling. I shuffled over to him, pulling the IV pole with my left hand.

"You need any help?" he asked, with his hand stretched out to me.

"Nah," I replied, shaking his hand with my own. "I'm good. Take a seat." I motioned to the chair on the right side of the bed, and walked around to the other side, and lay down on it. "What are you doing here in the middle of the day?"

"We had a hearing in front of Judge McKenna down at 500 Pearl Street," Jim said, referring to the federal courthouse downtown. He took off his suit coat, and sat down in the chair next to the bed. "I was on my way back to the office, and I thought I would stop by for a visit.

"Well, thanks." To my surprise, my friends continued to visit me frequently during my second session. At least one new visitor came every night.

Jim pointed to my head. "Your bald look doesn't look that bad."

"Yeah, but it's still weird. I'm constantly touching it. I can't believe there's no hair or stubble there." I rubbed my head with my right hand to demonstrate. "I mean, it's completely smooth. And it's not just my head; all my facial hair is gone, too."

"Really?" asked Jim, surprised. "So you don't shave anymore?"

"I haven't shaved in a week." That development had been a big surprise. One morning, before work, I had looked at myself in the mirror and was shocked by the change in my face. There was no stubble whatsoever on my face. It was pale and untouched like a child's face. The feel of it was shocking, too. I had had stubble on my face for so long that I had forgotten what a smooth hairless face felt like.

"Wow. That must be weird. But you still have your eyebrows."

"Yeah. I think they're a little thinner, but they are still there. I'm hoping that I don't lose them altogether."

"How have you been feeling?" He asked, with a concerned look on his face.

"Eh. Today, I feel like one of those passengers who had the fish." I pointed to the TV screen, where Julie Hagerty was trying to inflate the autopilot.

"You should've had the steak," said Jim.

"Actually, I had the lasagna," I replied, paraphrasing Leslie Nielsen's joke from the movie. Jim chuckled. "Mainly, though, I'm tired."

"I can go if you want …"

I interrupted him. "No, it's fine. I can't sleep anyway, so feel free to stay as long as you would like. Anyway, I just have a few more days left and within a week, I'll be back to normal."

"I hope so," said Jim. "Then it's back to work. At least you'll get one last slow week of August."

For lawyers, the month of August is usually much slower paced than the other months of the year. A number of people are on vacation, especially judges, who generally are loathe to schedule hearings or trials during that time. Unfortunately for Kyle, the judge on his case was not one of those judges. Hence, he was in Boston in August for the Qualtech trial. "I wish. I was busy for the first two weeks. I had to draft a ten page reply brief that we filed just before I came in here. Then I had another matter where we had to get some document requests out." I stopped to think about how crazy that week had been. "But forget about work, how was your vacation? Didn't you and Donna go to California?"

"Yeah, we did, for two weeks. It was great. We started in San Fran, spending some time in the wine country. Then we drove south down Highway One, stopping off at Pebble Beach to play a round of golf. After that, we drove to Los Angeles and spent some time there."

"Wow. That sounds like a great trip," I said. I had never been to California, or, for that matter, anywhere west of Minnesota. My impressions of California were based solely on television and movies.

"It was," Jim said. "And we both needed the vacation."

"So things are getting pretty serious," I said. I felt a sudden lurch in my stomach. Luckily, it wasn't strong enough to make me run for the bathroom.

"Yeah, they are. We've had all the serious talks too, you know? Like how many kids we want to have, or what their names would be, or where we would live if we got married."

"So are you, you know, going to marry her?"

"Yeah, dude, I am," said Jim with his familiar big smile. "I decided on the trip. We were driving down Highway One in this convertible we rented, and we were talking and laughing, and I couldn't stop thinking about how great the vacation was going.

Then I started thinking about where we should go on our next vacation, and then the one after that. That's when it hit me. I wanted to be with her, and do things with her for the rest of my life. You know what I mean?"

Unfortunately, I didn't. I had never felt that way about a girl before. I had been in love with two women before: my high school girlfriend, Kara, and Sarah. Although I had loved both, my relationships with them ended before they became that serious.

To cover my ignorance, I mocked Jim. "It sounds like you're whipped," I said, with a smirk.

"Fuck you," he said, with a laugh. "I'm happy. You know, that's the other thing that hit me on the trip: how happy I am, and have been ever since I started seeing her."

"You didn't know that you had been happy?" I asked.

"Not really," he replied. "I mean, I felt it, but I never really acknowledged it, you know? It's like, if you had asked me before the trip, I would have said that seeing Donna hadn't changed anything, really. But when I really thought about it, I realized that I'm probably happier than I have ever been in my life. Haven't you ever had that happen to you?"

I thought a little bit and realized that I had during a two month period in the winter of my sophomore year in high school. Only I wasn't happy; I was depressed. I was doing well academically, but other things had been weighing me down. Kara had dumped me, although we would be back together a year later. Of course, teenagers think that getting dumped is the worst thing that will ever happen to them. On top of that, I was playing junior varsity basketball, and playing poorly. In the past, my poor performance wouldn't have bothered me, but, after a surprisingly successful season of varsity football, I thought I would do better in all sports. When I didn't, it ate at me, in a way it never had before.

At the time, I probably would have said that things weren't great, but I didn't know how bad I felt until one night in January.

That night, the JV team suffered a tough loss and I had turned over the ball more times that I cared to count. I had come home, after a friend had dropped me off, to find Mom sitting in a chair in our family room, tears in her eyes.

"What's wrong, Mom?" I asked, suddenly concerned.

"That's what I was going to ask you," she said. "Jack, why are you so depressed?"

I had replied with what I thought was a small white lie, saying I was fine. I did not realize how big a lie it was until she told me that everyone had been worrying about me. She had spoken to my sister and father, my teachers and coaches, and all of them had noticed that I had been moody, and distant for weeks. I had not been smiling nor had I been my usual self. Mom told me that she was worried that I was thinking about suicide. My first thought was that she was being overly dramatic, and then I remembered that the year, before a junior at our school had hanged himself. Mom then asked me again, why I was so depressed.

At that moment, I had realized that she was right; I had been depressed. I was not suicidal, though, so I quickly dispelled that idea. However, I was feeling worse than I had ever felt before. After that, slowly, and hesitantly, I told her what had been wrong. We talked for a while that night, in a way that we never had before.

After my talk with Mom, things got a little better, day by day. I played basketball a little better, and my failures weren't as important as they were before. I thought about Kara less each day, and when I saw her at school, it hurt less each time. In the end, recognizing I was unhappy helped me to deal with the unhappiness.

Remembering that winter, I said to Jim, "Yeah, that's happened to me. Sorry, I was just being a wiseass." I suddenly felt bad about the whipped comment as well. "I'm happy about you and Donna. Have you thought about when you are going to propose?"

"I think I'll do it in December. Her birthday is December 8th, and that's right around the time we started dating. I've got some money saved from the last bonus, so all I need to do is buy a ring."

"That's great, Jim," I said.

"Yeah," he said, "it surely is." He looked down at his watch. "Shit, it's already 3:30."

"Do you need to get back to the office?"

"Yeah, I should get going, and it feels like I just got here. Is there anything I can get you before I leave?"

"Nah, I'm good. Thanks for coming," I said.

"No problem." Jim stood up, picked up his coat, and put it on. "If you need anything or want the company, just let me know, okay?"

"I will."

"And when you get out, and feel better, give me a call. I'd like you to have dinner with Donna and me some night."

"Sounds good. I'll see you." We shook hands before Jim grabbed his litigation bag and walked out the door. *That's another one down*, I thought with a sigh. I was happy for Jim, but was feeling sorry for myself. Other than Sarah, Jim was the last single friend I had left. He was going to get engaged, and from the way that I had seen Dan look at Sarah at the party, Sarah was not far behind Jim. I, on the other hand, was far, far behind.

My self-pity was suddenly interrupted by the overwhelming urge to vomit. I quickly, but carefully, stood up and headed for the bathroom, hoping for more than another dry heave.

⚊⋅⊹⋅⚊

"Are you feeling any better today?" asked Mom, her concern, as always, evident on the other end of the telephone.

"Yeah, a little bit better. The nausea is not as bad as it was yesterday," I responded.

It was Thursday afternoon, and before Mom's call, I had been in my bed, lightly napping, listening to *The Beatle's Greatest Hits*. It had taken some time to settle my mind down enough so that I could fall asleep. Unfortunately, I had only been asleep for about fifteen minutes when the phone rang, interrupting my sleep and *Eleanor Rigby*.

"Good," Mom said. "Are you eating anything?"

"I had most of the breakfast, but only a little bit of lunch. My stomach is feeling a little better, but my appetite is still pretty low."

"Are you getting any sleep?"

"I had a nap before you called," I replied.

"I didn't wake you, did I?" Guilt mingled with the concern in her voice.

"No," I lied. On our calls, Mom often said that she felt guilty that I, her only son, was in a hospital a thousand miles away alone. I did what I could to lessen her guilt. "I was up for a little bit."

"Okay, but if you need to sleep, I can call back later."

"Nah, I'm good. What's going on there?"

"Not much. Your dad's running errands and I'm minding the store. But there aren't any customers, so I thought I would call early today."

"That's fine."

"Have you had any visitors today?"

"No, but I think Rachel's going to be coming in a little while."

"That's good." There were a couple moments of silence before she began speaking again. "So I think I should come out for your last chemo session."

"Mom, we've talked about this …,"

"You should have some family around you when you are in the hospital," she interrupted, her voice cracking. "I feel like a horrible mother sitting here while my only son is laid up a thousand miles away."

"Mom, you're not a horrible mother." I reassured her. "Tickets are expensive, and it's not like I'm seven years old and alone. I'm 28 years old. And there's not much you can do here anyway. You would just end up sitting here bored. And I have people here to keep me company."

At that moment, I heard a knock at the door and saw Rachel there. She was wearing a black suit coat with a matching skirt, and a red blouse. She was holding an expensive leather portfolio bag that Kyle had given her for her birthday. I waved to her to come in, which she did, walking over and sitting in the chair next to my bed.

"I know you have some good friends," Mom replied. "I thank God every day that you've made such good friends, but they are only there for a little bit each day. You should have someone there for the whole day every day."

"Mom, you know me. I prefer to be alone most of the time." A thought occurred to me. "Listen, Rachel just arrived. Why don't you call me tonight around seven, your time? I'll think more about you coming out, and we can talk about it then."

"Do you promise?" she asked, hopefully.

"Yes, I do."

"Okay, I will call you then. Say hi to Rachel for me, and thank her for being such a good friend."

"I will, Mom. Goodbye."

"Bye."

I hung up the phone and turned to Rachel. "My Mom says hi, and wanted me to thank you for helping me out."

"When you talk to her tonight, tell her she's welcome. I take it from the phone call that she wants to fly out here?

"Yep, that pretty much sums it up."

"Why doesn't she fly out then?"

"The tickets are pretty expensive, and money's a little tight for my parents this year."

"You can afford to help her out, can't you?"

"Easily, but I don't think she should come out."

"What?" Rachel asked, her eyebrows raised in disbelief. "Why not?"

"Because I know how hard it would be on her. She'd see me, like this," I motioned to my head, and then to the IV in my arm, "and it would hurt her. And she would just be sitting around here all day, unable to do anything. I don't want to do that to her."

"Don't you think, that being at home and imagining what you are going through, and not even being here with you would be worse for her? At least here, she would know how bad it is, and would know that she's doing something, even if it's keeping you company."

I thought about Rachel's points before responding. They made sense, but I thought there were other factors involved. "I guess, but at least she's got my dad and friends at home to help her. Here, she'd be by herself. She would have to get around the City and stay at my apartment by herself."

"You don't think that she's thought about that?"

"I guess. I don't know."

"And what about you? Don't you think having her here would help you? I mean, I know you have visitors at night, but aren't you lonely all by yourself during the day?"

That was a question I had not thought about it. "Maybe. I don't know. It's not that big a deal."

Rachel raised her right eyebrow, and then she looked over at the window, obviously lost in thought. A few seconds later, she broke her silence. "Okay, that's up to you to decide, but I think you should change your mind. I think your mom being here would help you more than you know. I can tell just by looking at you that the chemo is doing a number on you, and this is only the second session. And I don't believe for a second that you're not really lonely. Just promise me that you'll think about it, okay?"

"Okay, I promise." I meant it, too. I would think about it, but, sitting there, I already knew that my decision was not going to change. "So how are you and Megan doing, with Kyle in Boston? It's been two weeks right?"

"Yeah, and unless they settle at some point soon, it could be another month. So far, it's not so bad. The way you guys work, we usually don't see much of Kyle during the week anyway, and we have the nanny and both of our parents to help out. It's the weekends that are tough. That's why Meg and I are going to take a trip up there Friday night to be with him this weekend."

"How's he doing?"

"I think he's enjoying the work, and it sounds like it's going pretty well. The other side is still putting on their case, but it sounds like his team did a good job of cross examination on a couple of their witnesses. Kyle's getting tired, though. They get up early each day, work all day, and then work late each night, preparing for the next day. I think the fun is going to wear off soon."

"Well, when you talk to him, tell him good luck for me."

"I will. He wanted me to say hi too, and that you should keep your strength up."

"I'm doing my best."

"Are you hungry? I think I need a slice or something."

"Why don't you go home to Meg and eat with her? You don't need to stick around."

"Naw, it would be nice to have some adult, non-work conversation tonight. I've been hanging out with Meg, and Meg alone, for the last three nights. You may not get lonely without adult company, but I do. Plus, my parents are watching her now."

"Okay, well, I guess I could eat a little bit. I had a decent breakfast, but I haven't eaten much since."

"Should I get some slices?"

"Not pizza. I'm not sure how my stomach will handle the grease. There's an Ess-a-Bagel near the pizza place. Maybe a toasted bagel with some strawberry jelly. I can pick at it tonight."

"Okay. I'll be right back." Rachel stood up from the chair, leaving her bag behind. After she left, I carefully stood up from the bed. I had been lying down for a couple of hours, and needed to stretch my legs. I walked to bathroom sink and turned the cold water handle on the faucet. I splashed some water on my face, and looked in the mirror.

Rachel's question suddenly popped in my head. *Aren't you lonely all by yourself?*

Staring at myself, I didn't know the answer.

When I think back to my chemotherapy sessions, I remember that the worst moments weren't during the time I spent in the hospital, with drugs pumping into me. No, the worst moments were those spent at home in my apartment, recovering from my chemotherapy treatments.

The first recovery period wasn't that bad, but the others were. Early on during the second period, I knew something was different. I had left the hospital Saturday morning feeling exhausted and nauseous. Sarah rode back with me in a taxi, and when we arrived back at my apartment, I told her that I was tired and needed a nap. After she left, I went to bed, and lay there for about an hour, unable to sleep. My mind was a jumble of non-stop thoughts, fueled by my chemo brain and the cabin fever that I felt after spending five straight days in the hospital. I tried to calm my mind, visualizing things in the past that had soothed me: the New York skyline, the sound of rain on my parent's roof at night when I was a kid, the feel of a woman in my arms. None of it worked. I would achieve a moment or two of serenity, and sleep would seem in reach. But then the thoughts would return, churning my mind, keeping me awake.

After an hour, I realized that sleep was hopeless. I thought about watching some television, but I suddenly wanted to be out of my apartment. After getting dressed and grabbing my iPod, I left my apartment and walked around the Upper East Side for a while, hoping that the sights and sounds of Manhattan would help. I listened to some music, and again, for a little while, it seemed to work. After about thirty minutes though, I grew tired, and needed to rest. I continued to walk as I explored my options.

I refused to return to my apartment, and I wasn't hungry, so lunch was out of the question. I thought about spending some time at the Barnes and Noble store on 86th street, but, then I passed the movie theater on 3rd Avenue, and saw that the movie *Underworld* was playing. The next available showing was in twenty minutes. Figuring that the movie would be a good way to kill two hours, I bought a ticket.

The movie wasn't great, but it wasn't all that bad either. At least, that was my impression of the first half of the movie. About thirty minutes after the film started, I was watching Kate Beckinsdale doing some very athletic fighting moves, which, given her skin-tight outfit, should have been impossible. My focus on the supernatural aspects of her clothing was soon interrupted by a feeling of overstimulation, as if I had drunk a combination of Red Bull, Mountain Dew and espresso. I started to fidget in my seat, crossing my legs one way, and then uncrossing them, and re-crossing them another way. I moved my arms and hands from lying on the armrests to crossing them to putting my hands in my lap and then putting them on the armrests again. I spent the next twenty minutes that way, and lost track of the movie. At that point, I decided that I could not sit there any further and left the theater.

Tired, anxious and frustrated, I went back to my apartment. Once there, I went from one activity to the next. I brought some dirty clothes down to the laundry machines in the basement, and then started to play *Halo* on the Xbox. My restlessness didn't stop, and fifteen minutes later, I was cleaning my room. Fifteen minutes after that, I tried watching TV, and then, when I couldn't stand that any longer, I walked down to the basement and put my laundry in the dryer. After that, I tried again to nap, but fifteen minutes later, I was pacing my apartment, walking from one side to the other, back and forth, until I decided to clean my bathroom.

The rest of my day followed that same pattern, as I went from one activity to the next, my restlessness acting like an ocean tide. With each new activity, the nervousness would ebb for a short time before it would rise again, washing out any peace that I had achieved. Eventually, around seven o'clock that night, after I had eaten a couple bites of penne ala vodka from a nearby pizza place, I lay down. My exhaustion overcame my restlessness, and I fell asleep.

When I woke up late Sunday morning, I did not feel that much better. I was still tired, and my appetite had not returned. My chemo brain was still active, and I spent Sunday in much the same way that I had spent Saturday. I spoke to some friends and family on the phone to help break up the day, but most of it was spent pacing from one activity to the next, feeling anxious, depressed and tired.

Despite all of that, the worst part of the weekend was Rachel's question, which my mind asked over and over. *Aren't you lonely all by yourself?* The question in my mind made the chemo-induced ADD that I was experiencing ever more unbearable. At first, I couldn't answer the question, but as it repeated in my mind, I couldn't deny the truth any longer. Just like Jim, I hadn't realized what I had been feeling until I faced the truth. I was feeling lonely; very, very lonely in fact.

What depressed me even more was that I realized that I had been feeling lonely for quite a long time, long before Sarah found the lump.

CHAPTER THIRTEEN

"**F**uck," I muttered, as I stared at the letter that I had drafted the night before. The draft was a response to a letter written by our opposing counsel in the King Industries case. In their letter, which was sent to the judge and our firm, counsel accused our firm of misrepresenting certain facts in our discovery responses, and requested that the judge impose penalties against us. My draft disputed that we made any misrepresentations, and accused counsel of their own misrepresentations. When I emailed the draft to Lauren Kaspar late the previous night, I knew that it was not the best thing I had ever written, but I thought that it was still good.

I was disabused of that notion when I saw the letter in my inbox at 4:30 the next day. Laura's comments, in red ink, covered the letter to the point where it had become the punch line to the question "what's black and white and red all over." She had crossed out words and, in some cases, whole sentences. She had written question marks next to the points that were not clear, of which there were, apparently, many. She also pointed out several facts and arguments that I had forgotten. After one review, it was clear that, while the letter was not the worst thing I had ever written, it certainly was the worst thing I had written in quite some time. It also was clear that I would be working late again, revising the letter.

"Fuck," I said again, and sat back in my chair, as the acoustic version of Colin Hay's *Overkill* played through my office speakers. It was September 10th, and in the last month, I had experienced many late nights, all by choice. After realizing that I had been feeling lonely for years, I had reached the conclusion that I needed to surround myself with people as much as possible. Every Saturday night, I was out with friends, often as a third wheel to Jim and Donna or Sarah and Dan. Throughout it all, I was out late, never arriving home until after midnight.

The rest of the nights of the week were spent in the office. Being at work meant doing more work, but it also meant being around people more often. Rather than working from home after eight p.m. each night, I would stay in the office to work, taking breaks here and there to chat with people. I wasn't able to hang out with Kyle, because he was still in Boston on trial. However, I spent a lot of time with other colleagues, like Wayne and Hal, eating lunch or dinner with them as often as I could. I did anything I could to make sure I was not alone, especially alone in my apartment.

By September 10th, though, I was exhausted. I did not know how much of my exhaustion was an after effect of the chemotherapy treatments, but I knew that, even without the chemotherapy, I still would have been tired. There had been too many late nights, and not enough sleep, for me to feel otherwise. Because of that exhaustion, I was making mistakes. The letter was not the first time in the previous three weeks that I had delivered a bad work product.

The end result was that I was miserable, probably even more than I had been three weeks before. It wasn't just the loneliness, the exhaustion or the mistakes. I was also freaked out because, in four days, I would be back in the hospital for my third round of chemotherapy. I dreaded that more than anything else, because I knew that round would be worse than the other two. I would be more tired, more nauseous, and more constipated than I had been before. I feared the three days after the treatment the most when my chemo brain ADD would kick in.

"FUCK!" I said, this time louder.

There was a knock at my door. Elizabeth was standing there, with a concerned look on her face. "Is something wrong?" she asked.

I shook my head. "Sorry, just letting off some steam," I said, pushing down the misery and putting up a façade of wellbeing. *I need to be stronger than this.* "I made some mistakes on this letter for Lauren Kaspar, and I'm not happy about it. Come on in."

"Are you sure? I can just email you …," Elizabeth said.

"No, I'm good." I turned off the mussic, and put the King letter to the side of my desk.

"Okay," she said and walked into my office and over to the chair in front of my desk. "We just got word from Judge Metron's clerk that he's scheduled an oral argument on our motion to dismiss for October 21st at 2 p.m." Judge Metron was the judge in the National Mutual case. "Mike wanted me to check with you to see if you would be in treatment that day."

"I think that's my last session, but let me check," I said. I accessed the calendar on my laptop. "Yep, I'm in the hospital all that week."

"Crap," Elizabeth said. "Listen, you did the lion's share of work on both of our briefs, and Mike and I thought it was important that you're there to watch the argument. I'm not sure if we can, but if you want, we can see if we can postpone it for a week."

I thought about her offer for a couple of seconds. It was a nice, and, at any other time, I would want to be at the hearing. However, at that moment, my interest in my work was at an all-time low, and I really didn't care whether I was there or not. "Thanks for the offer, Elizabeth, but that's okay. I don't need to be there. I should be able to help you guys prepare the week before though."

"Well, if you're okay with it, we'll go as is. It may not be that big a deal anyway. Metron may only hear the arguments and reserve a ruling for later."

"Well, if we win that day, you'll need to come by the hospital and we'll celebrate."

"Will do," she said, as she stood up from the chair. "By the way, if I don't see you tomorrow, good luck with your session next week."

"Thanks, Elizabeth. See you later." Elizabeth walked out of my office, and I turned the music on. I wasn't ready to start work on the King draft yet, so I opened up the internet browser on my laptop, and went to yahoo.com to check on the news. There were a number of articles about the anniversary of 9/11 and the ongoing terrorism threat from al-Quaeda. There was also an article about the debate held the night before between the nine Democratic candidates for President in the 2004 election.

In the local news section, I noticed a link that stated "Sportscaster Sean Kimerling Dies at 37." Having watched Kimerling often on the WB11 news, I curiously clicked on the link. The article that came up was a short one, stating that Kimerling "died Tuesday of complications from testicular cancer. He was 37." I stopped reading, and tears started to well up in my eyes. *That's not supposed to happen anymore*, I thought. *Doctor Cross said that testicular cancer was the best type of cancer you could get.* I read some more of the article, trying to find some more information about his death. The only other details in the article were facts about his life and career. I started to surf the net frantically, searching for more information, but I was unable to find anything more than what the Yahoo article had posted.

Tears were pouring down my face, and my chest felt tight under my shirt. I didn't know Sean Kimerling personally, but having seen him on TV, and knowing he had testicular cancer like I did was too much for me. I started to take short, deep breaths and I felt the walls of my office closing in on me. I suddenly stood up from my desk and started pacing.

Just then, my phone rang. Without looking at the caller ID, I pressed the speakerphone button. "Hello," I answered, forgetting to announce myself as I usually do.

"Hey Jack, it's Sarah," Sarah's response was a little uncertain, probably because of the way I answered. "How are you doing?"

"I'm not good, Sarah," I said. I wiped my eyes. "I …, uh, I don't know what to do?"

"Jack, what's wrong?" Sarah asked, worried.

I sat down in my chair, and took a deep breath. "I just read a story about this sportscaster on Channel 11, Sean Kimerling. It says he just died of testicular cancer." My tears resumed as I said the words.

"Oh my God, Jack. What did the story say?"

"Not much. Just that he was 37, he had testicular cancer and he died from complications, I guess from treatment."

"That's horrible," Sarah answered. "How can I help you?"

I suddenly stood up from my seat. I knew what I had to do. "Sarah, I have to get out of here. I need walk to around, and process this."

"I'm leaving work now. Let me meet you. I'll walk you home."

"Alright. I'll be waiting outside on 57th street."

"I'll be there in ten minutes. Bye."

I packed up my work quickly, but had enough foresight to slip the King letter and my research into the laptop bag at the last second. I wasn't sure how I would do it, but I knew that I needed to finish the letter before the next morning. I'd have to work on it at home at some point. Once I was finished packing, I quickly left my office.

⇒⊰⊱⇐

When Sarah found me ten minutes later, I was pacing the sidewalk in front of my building. It was a very warm September night. The sidewalk was filled with people leaving work for the evening, which made my pacing a little difficult. I wasn't crying, but from the looks of people on the sidewalk, my agitation was clearly visible.

Suddenly, I spotted Sarah walking briskly through the crowd, dressed in a sleeveless black work dress and her white New Balance sneakers. Her face held a concerned look that grew in intensity when she saw me. She walked over to me, and gave me a hug, saying "Oh Jack." We held each other for a second, and then we separated.

"Why don't we walk through Central Park?" Sarah asked. "We have about an hour before it gets dark, and we can talk better there."

"Alright," I said, and we started to walk to the park.

We walked in silence for a while, threading our way through the throngs of people on the sidewalk. As we turned north onto Sixth Avenue, Sarah told me, "Tell me how you are doing."

"I'm a mess, Sarah, that's how I'm doing." The words came out of my mouth like water bursting through a crack in a dam. "There's just so much different shit going on in my head right now. I've been mess for a while, but I felt like I could handle everything, you know, but I was *just* hanging on, just barely. Then I hear about this sportscaster, and I simply … can't … deal anymore."

A thought abruptly popped into my head. *Am I having a breakdown? Is this what a breakdown feels like?"*

"Jack, it's going to be okay, we just need to talk about it," Sarah said, calmly. We crossed 58th Street, and entered Central Park. The Park was less crowded than the rest of the City, though a fair number of people were making their way through the Park. "When you saw the article this afternoon, what's the first thing you felt?"

I thought for a second. "Fear, and then sadness."

"So why were you afraid?"

"Isn't it obvious?" I said, angered that she would ask such a stupid, insensitive question.

"Yes, it is," she said, gently. "But, you need to say it out aloud to someone. You said that you've been miserable, but this is the first time I've heard it. I'm betting that no one else has heard it either, which, by the way, you and I are going to talk about later." As she admonished me, a little anger slipped into her tone and her eyes.

"You've been bottling your feelings in, Jack, not sharing them with anyone." Her eyes and tone became gentle again. "That changes now. I'm here to listen to you, so, please, tell me why are you afraid."

Feeling the sting of her rebuke, I released my own anger. "Alright, I'm sorry." I took in a deep breath and then let it out. "I'm afraid that what happened to Kimerling is going to happen to me. Today's the first time that it's really hit me that the cancer could kill me."

"You didn't realize that before?"

"Not really," I said, looking at the sidewalk ahead of me as we walked. "I mean when I first found the tumor, I thought that it could happen, but I didn't really believe it could." As we spoke, we kept walking northeast through the park, choosing pathways where no one else would walk by us, and hear our conversation. "I mean, the very first thing the doctor told me after telling me that I had cancer, was that testicular cancer was the best cancer to have. It was 95% curable. So all along, I've been thinking that death was a possibility, but it was so remote, I figured that it couldn't happen. It never really occurred to me until today that 95% curable means 5% fatal."

I looked directly at Sarah. "Sarah, for the last three and a half months, I've been afraid, afraid of life with one testicle, afraid of how the next chemo treatment is going to make me feel, but today's the first day I've been afraid I could die."

Sarah placed her left hand on my right shoulder, and returned my look. "Jack, it's okay to be scared. Hell, I've been scared for you this entire time. You just have to keep telling yourself the same thing I tell myself: you're going to be okay."

"Yeah, I know." I said. I had been telling myself the same thing throughout the treatment. Those words were just not as convincing as they usually were.

"You also said that you were sad?" Sarah noted.

"Yeah, I feel bad for Sean and his family," I said. "I know what I've been going through, what my family's been going through, and they were going through the same things. But now, he's gone. If I put my stuff away for a second, I feel incredibly sad for them."

"I know. I feel bad for them too." Sarah said, touching my arm again, as I wiped the tears from my eyes. We walked in silence for some time. In the silence, I felt some sweat drip off my forehead. It was a very warm evening, meant for walking in shorts and a t-shirt, not a dark blue suit. I took off my suit jacket and carried it in my right hand.

The motion roused Sarah. "So Jack, what's been going on in the last month? Why are you so miserable?"

I spotted a park bench, and pointed to it. "Let's sit down." When we did, I told her about my discussions with Jim and Rachel and how they had led to my realization that I was lonely.

"Jack, that's normal. Before I met Dan, I felt the same way you do. Heck, the very reason we hooked up in June was because I was feeling lonely. But twenty-four hours later, I met Dan. Once you get through the chemo, you'll meet the right girl. Everything will be okay."

"How can I believe that, especially after today's news? I was this close," I said, holding my right thumb and forefinger less than a half an inch apart, "to turning you down the night you found the lump. If I had turned you down, or if you hadn't found it, maybe I would never have found it."

"Or think about tomorrow. It's the second anniversary of 9/11. Look at all the people who went to work that day, thinking that there were bright times ahead in the future, and there weren't."

"Jack, that's true all of the time. Something bad could happen to us at any time. We just have to enjoy life while we can."

"Well, that's the other thing that makes me miserable," I said, "because I know that I'm not doing that."

"What do you mean?"

"Sarah, after the last treatment, I realized that I've been lonely and unhappy for a long time. Like, I haven't been really happy since you and I were seeing each other."

Sarah looked at me in surprise, and tensed up. "I don't know what to say."

"I'm sorry," I said, seeing that she mistook the meaning of my words. "That's not how I meant it to sound. I'm not making a play for you. What I'm saying is that when we dated, we had a connection that made me happy. I haven't had that type of connection since we broke up."

"But you dated that girl Jenny for a while a couple years ago. Are you saying that you didn't have a connection with her?"

"That's what I'm saying. I mean, yes, we had sex and we had fun, but in the end there was no connection. It's why I broke it off with her, and why I never considered staying friends with her afterwards."

"Well, she wasn't the right girl for you."

"Maybe," I admitted, "but maybe we didn't have a connection because I didn't spend enough time with her building one. I mean, for two people who were seeing each other for three months, we barely saw each other. Work kept getting in the way. We'd have two nights during the week, at most, where we'd see each other. For a relationship to build, you have to spend a lot of time with the person. And what time do I have? I'm always working. And because of that, in the last year, I've probably had five first dates, a couple second dates, and that's it. I've had sex with one person, and that was you. Shit, other than you, I haven't even kissed anyone in eleven months."

I took a look around and noticed that it was starting to get dark. It was also a little cooler. "We probably should get walking again."

"Okay," Sarah agreed. We both stood up and walked towards Fifth Avenue. "So you think work's getting in your way?"

"Yeah, I do."

"Would you like to know what I think?"

"Sure."

"Yes, you do work way too much but I think that you're part of the problem."

"What?" I said, surprised.

"Hear me out. You said that you need time to build a connection, to build a relationship, but that's not completely true. Time helps make a connection with another person, but you don't need it. What you need is to the desire to connect. You have to be willing to share yourself with the other person, to be vulnerable with them. The reason you think time is necessary, is because the more time you have with someone, the better you know them, and the more comfortable you feel in sharing yourself with them."

I stayed silent as Sarah talked.

"Your problem is that you have a hard time sharing yourself with people. You said that when we dated, we had a connection, and we did. But you forget that, at times, getting you to share certain things was like pulling teeth. In the end, it was one of the reasons why we broke up. You weren't sharing enough with me. I wanted a stronger connection with you, and you weren't willing to give that."

"I've gotten better at that, though."

"Really? In the past month, did you tell anyone, like Kyle, Jim or your family, that you have been so miserable?"

"No," I admitted.

"Why not?"

"Everyone's got their own things going on," I answered defensively. "Kyle's still on trial. You've got Dan, and I'm trying not to make things weird for you or him. Jim's got his things, and my family worries enough about me. I don't want to upset them more."

"Come on, Jack. That's not the real reason, at least not all of it. You didn't want people to know you were hurting. Why?"

I struggled to answer Sarah's question. There were things that I was unwilling to admit to myself, much less admit to another person.

Sarah turned to me and stopped walking, and I did the same. We had crossed Fifth Avenue and were standing in front of an apartment building on 73rd street. "Jack, I'm your friend, and I care about you. None of that's going to change, regardless of what you tell me."

"I guess …, it's just that I don't want people to know how weak I am, Sarah," I said, trying to maintain my composure. "It's pretty much why I've done everything the way I have in the last three months. I've been working my ass of at work, so that people don't think that cancer is beating me. I told my mom that she shouldn't come out, because I don't want people to think that I'm some guy who needs his "mommy" to take care of him. I don't want anyone to think that I'm less of a man, even if …" I faltered, unable to utter my thought.

Sarah was not so constrained. "Even if you only have one testicle," she said.

"Yeah," I said, looking at my feet, trying to avoid her gaze.

"Oh Jack," Sarah said, giving me a hug. "We talked about this. You're still a man, whether you have one or two testicles. You're also not any less of a man if you tell your friends that you're afraid, or sad, or lonely."

"I know what you told me, Sarah, and I wish I didn't have this fear, but I can't shake it." I looked around and noticed that the sun was setting and the street lights had come on. I also noticed an older couple passing us. Both of them had a strange look on their face as they saw us. "Come on, we should get going."

We started walking again, east on 73rd Street. "Is there anything I can say to convince you that I don't think you're any less of a man?" Sarah asked.

"I don't think so. It's just going to take me some time."

"You know, I'm half tempted to take you to bed just to show you how much of a man I think you are," Sarah said, with a slight smile on her face.

Despite my mood, I couldn't stop the barest hint of a similar smile appearing on my face. "We both know that's not going to happen. You've met 'The One,' remember? You're as good as married."

"It's only been three months, Jack."

"It doesn't matter," I said. "Remember when you were dating that tool Dean? You saw him for six months, but all along, I knew that eventually we'd have sex again. I knew that you and he were going to break up eventually. Mostly because he was such a tool, but also because I could tell by the way you guys looked at each other. But, that night after I had my head shaved, when I saw you and Dan together, I knew that we were no longer 'buddies,' as you called it. I know we're never going to sleep together again."

Sarah didn't say anything. She couldn't dispute the fact. She looked at her feet and looked a little sad.

"We're still friends, though," I said. Sarah looked back at me. "Don't get me wrong, sometimes, I still picture you naked." Sarah gave me a small punch to my right arm, but a smile appeared on her face. "But, you're my friend. Hell, you're the girl who may have saved my life. You'll always be my friend."

We continued to walk towards Sarah's apartment building. Night had arrived and the air was much cooler. The sidewalks remained packed with people, most of whom were probably heading home to loved ones, or on their way to meet someone for a date.

"Dean really was a tool, wasn't he?" Sarah asked.

I had to smile, despite my mood. Sarah always knew how to lift my spirits, if even a little.

"Take it from the son of a hardware store owner," I said. "Dean was a Black and Decker, ten in one, multi-purpose tool."

Sarah chuckled. "Are you going to be okay, Jack?"

"Well, I felt like I was having a breakdown before, but I feel a little better now."

"So what are you going to do?"

I shrugged my shoulders, as I stared at the sidewalk ahead of me. "I'm going to head to my empty apartment, eat some Chinese delivery, and then work on a letter that needs to be done finished tonight. Then, tomorrow, I'll do all the things that need to be done before my chemo treatment next week." I turned and looked Sarah in the eyes. "I told you, Sarah, I never have time."

"What are you going to do about that?" Sarah asked.

"As long as I'm at this job, I'm going to be lonely. And if I leave the job, I feel like I'm basically throwing away the last three years. Plus, there's no guarantee I'll meet the right person anyway. I may be lonely for the rest of my life."

"Things will get better, Jack."

"We'll see," I said, with no belief whatsoever in Sarah's words. What I thought was that things would only get worse.

CHAPTER FOURTEEN

I rubbed at the swollen lump on my left arm, hoping the pressure would cause the chemotherapy drug in the skin to dissipate. It was late on Wednesday morning, September 17th, and I had been in the hospital for two days. Twenty minutes earlier, while attempting to insert the IV needle into a new vein, the attending physician had unknowingly missed the vein, and had inserted the needle directly into my skin. For almost fifteen minutes, the drug had pumped into the skin, causing the flesh to bulge. When I finally noticed the swelling, and called the nurse, it was the circumference of a silver dollar. When the nurse, a tall woman in her early fifties, saw the lump, she swore under her breath, and advised me that I should never let a doctor do simple things like inserting an IV needle or taking blood again.

In the doctor's defense, by that morning, it had become difficult for even the nurses to find any viable veins. The veins in my wrists, the back of my hands and in the crooks of my elbow were all stiff from my earlier chemo treatments. They bulged out of my skin, looking, and feeling, like electric wires. The nurse had to hunt for a while to find a good vein, but once she found it, she inserted the needle easily, and fastened it to my arm with some translucent tape. She also informed me that the swelling on my arm would eventually subside. While the nurse didn't tell me to constantly rub the lump, I figured the instruction was so obvious that she knew that she didn't need to say it out loud. So, I continued rubbing.

Unfortunately, the rubbing could not lift my spirits, which remained low. Talking to Sarah about my issues had not helped, and I had not told anyone else. Nor did I intend to do otherwise. I needed to hold it together for another month, until my last chemo treatments were over. Once that was done, I would figure out my life.

After another five minutes of rubbing, I gave up. I couldn't tell if the lump had shrunk, but I was tired of the rubbing, and I was pretty sure that the other two patients in the room, two women in their fifties, were thinking that I was schizophrenic. I was just about to recline my chair and rest my eyes, when a little girl and an adult woman walked into the room. The girl was wearing a white t-shirt with a red heart on it and blue jeans. She appeared to be about seven or eight years old, although it is always hard to tell the age of a cancer patient. Like me, and the other two women in the room, the little girl was bald with pale skin, and walked with a portable IV pump and stand. Despite her condition, the girl had an incredible smile and light in her bright blue eyes. I was suddenly captivated by her smile. It was a brilliant sign of life amongst illness.

Due to her resemblance to the girl, I figured that the woman was the girl's mother. She was a well-dressed, attractive raven-haired woman in her early thirties with a large yellow handbag hanging from her left shoulder. She watched her daughter carefully, with an obvious mixture of love and pain. She had a small smile on her face, but her blue eyes did not hold the same life that her daughter's did. Instead, her eyes held something that I saw every time I looked in the mirror. It was a look of someone under incredible emotional strain.

Pulling her IV pump, the girl walked over, and stopped two chairs to my left, on the opposite side of a small table. The girl pointed to the chairs. "Mom, can we sit here?"

The mother turned to me. "Do you know if anyone is using these chairs?" she asked politely.

"No, they're open."

"Thank you," replied the woman. "Okay, Courtney, you take that one." She pointed to the chair furthest from me. When Courtney sat down, her mother sat down in the other chair. "Do you want to color again today?" She started reaching into her handbag, before Courtney answered.

"Yeah!" Courtney took a drawing pad and crayons from her mom and immediately began drawing. Watching Courtney and her mom, I suddenly thought of my sister Jesse and her daughters, Libby and Belle, both of whom were younger than Courtney by a couple of years. I suddenly imagined my nieces Libby or Belle in Courtney's place, and Jesse in the mother's place, and the thought broke my heart. I tried to get the image out of my head by closing my eyes, and lying back in my chair. That didn't work very well, so I put my headphones on and listened as *My Hero* by Foo Fighters started to play.

A couple of songs later, I felt a tap on my left shoulder. I opened my eyes, and saw Courtney's mother looking at me. Courtney was standing in front of her mother's chair, facing me, with a piece of paper in her hands.

"I hope I'm not waking you," said Courtney's mom, after I took out my earbuds.

"No, I was just resting my eyes."

"Well, I'm sorry if we're bothering you, but my daughter, Courtney, has something to share with you, if that's okay."

"Um, sure," I said, with a little uncertainty.

With a shy smile on her face, Courtney handed me the paper, and said, "I hope you like it." The paper in purple crayon said, "Feel better." Below the words, Courtney had drawn a large sun, and a tree. Next to the tree, she had drawn a very simple picture of me in my red Flash t-shirt and gray Nike athletic shorts.

"Thank you, Courtney," I said, touched by her gesture. I also felt a little ashamed. I had sat in the chemo room with other patients over ten times, and I had never sought to interact with any of them, much less do anything to make them feel better. I was too wrapped up in my own situation, unlike this smiling girl who thought about others. "I'm Jack, by the way. This is a great picture. You're a very good artist for your age."

"Thank you," said Courtney. She pointed to the lightning bolt on my T-shirt. "Is that a Flash t-shirt?"

I had not expected that question. "How do you know the Flash?"

"Sometimes I watch the Justice League cartoon with my brother, and the Flash is on that.. Also, my brother has the Flash action figure, and Batman and Superman."

"Well, I watch that show too, but I don't have any action figures. Yes, it is the Flash symbol. Do you like that show?"

"It's okay. I wish they had more girl super heroes. They only have Wonder Woman and Hawkgirl on it. Isn't there any other girls in the Justice League?"

I thought about the various female superheroes that I could describe to Courtney. Suddenly, a thought occurred to me.

"There's a bunch they could have, like Supergirl, Black Canary, and Vixen, but there is another one that I bet you would like. Have you ever heard of Stargirl?"

Courtney shook her head.

"Well, Stargirl is this teenage girl who has a belt and staff that give her all kinds of powers, like flying. She's on a superhero team, although it's called the Justice Society. She's pretty cool and brave. And, guess what? Her real name is Courtney."

Courtney's smile grew bigger. "Really? That's my name. What color hair does she have?"

"She has long blonde hair."

"That's what my hair is!" Courtney said, excited. Then, her smile deflated a little. "At least, it is when I'm not doing chemo."

"Courtney," her mother said, "you probably should bring the other two ladies their drawings."

"Okay," said Courtney. "Thanks for telling me about Stargirl, Jack."

"You're welcome. And thank you for the drawing."

"You're welcome." Courtney went back to her seat and grabbed two other pieces of paper. She walked over to the other two women, who had seen our interaction, and appeared to be ready for their own drawings.

Courtney's mother stayed behind in her seat. After watching Courtney talk to the women for a few seconds, she turned back to me, and held out her right hand. "I'm Barbara, by the way, Barbara Stern."

"It's nice to meet you, Barbara," I said, shaking her hand. "It was really nice of Courtney to draw these pictures," I said. "You must be proud of her. She seems like a great girl."

"She is," said Barbara, as she lovingly watched Courtney talk to the two other patients. "I'm sorry I interrupted but I didn't want her to think too much about missing her hair."

"I understand," I replied. "That makes sense."

"You know, you talked about superheroes, but the real life version is right there. I'm constantly amazed by how strong she is. She's nine years old, and has leukemia, and has to go through these awful chemo treatments. But she rarely complains, and she always wants to do this type of thing for other people."

"Is …," I started to ask, uncertain whether my question would be appropriate. "Is she going to be okay?"

"We hope so. When Courtney was diagnosed last year, the odds of her making it through this were 70%," Barbara said, her eyes moist with tears. "She went through chemo for two months last year, and we thought the cancer was gone, but it came back about a month ago. This is her second chemo visit for this round, and she has two more to go: one in two weeks, and another two weeks after that. Hopefully that will get rid of the cancer for good, because I don't know if I can watch her go through this again."

"The last year must have been very tough for you."

"More than I could ever have imagined," Barbara said. She turned to look at me. "Do you have any kids, Jack?"

I shook my head.

"I wish I could describe what it's like." Barbara sat for a couple of seconds looking at Courtney, and then she turned back to me. "When I was a kid growing up, my mother frustrated me. She was always worrying about everything, and, well, mothering me. She always said she acted that way because she loved me, but I couldn't understand it, because I loved her, and I figured the love I had for her had to be the same as the love she had for me. And I wasn't that dramatic, so why did she have to be that way?"

"But, then I had my son, Pat, and then Courtney, and I finally understood. When you're a parent, you feel so much for your kids, far more than you can feel for your own parents, and for anyone else for that matter. When they're happy, the happiness you feel is incredible. But when they're in pain, the pain you feel is unbearable. It's torture. The thing is, I look at her, and I still see the baby girl I gave birth to. And watching my baby girl going through what she has, well, it's like someone is tearing into my soul. And I don't think it will ever change. When she's my age, I'll probably still see her as my baby girl, and her pain will still be torture to me."

Barbara stopped talking for a second to wipe her eyes. Then, she dropped a bomb on me. "Of course, it would be worse if she was going through it, and I wasn't here to help her."

Barbara's last sentence was like ice water thrown in my face. I suddenly realized what my mother must have been going through over the last three months. There I was, her youngest child, sick from cancer and chemotherapy drugs, and I was half a country away. She was unable to help to me, even for a short time, because she couldn't visit me – because I wouldn't let her visit me. All along, I had told myself that I was reducing her pain. I realized that I may have done the opposite. Suddenly, I felt like the world's biggest ass.

Trying to rid myself of that guilt, I turned back to Barbara. "Well, it's clear that you're helping her," I said. "I know a little about what she's going through, and for her to think about others when she's here, well, it has to be because of you and your husband."

"That's very sweet of you," Barbara said, wiping the tears from the corner of her eyes. "Look at me. I'm complaining about how tough it is to watch someone deal with cancer to someone who is actually dealing with cancer. I'm sorry, that's so insensitive of me."

"There's no need to apologize. You have every right to vent."

Just then, Courtney came back over to her mother. "Mom, one of the ladies is the grandma of one of the kids in my class. Come on, you should talk to her."

"Alright, dear." Barbara stood up, and looked at me. "Jack, it was nice talking to you."

"Same to you. And Courtney, thanks again for the picture."

"You're welcome."

I watched as Courtney and her mom walked to the other side of the room. From what Barbara had said, it sounded like Courtney's last chemo treatment would coincide with mine. I decided that, during that last treatment, I needed to repay Courtney's gesture with one of my own. I began thinking of ways to do that.

Five minutes later, I took a look at the clock, which read 11:15 a.m.. It was time to go back to my room. Lunch, or at least what the hospital called lunch, would be arriving in my room soon, and, despite the low level of nausea I was feeling, I needed to eat. With my right hand, I waved to Courtney and Barbara, carefully moving my hand so as not to damage the drawing. My left hand pulled my IV stand as I shuffled along. I walked out of the chemo room and looked down at the swelling on my left arm. It appeared to be a little smaller than it was before.

When I arrived back in my room, Kyle Robinson was sitting in the chair next to my bed, watching SportsCenter on the television. He was dressed casually, in a Polo shirt and khaki slacks, as if he was headed to the golf course. When he saw me, he stood up and said, "Smalltown!"

"Dude!" I said, a smile breaking out on my face. "Rachel didn't tell me last night you would be back."

I walked over to him, and did the handshake and one-armed hug used as a greeting by virtually all guys my age, and absolutely no women. "That's because she didn't know I was coming home," he said. "You should have seen the look on her and Megan's faces when I walked into the apartment last night."

"I bet they were surprised. So, wait, is the case settled then? Or did you get a break?

"We settled. Right before the judge sent the case to the jury, the other side offered to settle the case at 35% of their demand. Before, they never got lower than 75%. We ended up settling at 20% of their demand, and the client is ecstatic."

"That's great!" I said.

As he was talking, I walked around to the other side of the hospital bed, and laid down on it. "I bet you're glad to get home," I said.

"I am, and I'm taking a week and a half off to decompress. So is the rest of the team."

"It sounds like you need it. A month and a half away from your family: that's rough."

"Yeah, it was," said Kyle, his eyes on the TV. "I've heard that the last month has been pretty hard on you too."

I looked at Kyle in surprise. I hadn't shared anything with Rachel about how tough things had been. He must have spoken to …

"Sarah. Sarah told you," I said. Kyle turned to look at me, and nodded. I was surprised that my friends had been talking to each other. We did not hang out as a group together. In fact, as far as I knew, Kyle and Rachel had only met Sarah two, maybe three, times. They were two separate groups of friends that didn't usually mix. "What did she say?"

"She told me about how you felt like you were having a breakdown after hearing the Sean Kimerling news. She said that you were lonely and depressed. She said you thought you may have to quit your job. "

"She just called you out of the blue, and told you?"

"No, Rachel and I have been in touch with Sarah and your friend Jim ever since we found out the cancer had spread."

In retrospect, I can't explain why that information made me angry, but it did. "So you guys have been talking about me behind my back?"

Kyle turned his chair to face me. As he did so, he responded to me, patiently and gently. "No, Jack, we weren't. We were making sure that you were getting the support you needed. After you were diagnosed, I knew, maybe more than anyone else you know, how hard this was going to be on you, and that you would need our help"

"What do you mean, you know more?" I said, still angry.

"I should have told you this earlier. In fact, Rachel's been on my case to tell you since Day One. She said that she almost told you herself last month, when she was here." He stopped talking for a second, and took a breath. "Anyway, when I was fourteen, my dad found out that he had a brain tumor. He went through surgery, chemo and radiation, but about a year later, he died."

After I initially found out that I had cancer, a number of people, like Mike and Jade, had shared with me stories of friends and family who had had cancer. In some ways, I had become used to the idea that virtually everyone had been impacted by cancer, in one way or another. Even so, I was still stunned by Kyle's news. Kyle rarely spoke about his parents, and I had never met them. The anger I felt suddenly melted away.

"Kyle, I didn't know," I said, ashamed. "I'm so sorry."

"I know, dude. Don't beat yourself up. I'm not telling you about my dad to make you feel bad. The reason that I'm telling you is because I learned a lot from my dad's death. That year was very tough on me, and it was tough on my dad, but he handled it a lot better than I did."

"What do you mean?"

"Well, throughout that year, he always thought that things would turn out for the best, like when we discovered he had cancer. One Sunday night, he had a seizure, so my mom rushed him to the emergency room. In the CAT scans, they noticed that he had a brain tumor. Anyway, the next day, I spoke to him and he kept telling me how lucky we all were. He said that he could have had the seizure ten minutes earlier when he was driving all of us home on the Long Island Expressway. And he was a speeder. If he would have had a seizure then, my entire family probably would have been killed."

It occurred to me that Kyle's dad's words about being lucky were similar to what Kyle had told me the day after I discovered the tumor. He had told me then how lucky I was that Sarah had found the tumor when she did. My guess was that the consonance had been intentional.

"Throughout that year, he kept telling us that he had been given a gift, even after we knew that he only had a little time left. His family was alive, and he had been given more time to spend with them. He said things like that all the time, and he always thought that things would turn out okay. Even when he knew he was going to die."

Hearing about Kyle's dad stirred up the feelings of inadequacy that I had felt in the chemo room earlier. I had been unable to reach out to others like Courtney had done, or stay positive like Kyle's dad. I feared that I simply was not as strong as they were. "How'd he do it, Kyle? How'd he stay positive the whole time?"

"I didn't know for the longest time, Jack. I wish I had known, because I didn't handle it well at all. I mean, I was a teenager, and he was my hero. I didn't see it as a gift. The way I saw it, my dad was being taken from me." Kyle's eyes were teary, and every so often he would pause as he spoke. "When he died, I went over the edge. It was the start of the summer, and I was supposed to play summer baseball, and go to camps. Well, I quit the team, and told my mom I wasn't going anywhere. Instead, I spent all my time in my room, refusing to talk to anyone including my friends. I even stopped watching Yankees games. Everything reminded me of my dad, and it hurt so much to think I would never see him again. And then every night, I would have nightmares, where I saw him dying, looking bald, pale, and sick."

Like I do now, I thought. At that moment, it occurred to me how tough it probably was for Kyle to be around me. He probably was remained of that last year with his father every time he saw me.

Yet, he had gone above and beyond what was necessary to help me. I suddenly felt an incredible sense of gratitude for his friendship.

"One night," Kyle continued, "I had a different dream of dad. He still looked sick, but he told me to go play catch. It was such a powerful dream, that the next day, I did just that. I called my friend Tony, and told him I wanted to play. I didn't want to talk. I just wanted to throw and catch a baseball."

"And we did. And it was tough. But when it was over, I felt a little better. That night, I didn't dream about my dad at all. The next day, we played catch again, and started to talk, just about baseball, but it was something. We played again the day after that, and the day after that. And eventually, I watched a Yankees game again with my friends. It was a good game. Don Mattingly hit a grand slam, and the Yankees won. It was still tough, though. I kept looking to my dad's chair, waiting to hear him say something about the game."

"Anyway, that night, I had another dream of my dad. We were at Yankee Stadium, and he wasn't sick. He looked fine; like he did before he got sick. We were watching the game, and he looked at me and said, 'Did you see Mattingly hit that grand slam, Kyle? Wasn't that great?'"

A tear ran down my face, as Kyle told his story. Captivated by it, I forgot about myself and how I was feeling.

"After that, things were better. I was still sad a lot, but I knew I wouldn't feel that way forever, and that things would get better. And that's when I knew why my dad was able to stay positive. For one thing, he had his family and friends constantly at his side supporting him. When I let my friends and family in, and talked to them, they were able to help me too."

Kyle pointed at me. "That's where you've been at a disadvantage, Jack. Your family lives in Minnesota, and you don't have a wife or a girlfriend or kids around. You have a support group here, but we have our own lives and responsibilities. When you were diagnosed,

I realized that your friends all would need to work hard to make sure you had the support you needed, like having someone visit you every night in the hospital, or calling you, or being with you when you had your head shaved. So, I called all of your friends early on. We've been staying in touch and coordinating ever since."

I felt ashamed at my earlier outburst at Kyle. At the same time, I was amazed at my friends' thoughtfulness and compassion. "I'm sorry I was angry, Kyle," I said. "You guys did the right thing."

"It's okay, Jack. The other thing I learned was that a person can't see how good life can be if they don't take the time to enjoy the good things in their life. When my dad got sick, he did his best to enjoy his life. He was a lawyer, too, and before he got sick, he was always busy. Afterwards though, he spent more time with my mom, my sister, and me. He went to all of my baseball games, and took me to a bunch of Yankees games. We went on at least three vacations that year. A little bit before he died, he said that the best times with his family were during that year."

"I made a mistake when I shut myself off from everyone and quit baseball," Kyle admitted. "When I started doing the things I enjoyed, the things that reminded me of the good times with dad, I saw how good life was."

"Okay," I said, not knowing exactly how his point applied to me.

"You've made the same mistake, Jack. You haven't shut yourself in a room, but you also haven't been taking care of yourself. When I was in Boston, I kept in contact with people at work. They said that, other than the days you've been in treatment or recovering, you've been at work. In fact, they say that you've been working as hard as you were before you got sick."

"Kyle, I worked because I felt good enough to work," I said, defensively. "I'm not going to let cancer affect my life any more than it has too."

"Ok, during that time, you were fine physically. But about mentally? I told you over three months ago that you needed time off from work. Since then, you've been diagnosed with cancer, had surgery, and been through chemo treatments, and the only time that you haven't been working is when you've been in a hospital room or recovering. Look at me, after the trial, I definitely need time away from work, and you need the time off more than I do."

I didn't know what to say to Kyle. I wanted to defend the decisions I had made and what I had done, but I couldn't see how I could.

"You're burnt out," Kyle said, "and you haven't taken any time to enjoy life. Of course, you're not going to see how good it can be."

"So, what, I should take some time off?" I saw the logic in Kyle's words, but I remained convinced that doing so wouldn't change anything. After all, I thought, the facts are the facts. Vacations were temporary. Afterwards, my career would still take up most of my time, and I would be alone.

"Hell, yeah," Kyle answered, enthusiastically. "Take two weeks off at the least. No one at work is going to say no. Go to Minnesota and see your family. Get drunk and find a woman to s*chtup*; maybe one of those Minnesota milk maids you grew up with. Read some comics or watch some of those sci-fi movies or shows that you like. If you stay here, you and I can play some rounds of golf. Just do things that make you happy. Once you do that, it's going to be easier to handle your last chemo session or decide what to do with work."

"Alright," I said. "I guess it can't make anything worse. I'll call in to work this afternoon and let them know."

"There you go," said Kyle, leaning back in his chair. "Trust me. Things will be easier afterwards."

I was pretty certain they wouldn't be, but I would give it a try. "Okay," I said. "Are you going to stick around here, or are you going to head home to Rachel and Megan?"

"Since I haven't seen you in a while, I thought I'd hang out here for a couple of hours."

"Cool," I said. "Why don't you tell me more about your dad, I mean, if you want to."

"Sure," Kyle said, nodding. "I'd like that."

For the rest of the afternoon, Kyle told stories about his father. Listening to them, I was humbled by how Kyle's dad handled both his sickness and his impending death. Still, a voice in my head kept pointing out that his death was proof that things don't always change for the better.

After Kyle left, I realized that I had not rubbed my left arm since he and I had started talking. When I looked at the lump though, the swelling was gone.

CHAPTER FIFTEEN

I gazed out of the window from the passenger seat of my sister's Honda Accord. The Central Minnesota landscape passed by as we drove north on Interstate 94 to Oak Lake. Every ten miles or so, small towns appeared along the highway. Dairy and turkey farms covered the rest of the landscape. On the dairy farms, Holstein cows grazed in pastures, next to bare corn and alfalfa fields. I had seen the same farms hundreds of times in the twenty-two years I had lived in Minnesota. The environment was so different, though, compared to the urban landscape to which I had become accustomed in the last six years that it was also alien. The dissonance was one that I felt every time I traveled back to Oak Lake, but this time it was even stronger.

Jesse had picked me up at the airport an hour earlier, and had driven ever since. I turned to look at her in the driver's seat. My sister has the average height for Minnesota women, which meant she was 5'7" or three to four inches taller than the average New York woman. She was wearing black frame glasses and her hazel eyes were focused intently on the highway ahead of us. Her long dark brown hair hung to her shoulders, resting on her red fall jacket. Under that, she wore a gray St. Benedict's College t-shirt and blue jeans.

Two empty booster seats were in the backseat of the car. Jesse's daughters, Libby and Belle, had stayed home with Jesse's husband Rick, but they would be traveling up to Oak Lake Friday evening. For most of the ride, we were relatively silent, listening to Depeche Mode's album *Violator* on Jesse's CD player.

As we drove, I imagined the surprised looks on my parents' faces when Jesse and I walked into their hardware store. Inspired by Kyle's surprise return to New York, I had kept my own visit home a secret from everyone, except Jesse. My parents were expecting Jesse to visit. She had told them that she had two days off and her high school friends were hosting a get-together.

The thought of my parents' shock upon seeing me was a pleasant diversion from the memories of my third chemo session. It was the Thursday after that session, and I was just starting to feel normal again. The session had been a bad one, with the only bright spots being visits from my friends, and my multiple conversations with Courtney and Barbara in the chemo room. I told Courtney more about Stargirl and other female superheroes, and had talked to Barbara about more adult things. The rest of the week was so bad though, that in Jesse's car, I refused to think about it.

"So, was your last session as bad as you thought it would be?" asked Jesse.

There goes that plan, I thought. "Pretty much," I responded, hoping that the answer would satisfy her curiosity.

"Did you get that ADD feeling again?"

Shit. "Yeah, it was worse this time."

"Don't want to talk about it?" She asked, finally getting the hint.

"No," I said. It suddenly occurred to me that I was repeating my previous behavior of shutting out the people who were concerned about me. "I'm sorry, Jess. It's just that the last month has been really tough on me, and I don't like to think about it."

"What's going on?" She asked.

I gave her the Cliff Notes version of my problems. "So, there you have it," I said. "Apparently, I'm a burnt out mess."

"I'm sorry to hear that, Jack," said Jesse, sympathetically. "Although, I have to say, I'm not completely surprised that you're feeling what you're feeling."

"What?" I asked, feeling the familiar sensation of annoyance at Jesse. No one had ever bugged me quite like my big sister.

"I didn't mean that I expected you to be burned out or a mess," she replied. My annoyance lessened somewhat. "What I meant is that I'm not surprised that you're bothered by these things now."

"And why is that?"

"I know you too well, little brother. There are two things that are important to you, your career and family. So far, your career has always come first. That's why you moved out to New York. You've wanted to build your own family, to be a husband, and a father, but on your timetable. You were only going to have a serious relationship with someone when you felt you had achieved a certain level of success in your career."

"But I've been dating for years, trying to find a girlfriend."

"Oh really?" She asked, sarcastically. "Then why do you rarely have girlfriends? Look at how many people have multiple long term relationships in their lives. Look at me. Before I met Rick after college, I had two relationships that lasted over a year. You've had, what, one serious girlfriend since high school, and that lasted for what, five months? You're an okay looking guy, and with a reasonably decent personality, and you live in New York." Her smile let me know she was joking a little. "There has to be at least one or two girls that you've met, even during law school, who could have been your girlfriend. So why haven't you had any serious relationships?"

Jesse's theory bugged me, but I didn't know how to respond. I had always thought that the reason that I had not been in any long term relationships was because I had not met the right girl or because, like I told Sarah, that I had been too busy working to meet the right girl. Under Jesse's theory, the reason I was alone was because I wanted to be alone. If Jesse was right, not only was I wrong about what I had wanted, it also meant that I had been deluding myself for years.

In my silence, Jesse continued on. "I think you've never really wanted to be in a long term relationship with someone unless you thought the person could be the one you married. So if you weren't ready to consider being married, you wouldn't get serious with anyone at all. I thought that you wouldn't consider getting married until you were thirty. It looks like your experience with cancer moved that timetable up."

"Even if you're right Jesse," I said, finally finding the words. "And I'm not saying you are, but if you were, I'm still in the same place. If I want to find the right person now, I still need to find someone, which is harder than you may think. Even if I do, my job doesn't give me enough time to be with that person. So my life still sucks."

"I don't know what to tell you, Jack. You just have to believe that, if you meet that person, you'll make her a priority, and everything else will work out."

"Yeah, well, I'm having trouble believing that now."

Jesse took her eyes off the road and looked at me. Her eyes showed some disquiet and concern. "So are you going to tell Mom and Dad about this?"

I shrugged. "I don't know," I replied. "I'm pretty sure I know what Mom's going to say,"

"'Jack, you should move back to Minnesota, you know," Jesse said, in an exaggerated impression of our mother, "'and find a good Minnesota girl. That's what you should do, you betcha.'"

"Wow, you really have that Adelaide Ritter impression down pat," I said, smiling.

"I've had years of practice, Jackie," replied Jesse.

Just then, the car passed over a slight hill, and Oak Lake came into view. I could see some of the taller structures in town, including the water tower with "OAK LAKE" painted on it, the grain elevator, and the steeples of St. Peter's Church. Suddenly, excitement washed over me, and my worries fled my mind.

"Are you sure you're going to be able to handle staying here for ten days?" Jesse asked. "It's going to get boring after a while. Plus, going from the fast pace of New York to Oak Lake's is likely to give you cultural whiplash."

Jesse pulled off onto the exit ramp for Oak Lake. As we drove up the ramp, I saw the Hardee's restaurant at the top, next to the Mobil gas station. The Hardee's was the only fast food place in Oak Lake. The other two restaurants were all mom and pop places that had been in Oak Lake for decades.

"I'll be fine," I said, confidently. "I think the slower pace is what I need, at least for a little while. I brought some books, and I have the second season of *24* on DVD, too. Plus, I'm going to reach out to Will, Jason, and the rest of my high school friends and see if we can do a night or two out, this weekend or the next."

"So you didn't give them the heads up that you were coming in?" Jesse asked.

At the top of the ramp, Jesse turned left towards downtown Oak Lake. We drove past a new 7-Eleven that had not been there the last time that I visited. I stared at the new site. Things did not change often in Oak Lake, but they still changed.

I turned back to Jesse. "Are you kidding? If I had told them, at least one of them would have told their mom, and with Oak Lake's gossip network, it's certain that when I walked into the store, Mom and Dad would be waiting for me."

"I would say that was a sexist remark, but I know your friends' mothers," said Jesse. "They are all gossips."

She took a left onto Main Street. Our parent's store, Ritter Hardware, was a block down on the right, located on the nearest corner of the next intersection. Despite a recent paint job, it looked exactly the way it did when I was growing up. Jesse took a right at the intersection and parked her car near the side entrance of the store.

"You ready?" She asked.

I nodded and donned a Minnesota Twins baseball cap that I wore to protect my head from the sun. "Let's go."

Jesse walked through the side entrance, and I followed. We turned right and walked down the lawn care aisle to the middle of the store, where the register was located. Mom was there, waiting on a customer. She was wearing jeans with a white blouse and the green vest worn by store employees. She turned her head, and saw Jesse. A smile blossomed onto her face.

"Jesse, I wasn't expecting you for another …," she began, and then stopped as her eyes slid from Jesse to me. Her smile shrunk a little when she saw me. She appeared confused, as though she did not recognize me.

I took the hat off my head. "Hey, Mom," I said. "It's me."

For a brief second, a look of surprise and happiness crossed my Mom's face. It was the look that I had been anticipating. "Jack," she said, "is that …." Another look appeared on her face, a look of sadness as she looked at my bald head, and the rest of my appearance. She quickly moved from behind the counter and hurried to me, the tears starting to pour down from her face. When she reached me, she grabbed me and hugged me tight. I returned her embrace, as a few tears escaped my eyes.

We held each other for a while. Mom cried the entire time. "It's okay, Mom," I said. "I'm okay."

She released me and looked up into my face. "I'm sorry Jack. I'm just so happy to see you, and seeing you like that," she pointed to my head, "well, you know, it was just a shock." She wiped the tears from her eyes, and yelled, "Ed, Ed, see who's here."

"Addy, what is it?" Dad yelled.

"Just come here!" Mom yelled back.

"I was just re-stocking the work gloves," Dad said, as he emerged from the small tool aisle. Dad was dressed like Mom, a white golf shirt, jeans, and the green vest. He had a pencil tucked behind his left ear, like he almost always did when he worked at the store. He saw me right away, his face displaying shock at my presence. "Jack." He walked to me and hugged me.

As we embraced, Mom went back to the counter to assist the customer. I heard her apologize, saying that "our son from New York City is here on a surprise visit." I also heard the customer ask "New York City?" in exactly the same pitch and tone used for years on the Pace Picante Sauce television commercials that aired in Minnesota and elsewhere. Over the years, when I told people in Minnesota that I lived in New York City, about seventy percent of them responded in the exact same way. Some things will never change, at least as long as that commercial continues to air.

"How long are you here?" Dad asked, after he released me. His eyes were moist, which is something I have rarely seen. I told him I would be in Minnesota for ten days, until Sunday October 5th. That answer prompted a host of other questions from Dad, which I answered dutifully. Yes, the firm was okay with my absence. Yes, I would be going back to work for a week before my next session. Yes, I was going to get paid. I had used a mixture of vacation and short term disability days. No, I didn't have to pay for my airline ticket. I had never used the ticket I had bought when I thought I would come home for my high school reunion.

Mom soon finished with the customer, and walked back to where Dad, Jesse and I were. "Well, this is a great surprise," she said.

"Actually, I have one more, Mom," I said. "I decided that I would like your company during my last session. I even bought you a ticket for the flight."

Mom started to cry again, just a little this time. She reached over and gave me another hug. "Thank you," she whispered.

When she let go, she was smiling. She wiped her eyes, which suddenly grew very large. "Oh, gosh, I have to call your grandparents and tell them you're here. They'll want to see you tonight. And we'll need to have the rest of the family over this weekend at some point. Your old teachers and coaches will want to see you too. They're constantly asking about you. You'll need to see a lot of people this week, for sure." She walked back to the register counter and grabbed the phone.

I looked back at Dad and Jesse. Dad was smiling and Jesse was laughing to herself. "Welcome back, son," said Dad.

There goes my week of rest, I thought.

The next Tuesday afternoon, I walked into my parents' hardware store, singing softly to Barenaked Ladies' song *The Old Apartment*. I was meeting Mom for lunch, having spent the previous two hours walking around Oak Lake, as I had at least once a day for the past four days. Physically, I was feeling completely back to normal, and was contemplating running one or two miles the next day.

The last four days had passed pretty much as Mom predicted it would. Every night had been spent either at home, at a bar, or at my grandparents' homes meeting family and friends. Everyone expressed delight at seeing me, while their eyes expressed their worry over my condition. We talked about a variety of issues, including New York, the upcoming deer hunting season, and of course the Vikings. There was some excitement amongst Vikings fans in Minnesota at that time. Going into the Sunday game, the Vikes were 3-0, and on the first Sunday I was in Minnesota, they beat San Francisco 35-7. Of course, the excitement that I heard was a quiet one, and any optimistic talk was often qualified by statements like "but I'm sure that they'll screw it up somehow." Vikings fans were all too accustomed to having their hopes crushed in the past to express exuberant confidence in the team.

Other than the Sunday watching the game and walking around town, I spent my days relaxing at home and reading a book or watching television. I enjoyed the walks the most, though. My sojourns around Oak Lake temporarily washed my mind of the memories of the previous chemo session and immersed it in the memories of my youth. I walked by the library where I had read so many books, and the athletic fields where I had played sports. I went to the two parks where I had played as a child, and where I had spent time, in high school, making out with Kara. With each trip, I remembered more about the boy I was when I lived in Oak Lake.

When the hardware store door closed, I took out my earbuds, and walked to the computer register where Mom was sitting, reading the *St. Cloud Times*, a local daily newspaper. The store was otherwise empty.

"Hey Mom," I said. "Where's Dad?"

"He realized that he needed to pick something up in St. Cloud. He won't be eating dinner with us today."

In Oak Lake, as in other parts of Minnesota, the words they use to describe the meals of the day are different from those elsewhere. Breakfast was breakfast, but the midday meal was not "lunch," but "dinner." "Lunch" was often something eaten either between breakfast and lunch or in the afternoon (often after a wedding or a funeral), and usually consisted of ham and butter on white bread or sandwich buns. The evening meal wasn't called "dinner," but instead, "supper." When I first moved to New York, one of my more embarrassing moments occurred when, talking to Jim and Barry, I referred to lunch as "dinner." To this day, they still tease me about that incident.

"Are you ready to go?" I asked.

"You bet," she replied, putting down the paper. "Let me close up." She shut down the computer and grabbed her purse. I waited as she locked the side door. We then walked to the front door, where Mom placed the "Out for Lunch" sign before we left the store and she locked the door.

"How was your morning?" Mom asked, as we walked towards Bo's, a restaurant two blocks away. Mom and Dad often ate their lunches there.

"It was good. I've been walking around town most of the morning."

"Where did you go today? Oak Lake's pretty small. I bet you're running out of new places to see."

"Pretty close. I walked to the high school and around the football and baseball fields. Then I checked out the new Oak Lake Heights development. There are some nice houses up there."

We reached Bo's and walked in. The restaurant had two common areas connected by a hallway. The bar area was located in the first room. In that room, the heads of three bucks with large antlers were mounted on the bar walls. Various bass, walleye and other fish mounts hung next to the bucks. I recognized two regulars who were seated at the bar. They worked for the Oak Lake telephone company and were each enjoying a bottle of beer with their lunch while they watched the bar television. Mom and I walked to the dining room. It was painted white with dark wood paneling serving as chair rails. Wildlife paintings hung throughout the room. Because it was lunchtime, five of the seven tables were filled with customers.

Mom called to Katy Schmidt, who was one of the two waitresses on duty. "It's Jack and I for dinner today, Katy."

"Take whichever one you want, Addy," said Katy, as she poured coffee for two other customers. "I will be there in a minute."

"Thanks," Mom said, and we walked to the nearest empty table. As we sat, I wondered how long it would actually take Katy to come to our table. It wasn't that Katy was a bad waitress. On non-New York standards, she was actually quite good. Outside of New York, waiters and waitresses tend to move more "leisurely" (for lack of a better term) than their New York counterparts did. After six years, though, I was used to New York standards, and could not appreciate the more leisurely nature of the Midwest wait staff.

"Mr. Dodds called the store today," Mom said. "He said to apologize for being unable to see you, but he will be on vacation up north until next week." Michael Dodds, or "Mr. Dodds" as he was called in the Ritter household, was one of my math teachers in high school, although he was now retired. He was one of the two people most responsible for my application to Yale and my eventual move to New York. Mr Dodds was the one who had convinced me that I could attend an Ivy League school, and succeed anywhere. Without his efforts, I probably would have stayed in Minnesota all my life. Considering that fact, I wouldn't be surprised if the elder members of the Ritter household used a more derogatory name than Mr. Dodds.

"That's too bad," I said, sincerely.

Katy came to our table with two menus and two glasses of water. "Can I get you anything to drink?" She asked.

We told her that we both wanted Diet Cokes, and then she left to fetch our drinks. I looked at the menu, as if I didn't already know what it said, and what I would order. When I was at Bo's, I always ordered the California burger, which was the cheeseburger with tomato, lettuce, ketchup and mayo. I wondered, not for the first time, whether it was called the California burger because it had been invented in California or whether it was given that name because the inventor thought that Californians ate their burger that way. My money was on the latter.

"So, are you going to tell me what's bothering you?" Mom asked.

I looked at her, and wondered if Jesse had told her. *No*, I thought, *then she would have known what was bothering me.*

"How do you know that something is bothering me?" I asked.

"I'm your mother, and you've been moping since you got here."

"Moping?" I said. I was fairly certain that, despite everything, I had not been moping while I was in Oak Lake. Mopers did not walk two hours a day, or meet people every night.

"Alright, maybe not moping," she said. "You've gotten better over the years of hiding when something is bothering you, but from time to time, you've let your guard done, and I could see that something is on your mind. At first, I thought it was the cancer treatments, but from the way you have been looking, I would say that you've been trying to figure something out."

"That's pretty close," I said, and I told her what had happened over the past few months. I didn't share everything, but I told her about how I chose to fight the cancer, the Sean Kimerling news and my conversations with Sarah and Kyle. It was a lengthy tale, long enough for Katy to deliver our drinks and take our lunch orders.

"So that's it, Mom," I said. "I feel like I have to give up on everything I've worked for career-wise or give up having a family. And with everything else going on, I feel that no matter what I choose, things still won't work out. I mean, I may never meet someone I want to marry, and there's no guarantee the firm will make me partner."

Mom looked at me for a few seconds, with some pain in her eyes. Then she shook her head slightly. "Jack, it's going to be okay. You'll make the right choice and it will work out."

"That's it?" I said, in disbelief. "That's all you have to say?"

"What did you think I was going to say? You should move to Minnesota and be closer to your mother?"

"Well, maybe not that exactly," I lied, not looking her in the eye. I turned to see her give me the same look that she had given me in the hospital, signaling that she didn't believe my bullshit. "I just thought you would have more to say than I will make the right choice."

Mom looked me in the eyes. "Jack, let me tell you something. Do you know why I didn't want you to move out East?" I was pretty sure of her reasons, but I didn't say anything. "Yes, I didn't want you so far away, and I thought that New York was too dangerous. But there was another reason. I thought that moving to New York where you had no friends or family was the worst thing for you specifically, because of your personality."

"My personality?"

Mom nodded her head. "All of your life, you've always preferred being alone. Jesse was the outgoing one, playing outside with any kid she could find, but you preferred to sit in your room alone reading books or in the living room watching TV. Do you remember the fights we used to have when you were in elementary school? Remember all those times I yelled at you to go outside and make friends?"

"Yes." And vividly, I did not add.

"As you got older, you got better, and were able to make a few good friends, but, you know, you never made friends easily and you hated being in large groups."

Mom's assessment of my personality did not sound unreasonable. In fact, it was pretty accurate.

"And when things got bad, like they did when you were in 10th grade, you would completely isolate yourself from everyone. I don't know why you do it. Maybe you don't want to be vulnerable in front of people."

I started to panic a little bit. Mom had pretty much described what I had been doing before my psuedo-breakdown with Sarah. Suddenly, I was wondering if Mom had been right about my move to New York.

"When you were here, I always worried about you, but I knew that you had family around that wouldn't let you withdraw from everyone. When you moved to New York, you didn't have any friends there, much less any family. I worried that if things got bad in New York, there wouldn't be anyone there to help you the way family could."

"So why do you think I will make the right choice in the future?" I said, with the panic creeping into my voice. "I mean, I still do the same things. I tried to handle everything by myself again."

"Because, Jack, when you moved to New York, you did something I thought you would never do. You made a good group of friends who care about you, like Kyle, Sarah, and your law school friends. Yes, you isolated yourself again, but you had people who were looking out for you and caught you."

"But Mom," I said, "I made all the wrong choices in handling this. My approach was all wrong. I mean, I had this mantra to keep myself strong that I would keep saying to myself, but after a while I stopped because it wasn't helping. I worked when I should have taken it easy. And now I'm freaked out because of all of these mistakes. How can you be sure I'll make the right choice in the future that everything will get better, after the last few months?"

Mom reached out and put her right hand over my left. "Have you ever thought that the reason that you've been freaking out is not because you made some mistakes but because you have cancer? That maybe, no matter what choice you made, you still would be freaking out? If you had stayed in Minnesota, instead of New York, and were married here, and you went through this, you could have freaked out because you realized that life is too short to play it safe, and that you should have followed your dreams by moving to New York. You're going through a tough time right now, and you're hurting. But sometimes in life, no matter what choice you make, you can't avoid the pain."

"But other people have gone through cancer or worse and not freaked out. They ..."

Mom interrupted me. "Are other people. They aren't you. You are who you are, Jack. You have your own strengths and weaknesses. Sure, you freaked out, and maybe someone else wouldn't have, but who cares? As long as you make it through this, and learn from it, who cares if you freaked out or made mistakes along the way?

The panic receded as I listened to Mom's words. I wasn't sure that she was right, but I couldn't say that she wasn't.

"I don't know, Mom," I said. "I guess you may be right. I'll have to think about it."

"I know," Mom said, nodding her head. "Just know that I'm sure you'll make the right decision after you've thought about it." She paused, and looked around the room. "Now where is our food? It's awfully slow around here lately."

Well, at least I was right about that, I thought.

CHAPTER SIXTEEN

On Saturday night of that week, my last night in Oak Lake, I planned to meet my five closest high school friends. Every member of the group lived outside of Oak Lake, so we decided to meet at my friend Trish Rice's parents' home. It had been almost nine months since I had seen the gang, so I was excited to see them.

I was dressed and brushing my teeth in my parent's second bathroom when Dad stopped by. "Well, that didn't take long for you to get ready," he said.

I took out the toothbrush and turned off my iPod, which I had jerry-rigged to a small boom box. The Indigo Girls *Closer to Fine* had been playing. "Well, when you don't have to shave, or wash your hair, it doesn't take long."

"I suppose so," said Dad. "So you'll be at Bill Rice's house tonight?"

I nodded my head, and cleaned out my mouth. "Yeah. That's still okay, isn't it? I mean, I kinda feel bad about not spending my last night in Oak Lake with you and Mom."

"It's fine, Jack," Dad said. "You've spent almost the entire week with us. Besides, your Mom and I will be fine watching Libby and Belle while Jesse and Rick go out." Jesse, Rick and their girls had arrived on Thursday. Rick and Jesse had already left to spend the evening with some of Jesse's high school friends. Mom, Libby and Belle had left earlier for some ice cream.

"Cool," I said.

"Want to have a beer with your old man on the patio before you go?"

"Sure," I said, and followed Dad out to the patio. We grabbed our fall coats and went through the garage. Along the way, Dad pulled two cans of Miller Lite from the garage refrigerator. As long as I can remember, Miller Lite had been the only type of beer Dad would drink. After I had moved away from home, I tried to introduce Dad to other brands, like Leinenkugel's or Sam Adams. That changed one night, two years before, when I bought him a six pack of Sam Adams Summer Ale.

"I'm not going to drink anything other than Miller Lite," Dad said, after seeing the beer.

"But this beer is better," I said.

"But I'm happy with Miller Lite, so why bother?" I was about to respond when Dad interrupted me. "I'm also happy with your mother. If you found a woman that you thought was better for me, would you want me to switch then, too?"

That was the last time I ever tried to convince Dad to try another beer.

When we stepped out to the patio, it was early evening. The sun would be out for another hour or so, and the temperature was in the fifties. Dad had lit a fire in the circular steel fire pit that sat on the patio. We sat down on the chairs that surrounded the pit and opened our beers. There may be better tasting beer than Miller Lite but it still went down well.

"Your Mom told me what's been going on," Dad said after he took his first swallow of beer.

"I thought she would," I said. I had expected this conversation for the past three days.

"I'm sorry that I haven't talked to you before, but I've been thinking about your problem. I wanted to be sure that I said the right things."

"Okay," I said, expecting to hear the same things I had heard before.

"Your Mom said that you're struggling to make a decision between your career and family, but I don't think that's the problem. I think that, deep down, you already know what you want. You're just struggling to accept it."

"What?" I asked, intrigued by Dad's suggestion.

"When you found the tumor or when you were told you had cancer, did you ever wonder if this was it, if you're were going to die from this?" I nodded. "What was your first thought after that, Jack?"

At that moment, it felt as though the fog in my mind had rolled away. "I thought that, I was too young to die. That I hadn't gotten married, or had kids to raise and watch grow up."

"Did you ever think that you didn't want to die because you hadn't accomplished some career goal, like becoming partner at your firm?"

"No, not once."

"There you go, Jack," Dad said. "Deep down, that's what's you really want right now. It's what needs to be your priority."

I marveled at what Dad had done. Everything was clear. "So you think I should quit my job?"

Dad shook his head. "Hell, no. You've got bills to pay, you have to eat, and you need health insurance. Besides, you're still reeling from this whole cancer thing. This isn't some Hollywood movie.

You shouldn't make any big decisions until you're done with che-mo and the cancer is gone."

Suddenly, everything was blurry again. "But you just said that I already knew what I had to do. That I had to make my personal life my priority."

"I meant that you know what you want the most right now. But that doesn't mean that's the only thing that's important. You can't ignore everything else. Let's say you quit your job. Then what? You need to work, so where are you going to work? Do you know if that will be any better than what you're doing now?"

Dad had a point. "So what are you saying I should do?"

"I'm saying stay at work, at least for now, but at some point, whether it's in three months, six months or a year, you're going to need to act. Until then, you should think about your options, and you should live your life in a way that helps you get what you want. As long as you remember that this is what you want, when the time comes, you'll make the right decision."

"It's that easy?" I said, doubtfully, although Mom had said some-thing similar. "Things will be clear, and I'll make the right decision?"

Dad nodded his head. "Do you remember the night that Mom and I told you that we couldn't afford to send you to Yale?"

I nodded my head. Until the events of the last four months, it had been the worst night of my life.

"I do, too," Dad said. He took a sip from his beer and stared out over our backyard to the river behind it. "You were just crushed when we told you. You didn't even get angry with us. You just stood there, close to tears, and kept asking us questions to try to find some way to go. Then when you knew it was over, you had this look on your face. It was the worst I had ever seen you look. Then you went to your room, and closed the door."

I remembered the night clearly. I had thought that the life I wanted was over. I had wanted to break down and cry, but wouldn't allow myself to do it.

"Your Mom and I were so worried about you. Your Mom thought that you'd hurt yourself or something, so she called Kara and had her come over. I remember Kara going into your room, and staying there for what must have been two hours. I remember," Dad said, with a sudden grin on his face, "that your Mother was worried that the two of you were having sex."

"We weren't," I said. Instead, Kara had talked to me, reassuring me that everything would be okay.

"Part of me didn't care if you were, if it lifted your spirits. Anyway, at some point, the two of you came out, and you asked if it was okay if you went out. Kara told us that she would take care of you, and it was Friday night, so we said sure. So the two of you went out, and your Mom and I stayed home feeling awful. At two a.m., you came in, drunk for the first time. We were a little angry, but then Kara came in too and said that you needed to let loose a little, and that you were going to be okay. We decided not to yell."

It had been the first night that I had ever gotten drunk. Kara had taken me to her family's cabin on Little Bear Lake, where I drank a lot of beer. Kara and I talked for hours, and eventually made love. By the time we left the cabin, Kara had convinced me that my dream wasn't over; it had just been delayed a little. That night, Kara joined Mr. Dodds as one of the two people that I credited the most with giving me the confidence and will to move to New York.

That was the beginning of the end of our relationship. It didn't end right away. We went to prom together, went to movies, made out in the park, and used the cabin more than once during the summer after we graduated. At the end of the summer, though, we broke up. She went to the University of Minnesota and I went to St. John's. We decided that it didn't make much sense to try a long distance relationship, especially when ultimately I would likely be headed out East. It was the first time I sacrificed my personal life for my career plans.

"Anyway," Dad continued, "when you woke up the next morning, you were hung-over. Your eyes were completely blood-shot, but there was a look there, like you got when you went after a rebound in basketball. Then you told us what you were going to do. You were going to go to St. John's, work your ass off, and get accepted to a graduate school out East. At that moment, I knew you were going to be okay. All you needed was some time to clear your head and figure things out."

The sex and beer probably helped too, I thought.

"That's all you need now, Jack." Dad said. "You know what you want, and once you clear your head, you'll know what to do, and you'll do it."

"It'll be that easy?"

"I don't know if it will be easy, Jack," Dad said. "But I know if you really want something, if you really want to have a family and to live the life you want, you'll make it happen. I've seen you do it before. For you, a dream is just a future you haven't created yet."

I felt honored by Dad's compliment and his words were inspiring, but I was having a hard time accepting them. In the past when I pursued my dreams, I was young, things were easier, different. I didn't have over $100 thousand in student loans and I hadn't been knocked around like I had been in the past few months.

I lifted my Miller Lite can to take a drink, and realized it was empty. *Time to go,* I thought. "Thanks, Dad. "I'm going to walk over to the Rice's. It will give me some time to think."

"Okay, but remember, Mom and I have faith in you."

"Okay." I started to walk away, but then something occurred to me, and I turned back to Dad. "You know, if this was a Hollywood movie, like *Doc Hollywood,* I would have come home to Oak Lake and decided to stay here."

"Which one was *Doc Hollywood?*"

"You know, the one with Michael J. Fox and Winchester from *M.A.S.H.*. Fox is a big city doctor who ends up in a small Southern town, and realizes that he belongs there." Dad's face stayed blank. "You know, he stayed because he fell in love with that woman who walked out of the lake naked."

"Now, I remember," Dad said, recognition and a smile dawning on his face. "That was a good movie. Well, as much as I wish it was different, small town life is not for you."

"Yeah, I know," I said, and started to walk away again.

A second later, I heard Dad say, "Hey! Jack."

"Yeah, Dad?" I said, turning around one more time.

"Life isn't a Hollywood movie, but if you do see a naked woman coming out of the water, make sure you come and get me."

"Thanks, Dad." *Smartass,* I thought.

I didn't take the direct route to the Rice's. I needed to think about what Dad said before I saw the gang. I was hoping for a grand epiphany to get me out of the funk I was in. As I walked, I thought about the conversations I had with my family and friends in the past month. They all led to the same point: things would get better, if I had the faith and the strength to believe it. Yet, despite the logic behind the lesson, and the fact that I truly wanted to believe it, I couldn't. I wasn't convinced.

The trouble I had with it was similar to the trouble I had had writing the National Mutual brief the night I found the tumor. With the brief, I had written the logical points to my argument, but it was lacking that something extra to persuade and convince the judge. Walking to the Rice house, I knew that I had heard all the logic behind why things would get better, but I still needed to hear or experience something more to convince me. I just did not know what that could be. *Maybe getting drunk will help,* I thought.

With that, I headed for the Rice house. Trish's mom, Hilda, answered the door when I arrived. Trish's parents were about ten years older than mine, and both had retired. "Jack, it's so good to see you," she said. How are you feeling?"

"I'm okay. Thanks for asking."

We chatted a little bit about my treatments; her brother had been diagnosed with prostate cancer years ago. He had received chemotherapy and survived. "Well, I suppose Trish and the others want to see you," she said, and then walked me upstairs to the kitchen.

The entire gang, except for Kara, was in the kitchen. Skid Row's *I Remember You* was playing on a boom box on the counter. I knew that Trish was playing the tape of her favorite high school songs. She often played it at our get-togethers.

Trish and Sue Becker were standing on one side of the island counter. They were the same height, although Trish was auburn haired, and Sue was strawberry blonde. They both wore jeans, although Sue wore a gray sweatshirt, and Trish wore a yellow blue sweater. Across the counter, which held bowls and plates of food, stood Sue's husband, Jason, and Will Wagner. Jason was 5'11" and his blonde hair had receded a lot since I had seen him last. Will was my height, but had for the most part retained the brown wavy hair he had in high school. They both wore purple Vikings shirts and blue jeans.

Along with Kara, these four people had been my closest friends in high school. We had, for the most part, separated after high school, but we would meet up once a year or more during school breaks or holidays. Since I left for New York, my participation in the reunions was limited, but I usually always saw the gang once a year. I had spoken to each of them at least once since I was diagnosed, but on each of the calls, we had only spoken about my condition and treatment. I really did not know much of their lives since the previous Christmas, when we last saw each other.

During our get-togethers, significant others and spouses usually did not join. Sue (then Sue Koch) and Jason evaded that unwritten rule by dating each other three years after they started college at St. Cloud State. I figured that the first time they hooked up was after one of our group reunions.

They all saw me at the same time, but Trish got to me first. Like the rest of us, she had aged, but she did not look as if ten years had gone by. "Hey there," she said, and hugged me. "We missed you at the reunion."

Will hugged me next. Will had been the quarterback on the football team, and still looked to be in really good shape. "Dude, welcome back," he said.

Jason and Sue greeted me in the same way. Everyone gave me variations of the same look I had seen on faces during the previous nine days, happiness at seeing me, with a mixture of sadness at witnessing my appearance. The only difference was that Will and Jason were better at hiding it.

After the hug, Will came over with a drink. "Here, I made you a Jack Daniels and diet pop. Or should I call it soda?"

"Nah," I said, shaking my head, "when I'm home, it's pop. So, tell me about the reunion."

The group took turns telling stories from our high school reunion. They were the usual tales, like who had kids, who hooked up with whom, and who was wasted by the end of the night. The general theme though was the surprise everyone felt at how fast the years had passed and how much people had changed.

"Who changed the most?" I asked. "Was it Ken Kramer?" Ken had been the star running back on our high school football team. He also had been voted the Homecoming King, Prom King and the Most Attractive Male in class. I knew that he had played some football for the University of Minnesota, but I had lost track of him afterwards.

"Hell no," said Sue, smiling behind her glasses. "He's hotter than he was in high school. I think I may have married the wrong Oak Lake running back." Every now and then, Sue would make those jokes, but from what I could tell, it never bothered Jason. Like the rest of us, he knew that she only cared about him. She winked at Trish, and looked at Jason.

"Love you too, babe," replied Jason, with a smile. "Oh, hey Kara."

I turned around to see Kara Kane standing in the doorway to the kitchen. She had married Phil Waldman and took his name three years before, but she was always Kara Kane to me. For a frozen moment, I was the teenaged boy that fell for her over twelve years before, and my heart skipped a beat. Kara looked great. Her curly, raven-colored hair rested on her shoulders, though it no longer had the big, puffy look that was popular in the 80's and 90's, and was still popular in parts of New Jersey. She was wearing blue jeans, and a long sleeved pink blouse. She still had her swimmer's figure; well, except for her prominent baby bump. Then, time resumed, and I was back to being the twenty-eight year old I was.

"Oh my God," I said. "You're pregnant?" Kara smiled, nodded her head and walked over to me. She gave me a tight hug that lasted longer than with the others. It was like the hug that Sarah had given me the day I freaked out.

"Hey stranger," Kara said, into my chest.

"Hey," I said, softly and with emotion. We held each other for another second and then we parted. "Congratulations! How far along are you?"

"About six months," she responded, absolutely beaming. "I'm due on December 28th."

"Why didn't I know about this? I mean, we talked two months ago, and you didn't say anything. Plus, this is Oak Lake. The news should have made its way through the grapevine."

"Well, I can only speak for myself, but I thought with everything you were going through, it wasn't important."

"This is good news," I said. "It's probably more important to hear this type of news than it ever is."

"Alright you two, it's time to eat," said Trish. "Grab some food and come to the table."

"Hi to you too, Trish," said Kara, smiling. She walked over to give Trish a hug, before greeting the rest of the gang.

We all followed Trish's orders. For the next five hours, we sat around the Rice kitchen table, eating, drinking and talking about the old days and the new days.

Hours passed that way. I was having fun and drinking more than my fair share. I was drunk but not so much so that I was falling over or slurring my words. For the most part, I steered the conversation away from my treatment, saying only that it was tough, but was almost over. It was great to be back with my oldest friends, and with them, I mostly forgot about what I was going through. Every now and then, my mood would plummet, though, as I thought about the future. After one such moment, I stood up from the table and told the group than I needed some fresh air.

"The deck door is open," said Trish, pointing to the door.

"Thanks," I said, and, after grabbing a fresh drink, went out the door. The sun had set hours before, and the temperature dipped into the forties. I should have grabbed my coat, but decided that some cold air could help with my mood. I looked up at the sky, staring at the stars.

After a couple of minutes, I heard the deck door open, and Kara stepped out. She had been smart enough to don a thick sweater. "Hey," she said, "would you like some company?"

"Sure," I said, "come on out. I'm just looking at the stars. I won't be able to see them when I get back to the City."

Kara stepped out next to me, and gazed upwards. "I don't know how you do it. When Phil and I went to New York two years ago, I thought that it was a nice place to visit but I wouldn't want to live there. I mean, how do you deal with the smell of urine in the subways?"

"Well, that's only during the summer," I pointed out, "and it's no worse than the smell of cow manure and the turkey plant in the summer."

"I guess," Kara said. We stood in silence for a few seconds before she asked, "So, how tough has it been?"

I looked at Kara. Other than the time in tenth grade after she dumped me, Kara had been the person in high school in whom I confided everything. Although it was ten years later, I still sensed some of the bond that existed between us. I felt safe in sharing things with her.

"It's been a pretty tough couple of months," I admitted. "It's been much harder than I thought it would be."

"Have you had anybody out there to help you, friends or a girlfriend or anything?"

"No girlfriend, but I have a close group of friends who have been incredible. As much as things have been harder than I expected, my friends have been better than I could ever have imagined."

"Good," Kara said. "When you first told me that you had cancer, a part of me wanted to fly out there to help you."

"That probably wouldn't have gone over well with Phil," I said, with a smile.

"No kidding," Kara responded. "I get the sense, though, that it's not just the chemo treatments that have been tough. Is there something else?"

"Is it that obvious?" I asked. *God, am I just an open book?*

"No. It's just that you're not as talkative as you usually are, especially considering that you're drinking. As long as I've known you, you always talk more when you drink, unless you're brooding. Then you brood more. And I figured that, with only one chemo treatment left, you probably wouldn't be as 'broody' as you are. What's up?"

I sighed. "It's just that, this whole thing has made me reevaluate my life. Career-wise, I'm on track to get everything I've always wanted, but personally my life sucks, and I don't think it's going to get better if I keep following my current career plans. And as my Dad helped me realize tonight, what's really important to me is finding someone for myself, and raising a family."

"Okay," Kara said, obviously contemplating my answer. "So can you get another job, like at another firm or as an in-house attorney? Something that gives you more personal time?"

"Yeah, probably."

"So, isn't that a good thing?" Kara asked, sincerely. "You've realized what's important, now you can go get it."

"Yeah, I guess." I was about to tell her about the overwhelming feeling in my heart that no matter what I do, things wouldn't get better. I knew, though, that she would respond as everyone else had, things will get better. I was sick of hearing that response. I talked about something else instead. "It's just that I feel like I've failed somehow. I mean, I've spent years working toward this goal, and I've sacrificed so much. I moved away from my family. And the whole time, I've always chosen work over my girlfriends or my personal life." I looked away from Kara, trying to hide that she was one of those girlfriends. "After all of that, I realize that what I've been going for, it isn't for me. It feels like everything has been such a waste, and I'm a failure."

Kara put her hand on my shoulder. "Jack, you're not a failure. You just made it clear that you love New York, so moving there wasn't a mistake. And you graduated from one of the top law schools, right?" I nodded my head. "And your firm is really good, right?" I nodded again. "Well, it sounds to me like you're where you want to be, and you've gotten a great legal education and experience. How is that a waste? With that, you should be able to get a different job that gives you what you want. If you do that, then wouldn't everything have been worth it?"

"Yeah, I guess," I said, without much confidence.

"You're damned right it would," Kara said, emphatically.

"I get what you're saying, Kara. I guess my problem really is that I can't see that things will end up okay. It's clouding my perspective."

Kara put her hand on my arm. "I know. I've had some low moments over the years, too. Everyone tells you, it will be fine, everything is going to turn out, this too shall pass, blah blah blah. As if you've never heard that before. But eventually, with time, your perspective clears, and you realize things have already started getting better. You just have to be patient, and open to it."

"Thanks, Kara." I did feel a little better. Kara didn't solve any of my problems, but it felt good that someone understood me.

"Oh, and one more thing," She said, turning me around so that we were facing each other. "If you're blaming yourself for our break-up, don't. Remember, I was your friend before I was your girlfriend. And I knew, probably more than anyone else, what your dreams were, and where you would end up. And I knew that my dreams were different. We broke up because we reached the point where it was time to for us to break up, and go on with the lives we wanted. Neither of us made any mistakes, and I certainly don't regret any of it, okay?"

It felt like a weight had lifted off of me, and I felt even better. "Thanks, Kara, for everything. I mean it."

"You're welcome," she said, and we hugged again. "You coming in?"

"Give me another minute, okay?" I said. "I want one last look at the sky."

"Okay."

I watched as Kara walked back into the house and closed the patio door. I turned back to the sky and stared at the stars. They seemed to shine a little brighter than they had before.

⮜⊹ ⊹⮞

At 10:00 AM, the next morning, Jesse, her girls, and I left our parents' house in Jesse's Accord to drive back to the Twin Cities. Rick had left earlier in the morning in his car in order to meet some of his friends for the Vikings game. My flight was scheduled to depart at 3 PM, but the traffic was light, and Jesse had lead in her foot, so we had plenty of time.

Before we left, I said goodbye to my parents. Because I would be seeing Mom in two weeks, and Dad in two months at Christmas, my departure was not as dramatic as usual. Still, all three of us were emotional. It had been a great visit, during an incredibly hard time.

"Are you happy to get back to New York?" Jesse asked, as we drove onto the I-94 interstate. Her hair was in a ponytail again, and she looked a little hungover too.

"I feel pretty much the same way I feel every time I head back east," I said. "I'm sad because I'm going to miss you, and Mom and Dad, but …"

"What about us, Uncle Jack?" asked Libby from her booster seat in the back seat.

"Jess, did you hear something? It sounds like a munchkin talking." I took a quick glance at Libby and Belle. They were sitting in their booster seats. Libby, the six year old, was a virtual spitting image of Jesse at that age. Like her mother, her dark brown hair was in a ponytail, and you could almost count the freckles on her nose. Belle, the four year old, was more of a mix between Jesse and Rick. Her hair was in a ponytail, too, although blonde. Her light blue eyes twinkled as I looked at her. They both wore white pants with Hello Kitty shirts, Libby's was yellow and Belle's was pink. "Yep, there are two munchkins back there."

"Uncle Jack …" Libby whined as Belle giggled.

"Am I going to miss you two? Let's see am I going to miss you two waking me up at 7:00 AM, or rubbing my bald head every minute you are around me?

"Uncle Jack …" whined the two girls as their mother laughed.

"Sorry," I said. "Yes, I'm going to miss you two."

"We'll miss you too, Uncle Jack," said Belle.

After a little bit of silence, Jesse spoke again. "So you're going to miss us, but I thought I heard a 'but.'"

"Mommy said she heard a butt," Belle whispered to Libby, and they both giggled.

I smiled at Jesse, as she rolled her eyes.

"Yeah, I'm happy to get back to New York," I admitted. "Oak Lake's too slow for me. I need to get back, get a good slice of pizza, and feel some big City energy and excitement."

"Well, I'm not sure I could handle New York, but I know how you feel about Oak Lake." She looked out the window at the farmland we passed as we headed south. "So, are you feeling any better than you did when you got here?"

"I am," I said. "It felt good to relax, and spend time with everyone. Plus, I think my head's cleared a little."

"I hear another 'but' coming," said Jesse.

"But," I said, emphasizing the word, "there's still this gloom that I'm feeling. It's in the pit of my stomach, and I can't shake the feeling that things are going to get worse. I've been feeling it ever since I felt the lump. I feel like I'm living that Don Henley song, *New York Minute*. Life can go from good to bad, and when the good thing is gone, it's gone."

Jesse turned her head to me and gave me a peculiar look. "Jack, when's the last time you listened to that song?"

I thought about it for a second. "I don't know. Maybe a couple of years. The radio stations played it a lot around 9/11, but I'm not sure I've heard it since."

"Do you remember the last verse?"

"Yeah, it's the worst line in the song. It's like, 'Take my advice, hold on to your own, one day they're here, the next day they're gone."

"Do you have it on your iPod?"

I nodded. "I should. I burned all my CDs on it."

"Why don't you listen to it, because that's not how the song ends."

"You're wrong, but I'll listen to it." I pulled my iPod and earplugs out of my backpack, found the song, and selected it. It started exactly as I remembered it, right to the part I thought was the last verse. But then the song continued, to a verse that I had forgotten, and I heard the words I needed to hear:

> But I know there's somebody somewhere
> Make these dark clouds disappear
> Until that day, I have to believe
> I believe, I believe.
>
> In a New York Minute,
> Everything can change

Tears welled up in my eyes. I heard Jesse say "Jack, are you okay?" I nodded, and replayed the last verse. Closing my eyes, I listened closely, not only to the last verse but also to the final chorus. In the chorus, where I had previously heard Henley sing "everything can change" with sadness and resignation, I now heard him sing those words with hope.

That hope suddenly bloomed within me. When the song was over, I pulled out my earbuds, and looked at Jesse. "I'm sorry, Jesse, you were right. There was a last verse that I had forgotten."

"Are you okay?" Jesse asked.

"Yeah, I think I am," I said. "I don't know why, but suddenly I feel a lot better."

Years later, looking back at that moment, I know exactly why I felt better. Before I listened to the song in the car, I had been *absolutely* certain as to how it ended, just as I had been *absolutely* certain that nothing could get better. When I realized I was wrong about the song, I realized that I could be wrong about the future. I didn't believe that everything *would* change for the better. In fact, I was still scared that it wouldn't. Yet, suddenly, I knew that it *could* get better. The existence of that possibility made all the difference in the world.

CHAPTER SEVENTEEN

O n the morning of Saturday, October 11th, nine days before my fourth chemotherapy session, I stepped out of my apartment building to buy a newspaper and to eat breakfast at the Blue Moon Cafe. My iPod was playing Tom Petty's *Angel Dream No. 2* and I was feeling okay. After arriving back from Minnesota, I had continued to follow Kyle's advice, and spent my time doing the things I enjoyed. I went to the movie theater a couple of times, finished off season 2 of *24,* and read a bunch of comic books. I went out with my friends almost every night and even played a round of golf with Kyle. That week, and my time in Minnesota, had helped to relax me, and my head felt clearer, but I was still worried about my last chemotherapy session. I had a week of work before then, a week that would be spent mostly preparing for the National Mutual hearing, but it was the week after that still bothered me.

I walked to the newsstand on the corner of First Avenue and 90th Street, and picked up a copy of the *New York Daily News.* I reached into my pocket to pull out a dollar, but I fumbled with the money. There was one too many rolled up ones in my pocket.

Finally, I was able to grab just one and I placed it on the counter. As I waited for the newsstand worker to hand me the change, I felt a tap on my shoulder. I turned around to see the pair of ocean blue eyes that had dominated my dreams in the past four months.

Emma Murphy stood there, much like she had on the night we met, holding a dollar bill. This time, she was wearing casual clothes, a white blouse with blue jeans. She wasn't wearing any makeup, and her hair was pulled back with a blue hairband. She was still gorgeous. I quickly paused my iPod, and removed the headphones.

"Sorry, but you dropped this," she said, her smile as incredible as it was before, and handed me the bill.

"Emma," I said, stunned to see her again.

She looked at me for a second. "Jack?" she asked. She had not recognized me at first, but when she did, to my joy, she had remembered my name.

"Let me guess, I look different from the last time." The newsstand worker had my fifty cents, so I quickly turned around to get my change.

"Yes, you do," she said, as I turned back to her. "I didn't realize it was you at first. You've shaved your head, and ...." She stopped, clearly at a loss for words.

"Yeah." Another person stepped up to buy a newspaper, so I moved out of the way of the newsstand, and Emma followed. After we moved a couple of feet, I looked back at her. "Remember, when we met and I said something was going on?" She nodded. "Well, I have cancer. I've been going through chemo treatments for the past three months now. The day we met was the day after I found out."

Emma had raised her hand to her mouth at the mention of cancer, and put it back down to speak. "Oh, my God, Jack. Are you going to be okay?"

"Yeah, I think so." I quickly told her about the survival rate, and that I had one more chemo treatment left, although I didn't mention the type of cancer. I didn't know if I was ready to do that. "Hopefully, after my last session, I'll be clean."

"That's good, but the last four months must have been rough."

"I've had better times," I admitted.

"I can imagine," she said. "Well, now I know what your friend meant."

"My friend?" I said, puzzled.

"Yeah," Emma said, nodding. "About twenty minutes after you and I spoke at the Parker House, I ran into one of your friends, the tall blonde, in the bathroom."

"That must have been Rachel. She's the wife of my friend, Kyle."

Sarah nodded. "Now that you mention it, I think she did say that her name was Rachel. Anyway, she said that she was your friend, and that you really liked me, but thought you had screwed up your chance with me. She told me that you had a serious medical condition, but couldn't say what it was."

"'Serious medical condition?' God, I hope you didn't think it was herpes or anything like that."

Emma laughed. "Well, later, one of my friends wondered if it was an STD, but with the way you and Rachel acted, I figured it was something else. I didn't think it was cancer."

"Is that all Rachel said?"

"No, she said that as soon as things worked out, you would call me. She also said that you were an incredible guy; that you were smart and funny and a lawyer; and that you were someone that a smart girl would wait for."

"I didn't know she did that," I said. Knowing Rachel, I wasn't surprised that she would take matters into her own hands. On a normal day, the fact that she did would have frustrated me. That day, I was thrilled.

"Yeah, she must be a good friend." She bit her lip, and looked a little anxious. "And well, I am a smart girl, and it sounds like I won't have to wait much longer."

I thought for a second. I had gone through hell the last few months, in part, because I kept people at a distance. "Screw the wait," I said, "it was probably a dumb idea in the first place. How would you like to have dinner with me tonight?"

Emma smiled that bright smile again, and her blue eyes twinkled merrily. "Well, I had some plans to go out with friends, but I would rather have dinner with you."

"Excellent." My heart was leaping in my chest. I took a breath to calm it down. "How does Pinocchio's at 7:30 sound?"

"It sounds great. Shall we meet there?" she asked. I nodded. "Well, then I will see you there at 7:30. Bye," she said, and she walked south down First Avenue.

"Bye." I watched her go, and realized that she had a shapely behind. I laughed to myself, and walked happily to the diner.

I sat down at the counter, ordered a coffee and a western omelet, and started reading the newspaper. A couple of minutes later, the waitress came back with the coffee and said, "Reading something you like?"

"No. Why do you say that?" I asked, intrigued at the question.

"Sweetie, you have the biggest smile on your face. I guess you're having a good day?"

"Yeah, I am," I said, thinking about Emma. *Maybe the best day in a long time*, I thought.

⋈

Wearing a light blue v-neck sweater with a white t-shirt and pressed tan slacks, I walked into Pinocchio's at 7:25 PM. Pinocchio's is a small place, with no more than ten tables, and no bar area. It was darkly lit, making it a nice place for a first date. When Mark, the owner, saw me, he smiled and walked over. Mark was a tall, lanky Italian with dark, curly hair and glasses, and he always greeted the customers and took their orders.

"Good evening. Do you have a reservation?" Although I ate food from Pinocchio's twice a month, I rarely ate in the restaurant. Most of the time, I had the food delivered, which is why Mark was not familiar with me. I had not eaten in the restaurant since my parents had visited months before.

"Yes," I said. "Jack, for two at 7:30. I'm a little early if that's okay."

"Of course," Mark said. "Let me show you to your table." I followed him to a table for two, and I sat so that I could see the front door. "Can I get you something to drink?"

"Yes, please. I'll have a Maker's Mark and Diet Coke. Thanks." I sat and looked at the dinner specials on a chalkboard on the wall. After two minutes, Mark brought me my drink, and said "Enjoy." He then went back to standing near the kitchen where he could watch the restaurant.

At about 7:35, Emma walked into the restaurant. She was wearing a black and white patterned dress and looked incredible. She smiled when she saw me, and walked over to the table.

I stood up, and said, "Wow, Emma, you look great."

"So do you." She leaned in for a peck on the cheek, which I gave her.

We sat down at the table. Mark came over to her and said, "It's nice to see you again. Can I get you a drink?"

Emma smiled, and said, "Yes, a Cosmopolitan, please."

When Mark left, Emma looked back at me and said, "Okay, I have a confession. I've been to Pinocchio's with my roommate a few times since we met. I was hoping that perhaps I would run into you."

I smiled. I was thrilled that she thought of me in the months since we met. "Usually, I only do delivery from here, so it's not surprising that we didn't see each other."

We sat there for a second, in that nervous, uncomfortable silence that occurs often on first dates. Luckily, Mark was an efficient drink master and came back quickly with Emma's drink. We both said "cheers" and took sips from our drinks.

I decided to break the ice. "So, do you think it's weird that both times we met, I dropped a dollar, and you were there to pick it up?"

"Yeah, about that," Emma said with a sheepish look on her face. "I have another confession. The first time, you didn't drop a dollar. It was mine."

"Wait …, what?" I said, confused.

"This is so embarrassing," she said as she brushed her hair back behind her ear. She took another sip of her Cosmopolitan and continued. "I'm not really comfortable approaching guys. I guess, it's sort of a confidence thing. Anyway, when we were at the Parker House, I saw you and was really interested in you. But you weren't coming over to say hi. So one of my friends told me about a trick that she uses sometimes. If the guy is buying something at a bar or store, and pulls his wallet out of his pocket, you can pretend that he dropped a dollar and give it to him. She said it was a good icebreaker, and doesn't make the girl look too forward or desperate. So, when you went up to the bar, I decided to try it out."

I laughed. "Well, I think it worked. I had no idea. I guess I owe you a dollar."

"That's okay. You can buy me dinner." She said, with a smile that could brighten any room.

"Deal. What about this morning? Did you do the trick again?"

She shook her head. "No, you really did drop a dollar."

"So you weren't interested in my looks this morning?" I said, with some mock indignation.

From the look on her face, I could see that she knew I was joking. "I hadn't seen your face, when you dropped the dollar. But you do look good, despite everything. I think you look better with hair, but you can pull off the bald look."

"Thanks."

At that point, Mark came over and asked us if we wanted to hear the specials. We both knew what we wanted to order. We ordered the fried calamari as a shared appetizer, and Emma ordered the rigatoni bolognese. I ordered the "Tortellini Pinocchio," which was a bowl of cheese filled tortellini with prosciutto, mushrooms, and peas in a light cream sauce. It was my favorite Italian dish.

"So, I'm not sure if it's the best first date conversation," Emma said, after Mark had left, "but I was wondering if you wanted to talk about what you are going through, you know, with the cancer."

If Emma had asked me four months earlier, I would have said that we should talk about something else, and would have kept the conversation to small talk. However, I remembered my conversation with Sarah, when she said that I didn't need time to make a connection with Emma; just the willingness to share myself with her. As a result, I decided to be open and honest. I told her that I had testicular cancer, and that I had my right testicle removed. It took a little effort to tell her that. While I had told a number of people that I had testicular cancer, only my closest friends knew that I had more than just a tumor removed in my surgery. I talked and I talked, and shared things that I had not shared with anyone else. About ten minutes in, a waitress came by with the calamari, and between bites, I continued to talk.

As I unburdened my soul, Emma listened attentively. She asked questions here and there, and reassured me when I choked up. When I talked about my recovery days, which I had not described to anyone before, she put her right hand on top of my left hand, which had been resting on the table.

After a little while, a waitress came with our entrees, and a second round of drinks, and I realized that I had been monopolizing the conversation for a while. "I'm sorry. I've been talking about myself this whole time."

"That's okay. I know what it's like when you need to get stuff off your chest. And I am enjoying myself." We each started eating. We sat for a minute or so in a comfortable silence as we ate.

"Can I ask you a question?" I said.

"Sure."

"Well, don't take this the wrong way, but why did you agree to dinner? I'm incredibly glad that you did, but you are sort of jumping into a lot of serious crap here. I mean, I'm not sure I would have done the same in your position."

She looked at her hands for a couple of seconds, and then looked at me. "That's not a bad question. In fact, my roommate and my sister asked me the same thing today. I guess there are a couple of answers. The first one is short and simple. I like you a lot, and I think we hit it off when we met. I've done the dating scene since college and been in some relationships, but I have never hit it off with anyone that way before. So, I've been thinking about you since we met, and I knew that if I had got another chance see you, I was going to take it."

"Okay," I said, nodding my head. "In a way, that's the same reason, I asked you."

"The second answer is a little longer and more personal." She paused for a second, as if she was debating whether to share the story.

"If you don't want ..." I said.

"No, you were incredibly open with me tonight. I owe you the same. Besides, if we continue seeing each other, you would find out anyway." She paused again, and drank some more of her Cosmo. "Okay, third confession. When you asked me about Pinocchio's at the Parker House, you may have thought, because of the way I reacted, that I had never been here before." I nodded my head in confirmation. "What I didn't tell you was that I had been here before. My brother, Collin, used to take me here."

Tears started to form in Emma's eyes, and I knew then that what she said next would not be good.

"I say 'used to' because Collin was killed on 9/11."

"Oh my God, Emma." My tears, which had been just below the surface when I told my story, pooled in my eyes as well. "I'm so sorry."

"Thank you." And then, through her tears, she told me Collin's story. Collin was Emma's only brother, although she had a younger sister named Shannon. On 9/11, Collin had been 28 years old and had been working for an investment bank located on the 83rd Floor of the South Tower of the World Trade Center. Collin and Emma had always been very close, and he would often treat her to dinner, many times at Pinocchio's.

On 9/11, Emma had been working on the trading desk of her firm in Midtown Manhattan when the planes had hit. The desk always had television monitors in their office to watch the business channels and news. Emma started to panic when news came in about the first plane hitting the North Tower. She tried to speak to Collin, but her calls didn't get through. Emma's father called her soon thereafter to tell her that that he had spoken to Collin, and he was okay. That was the last time anyone in the family spoke to Collin.

When Emma saw the second plane hit the South Tower, she completely lost all the composure she had. Her co-workers had tried to reassure and console her, but, as Emma put it, what could they do for someone who knew she had just seen her brother die? Two of her co-workers took her home to her parent's house on Long Island. She spent the rest of the day with her family and other friends watching the news, hoping for a call from anyone telling them that Collin was okay.

Over the days to come, Emma and her family had waited anxiously for that phone call. However, because the point of impact from the plane included the 83rd floor, their hopes were small. Emma said that she had given up hope after the second day, although even two years later, she still had some dreams where Collin would show up on their doorstep claiming to have had a head injury and not knowing who he was for a long time.

Emma had talked for a while, as long as I had, and when she finished, our food and drinks had been long gone. We had declined dessert, and the bill was on the table. We had been in the restaurant for a while, although neither of us felt any hurry to leave.

"I was single when Collin died, and afterwards, I really wasn't interested in dating anyone for a while," Emma said, wiping the tears from her eyes with her napkin. "When I saw you at the Parker House, you were pretty much the first man I liked since 9/11. I'm not a religious person, but as I walked over to you, I said a prayer to God, and to Collin, that you and I would hit it off. And I asked for a sign. When you said you lived two blocks from me, I thought for a second that was the sign, but then I chalked it up to coincidence. And then you asked me about Pinocchio's. That was the sign, Jack. Because the last time that I saw Collin was the night before 9/11, and he took me here for dinner."

My mind reeled at the odds of those events. There were thousands of restaurants in Manhattan, and a maybe a hundred or two in the area where we lived, most of which were appropriate for a first date. The fact that I suggested the last place where she saw her brother was unbelievable. I had never put much faith in signs myself, but the odds of everything seemed so small, I could not dispute Emma on it.

"Now when you said you couldn't call for a while, that shook me, but then your friend Rachel came over, and reassured me. And I knew we would see each other again. And then this morning, I ran into you, and I … ." She stopped for a second, and then sat back with a sardonic grin. "God, don't I sound like Ms. Psycho-Stalker Chick right now?"

I laughed. "No, you're not." She then gave me the same "don't bullshit me" look that Mom had given me two weeks before. All women must learn that look at some point. "I mean, it's not something you usually hear on a first date, but then testicular surgery and chemo treatments aren't a typical topic of first date conversation either."

A small smile appeared on Emma's face. "Okay. Anyway, I'm not saying that the signs mean that we're meant for each other or that you are 'The One.' I just think that you and I are meant to be in each other's lives right now. In fact, from what you've told me, I think I could help you get through this last month. I can't imagine going through what you have without your family around. It's the only way I got through my brother's death."

"Well," I said, "my friends have been incredible. But, what I'm going through doesn't compare to losing your brother. I have no idea what you went through."

"No, you don't," Emma said, shaking her head. But then she turned to me, looked me in the eye, and reached out to grab my hand. "But you know what? I don't know what it's like to find a lump on my body, have the surgery you did, and then go through chemo for a week at a time for three months straight." She squeezed my hand and smiled. "What I do know is that we have both been through some bad times, and have suffered. It doesn't matter who had it worse."

At that moment, I wanted to kiss her, but we were at a restaurant, not more than two feet from two other couples. "We should pay up and leave so that Mark can have the table," I said. "Would you like to go to a bar for a drink or two?"

"Yes, I would," she said with her smile.

We paid the bill, and thanked Mark. We walked out of the restaurant and headed south, holding hands, to Marty O'Brien's, a nearby Irish pub. It was one of my favorite bars in the area because the bartenders treated their regulars very well, by buying them a free round at least once a night. O'Brien's also had a jukebox that played a great mixture of traditional and modern Irish songs and alternative American music. When we arrived, *Galway Girl* was playing on the jukebox.

"This is my dad's favorite song," said Emma, as we entered. "This looks like a proper Irish bar."

To our luck, there was one empty bar table. We sat down next to each other, ordered some drinks, and started talking. We talked about our lives before 9/11 and before cancer. I told her about growing up in a German Catholic family in Minnesota, and she talked about growing up in an Irish Catholic family on Long Island. There were some similarities in our backgrounds, and some big differences. For instance, she had never milked a cow or picked rocks from a corn field.

We found out that we had the same two favorite television shows: *24* and *Alias*. We talked about *24* more, because I had just finished watching the second season. We both agreed that the first season was better. I had not yet seen the second season of *Alias*, but Emma had. She promised me that it was better than the first season.

Every so often, one of us would touch the other, a finger grazing an arm here, a hand touching a thigh there. The tears were behind us, and we smiled, laughed, and drank.

We talked for a while, and at one point, when the jukebox was playing Matthew Sweet's *I've Been Waiting*, I looked at my watch. To my surprise, almost five hours had flown by.

"Emma, do you know that it's almost 2:00 AM?"

"No way, you're lying." She grabbed my arm to look at my watch. "Wow, that flew by."

"Yeah, we probably should get going."

"Yeah." She stood up from the table and looked around. "Can you walk me home?"

"Absolutely."

We walked down the street, again holding hands. When we arrived at her apartment building, a small one not too different from mine, she stopped and looked at me. "Well this is it." I stood there, with the uncertainty I felt at the end of many first dates, wondering whether to give the girl a kiss, a hug, a handshake or a nod of the head.

Emma broke the silence. "Listen, if it's okay with you, I would like to visit you in the hospital. Would that be okay?"

"Are you sure? I'm not going to be in great shape, and maybe worse, you'll have to meet my mother."

"Yes, I want to be there with you." Then she gave me that look and smile that she first gave me at the Parker House.

This time, I did not fuck it up. I pulled her to me, with my right hand on the nape of her neck, and kissed her. The kiss started off slow and soft with our lips almost barely touching. It slowly turned stronger, and she pulled me in closer. After a couple of seconds, we broke apart, and smiled at each other. I suddenly recalled one of the last lines from the movie *The Princess Bride,* about how the last kiss between Buttercup and Wesley left behind all other kisses in recorded history. Our kiss kicked that kiss's ass.

We stood there, holding each other for a while, until Emma asked, "Can I ask you a really personal question?"

"I think after everything we've talked about tonight, nothing's too personal."

"Well, um," she blushed a little as she spoke the words, "you said that the doctors said that your, um, equipment, would be normal after the surgery. Have you tested that yet?" Her eyes held a suggestive sparkle.

I laughed, a little nervously. "How do I say this? I've had a couple of successful solo practice runs, but I haven't conducted any …., um, you know, joint tests to confirm that everything is in proper working order."

"Well," Emma said, the sparkle in her eyes growing, "then I think we need to go up to my apartment and do those tests."

I looked deeply into her eyes. "Are you sure?" I knew that I wasn't. I hadn't been naked with a woman since the surgery and wasn't sure that Emma would be turned off once she saw me naked. The knowledge of what I had lost didn't bother her, but I was still afraid that the sight, somehow, would.

She held the look a couple of seconds, and then whispered in my ear, "Yes." She then led me up to her apartment, where we confirmed, to our mutual satisfaction, that my equipment still worked. Not too long after, I found out that Emma was a bit of a perfectionist, when she told me that we needed to confirm the results a second time.

So we did.

Later in the morning, after we woke up, we confirmed our findings a third time, this time under different operating conditions (the shower). Then, after a quick stop at my apartment for a change of clothes, we had breakfast at the Blue Moon Cafe. The same waitress who waited on me the day before took our orders. Emma ordered an everything bagel with cream cheese and a bowl of fruit. I had a sausage and cheese omelet with two strips of bacon. After the activities of the previous nine hours, I needed the protein.

"Would you stop that?" Emma said, with a smile on her face.

"Stop what?"

"You're smiling like you got laid last night," said Emma.

"Well, I did get laid last night, or more accurately, several times this morning." I said, grinning even more. I noticed the waitress looking at me, shaking her head and smiling. "And you have your own smile on your face, missy."

Emma giggled a joyful laugh. "I know. I can't stop."

"See? It's a natural, biological reaction."

"Oh, really? So you've had these smiles before?" she asked, playfully.

"Yes, but never as big of a smile as the one I have now."

"Oh, my God," Emma said, shaking her head. "My father warned me about men who were always ready with a compliment on their tongue." She picked up her coffee mug, and drank a sip. Then, she set the mug down, and smiled again. "But then again, he's been married to my mother for 33 years, and is always complimenting her, so who is he to talk?"

I laughed, and smiled some more.

"So what are you doing the rest of today?" Emma asked.

"Just enjoying a relaxing day," I said. In the past, in the times when I slept with a woman for the first time, I felt the need to spend some time by myself the next day. That day, I didn't feel that way. "Would you like to hang out with me for a while?"

"I'm all yours," she said. "At least I will be after I use the restroom. Excuse me."

"Sure." While I waited for her, in complete bliss, I realized something. I originally met Emma in New Jersey, but I wasn't supposed to have been there that night. If I hadn't found the lump, or if I hadn't been diagnosed with cancer, I would have been in New York, working on the National Mutual brief. If that had happened, I wouldn't have met Emma, and the previous night would not have happened. For the first time during the whole ordeal, I suddenly realized that something good, if not possibly great, had come out of having cancer.

A couple of minutes later, the waitress came over with the food. She looked at me, and said, "I guess you had a great night too, huh sweetie?"

I would not have thought it possible, but my smile grew even larger.

CHAPTER EIGHTEEN

"What do you mean, you have a girlfriend?" Mom asked, incredulously. "Three weeks ago, you were single and worried that you would never meet anyone."

It was Monday morning, and we were in my room at the NYU Medical Center. Mom had flown in the night before, just hours after Emma and I had ended our day together. Over the past eight days, Emma and I saw each other on all but two of the days. During the week, I worked at Garrick Knight, helping Mike and Elizabeth prepare for the hearing. Other than the Monday and Wednesday nights, I would leave work at 8 PM and have dinner with Emma at a different place. Each night, we ended up at her place, in her bed. We spent the entire weekend together, only separating just before Mom arrived from Minnesota.

I decided to wait until I was in my hospital bed, hooked up to an IV to tell Mom about Emma. I thought the setting would make the information easier for her to handle. It was a stupid, stupid thought.

"I know, I know," I said, holding up my hands. "But we originally met months ago, and I really liked her. But, that was the day after I found out I had cancer, so it didn't go anywhere. Then we ran into each other nine days ago, and ..."

Mom sat forward in her chair. "Wait, so you've only been seeing her for nine days?" she asked, in disbelief.

I was grateful that we were not in the chemo room for the conversation.

"Yeah, but our first date was great, and we spent most of last week together. She's been through a lot, too, probably even more than me. We really like each other, Mom."

At that moment, Mom did something I never expected: she laughed. The laugh was not a mocking one, but instead, joyful. "Jack, you may not fall for girls easily, but when you do, you fall hard."

"And why do you say that?" I said, confused.

"In all the years I've known you, I've only ever heard you talk about three girls, Kara, Sarah, and now Emma. Now, I know that you haven't been living the life of a monk ..."

"Mom!" I interrupted, in surprise.

"Are you going to tell me I'm wrong?" Her mouth was smiling, but her eyes challenged me to contradict her. When I didn't, she continued. "Anyway, the fact that this girl is only one of the three that you have told me about tells me that she means a lot to you. And I'm happy for you. I just want to make sure that you're not moving too quickly. It's not like you have been in the best mindset over the last few weeks."

"Don't worry. We haven't tattooed our names on each other, or moved in with each other. I mean, we talked about it, of course."

"Jack ...," Mom said, in the tone she used when I was being a wiseass.

"I'll be careful, Mom." I said and leaned back into my pillow. Mom was right though. I was falling for Emma. I was incredibly happy, and I was suddenly wondering whether, over the last two months, I had blown everything out of proportion. I thought that, perhaps, I was depressed and freaked out because I was going through a hard time and I was lonely. Maybe, like the swelling in my arm during my third chemo treatment, I didn't need to do anything for things to get better. I just had to trust that they would. I thought that it was possible that I didn't need to change anything about my job. Maybe, just maybe, I thought, I could have my dream career and my dream girl.

"So when is she coming by?" Mom asked, still smiling.

"Tomorrow afternoon. She didn't want to intrude too soon. Just remember to be nice to her."

"Ach, Jack! When have I ever not been nice to someone?"

"I can't remember one," I said, fairly truthfully. Mom was a true Minnesotan, and therefore a consistent practitioner of "Minnesota Nice." Sometimes, though, there is some passive aggressiveness under the Minnesota niceness.

"Well, then, why'd you say it?"

"I'm sorry Mom." I quickly changed the subject. "Can you reach into my backback and take out the picture that's in it? The backpack's between you and the bed."

Mom reached down, opened the backpack that I received at the last Garrick summer outing, and pulled out the drawing Courtney had given me. I had put it in a frame I had bought at Duane Reade after I flew back from Minnesota. "What's this?" Mom asked.

"It's a picture that a nine year old girl named Courtney drew for me, the last time I was here. She was diagnosed with leukemia last year, and she is going through a second round of chemo. I was sitting in the chemo room feeling sorry for myself, and she drew it for me."

Mom looked confused. "Why did you have it framed?"

"Because I need it to remind me what it means to be strong. Can you hand me the book in the bag, too?"

Mom remained confused. "Well that's different." She looked down into the bag and pulled out a paperback copy of Stephen King's *The Gunslinger.* "What's this box you have in here?"

"Well, that's a gift for Courtney," During my week off in New York, I spent some time looking for the perfect gift for her. The box held that gift. "She's supposed to have her final chemo treatment this week, too. Since she gave me something, I wanted to return the favor."

"Are you sure?" She said, as she handed me the book. "Is a nine year old girl going to like something like that?"

"I think she will, Mom." Mom did not look reassured. "Trust me." I sat back in the bed, opened the book to my bookmark, and began reading. I hoped to finish the book that afternoon, before the chemo brain kicked in. Still, it took a little while before I was able to fully concentrate on it.

When I woke up Tuesday morning, I could feel the effects from the chemotherapy drugs. I was extremely tired, despite sleeping well, and my stomach was unsettled, as if I had been riding a roller coaster for three hours. As the day went on, I felt the chemo brain kick in, and my concentration slipped several times. Luckily, I had finished *The Gunslinger* the night before, just before Kyle, Sarah and Rachel visited early in the evening.

Despite my physical unease, my mood was still pretty upbeat. I was happy that Mom was there. Even just sitting in a chair, reading her book while I watched movies, her presence comforted me. I was also looking forward to later that afternoon when Emma would visit.

She arrived just after 5:00 PM. She was dressed in a white blouse and blue skirt, and carrying a big Louis Vitton handbag.

She looked beautiful. She smiled at me, and then walked to where Mom was seated.

"Hi, Mrs. Ritter, I'm Emma," she said, extending her right hand as Mom stood. "Jack's told me so much about you."

"Please call me Addy," Mom said, shaking Emma's hand. Emma walked over to the other side of the bed, leaned down, and gave me a kiss. "Hey Jack."

"Hey Em," I said, her kiss left a smile on my face. I could sense Mom looking at us, while we talked.

"How are you feeling?" Emma asked.

"Eh," I muttered. "I'm not too bad."

Emma turned to look at Mom. "Is he just putting on a tough face?" Emma asked Mom.

"Just a little one," Mom responded, with a smile.

Emma sat down in the other chair, to the left of the bed, placing me in the middle of both of them. "Did you have a good flight?" asked Emma.

"It could have been worse," said Mom, and then she hesitated. "It would have been better if the man next to me didn't lean on me the whole trip."

"I hate when that happens," said Emma. "Did he talk your ear off?"

"No, thank goodness. I was able to read my book in peace."

They continued the conversation like that for a while, small talk at first, and then deeper conversation. Emma talked about losing her brother, and Mom listened. Later, Mom shared some personal fears about my living in New York after 9/11, things that she had never said to me. The conversation was a little awkward, but it went better than I expected it would.

It was still a surprise, though, when Emma suggested that she take Mom out for dinner when visiting hours ended. Mom declined the offer twice, saying she shouldn't and that she didn't want to put

Emma out. Emma was persistent, though, and Mom finally agreed after Emma suggested that they eat at Pinnochio's.

"You don't have to do this," I told Emma, while Mom used the bathroom. I was a little uncomfortable with the idea that Mom was going out to dinner with a woman who I had known for only ten days.

"I know, but I want to," Emma replied. "Your mom is in a strange place, and I know she doesn't know me from Adam, but she shouldn't have to eat alone somewhere unfamiliar."

"Thank you," I said, feeling extremely sleepy.

When they left, they each gave me a kiss, although Mom's kiss was on my forehead. After telling me to get some sleep (Mom) and take care of myself (Emma), they left.

Despite the fact that I was completely tired, and my concentration was shot, it took me a while before I fell asleep. The last thing I wondered was how bad the dinner would be.

I didn't sleep well that night. I placed most of the blame on the chemotherapy drugs, but some of it was due to my nervousness about Mom and Emma having dinner. All kinds of outcomes for the dinner passed through my head, from the benign, where the two had a pleasant, but awkward night, to the horrific, where Mom somehow found out that Emma and I had slept together and called her various synonyms for the word tramp. My anxiety was compounded by my concerns about the National Mutual hearing that would be held Wednesday afternoon. I had spent hours upon hours drafting the briefs and preparing Mike so that he could convince the judge to grant our motion to dismiss. The judge could make his decision later that day, while I was stuck in a hospital bed.

My nervousness continued throughout Wednesday morning with no respite, until Mom, looking happy, walked into my room.

When she arrived, I had managed to shower and get dressed, and was about to leave for my daily appointment in the chemo room.

"Good morning," she said. "How are you feeling?"

"Worse than yesterday," I said, wishing to appear disinterested in the events of the previous night. "Breakfast isn't really agreeing with me, so I had to rush to the bathroom a couple times. How was last night?"

"Last night?" Mom said, trying, but failing, to appear ignorant of the point of my question. "Oh, you mean the dinner between Emma and me? It was pleasant."

"Pleasant?" I asked, in annoyance.

The smile Mom had been trying to hide appeared in full force. "Alright, Jack. It was very nice. She spoke a lot about her family, especially about what happened to her brother. It breaks my heart to hear what she and her family went through, but she seems like a very strong woman. And she clearly thinks a lot about you."

"Really?" I asked. I wasn't surprised by Emma's feelings for me, only by Mom's recognition of them.

"Yes, really. She talked about how she wanted to see you again after she first met you. She thinks her brother brought you together."

"What do you think of that?" I asked.

"You know my faith, Jack. I know God has a Plan, but I don't pretend to know what He intends. Still, with everything that's happened, it wouldn't surprise me if this was part of His Plan."

"So you're not worried that I'm not thinking clearly about this?" I asked.

"I still don't want you to move too fast," she said. "But I think she could be good for you. And I think you could be good for her."

"Thanks, Mom."

"You're welcome. Now, aren't you supposed to be in the chemo room soon?"

"We have a little time," I said, after seeing that the time on the pump said ten minutes, "but maybe we should go up now."

"Okay," she said, and we walked out the door. The chemo room was on the floor above us, so we needed to take the elevator. As we walked down the hallway to the elevator another door opened ahead of us, and Barbara Stern walked out. She closed the door, and then saw us.

"Hi Jack," she said. She clearly had been crying. Her eyes were red and puffy, and her face bore remnants of the tears.

"Barbara, are you okay?" I asked, forgetting about Mom.

"No," Barbara said, her voice cracking and the tears resuming their path down her face. "Courtney's having a really bad morning. This is her last session, but the chemo is making her really sick, and she keeps saying she wants to stop now. Her dad is with us, so I left to get the nurse for help."

"That's awful," I said. "Is there anything I can do?"

"Thanks, Jack, but I don't think she should have any visitors right now."

"I understand," I answered. I thought for a second. "Um, I won't bother her, but would it be okay, if I gave you something to give to her? After she gave me the drawing, I felt that I had to get her something."

"That's nice of you, Jack, but you don't have to get her …"

"I know, but it's something I wanted to do," I said, interrupting her. "Her drawing, well, it's helped me. I really need to return the favor, if it's okay with you." For the past five months, I had received a lot of help and compassion from my friends and family, but it seemed to me that I had given nothing back to anyone in return. I needed to change that.

"Okay," Barbara said.

I looked at Mom. "Mom …," I said, and the realized I had not introduced her. "I'm sorry, Barbara, this is my mother, Adelaide Ritter. Mom, this is Barbara Stern. She's Courtney's mother." Barbara mumbled the politest hello her state would allow, and Mom offered her sympathies. "Mom, can you grab my backpack from the room?" Mom nodded her head, and returned to my room.

"This is very nice of you, Jack," she said, wiping her eyes. "And I'm sorry she can't see you. But she's a nine year old girl, and sometimes this whole thing is just too tough for her."

"Barbara, you don't need to apologize," I said, gently. "Sometimes this whole thing is too tough for me. I'm amazed that she's not like this every moment of every day."

At that point, Mom arrived back with the backpack. She handed it to me, and I opened it, pulling the gift out.

As soon as Barbara saw the gift, her eyes widened. "Oh Jack, this is too much."

"No, it isn't. Like I said, I need to do this, and I hope this can bring a smile to her face."

Barbara looked at me for a second. "I think it may. In fact, it may help more than any nurse could. Give me a second, okay?" I nodded my head, and Barbara went back into the room.

"That poor woman," Mom said.

"I know. I can't imagine what's she's going through."

"I can," Mom said, tears threatening to emerge from her eyes. I nodded my head and touched her shoulder.

The door opened, and Barbara looked out. "Jack, Adelaide, can you come in? It took some doing, but I convinced Courtney to talk to you. I told her that you had something for her, but I didn't say what it was."

"Okay," I said, and Mom and I followed Barbara into the room. Courtney's father was standing behind the chair by the bed. He was short and bald, but clearly fit. He was dressed sharply in a dark blue button down shirt, and charcoal slacks. He was clearly distraught. Courtney was in bed, still in her pink pajamas, watching me with sad eyes. Gone was the strong, smiling girl I had met a month ago. Suddenly, she was a sick little girl, going through something no child should ever have to endure. My heart broke.

When I reached the bed, Courtney's father nodded his head to me. He was a little stand-offish, which I understood. He was in a difficult position and I was someone he had never met, visiting his sick daughter to give her a gift. "Hi, Jack, I'm Mark Stern. Please, sit down." He pointed to the chair sitting next to the bed.

"Thank you," I said. As I sat down, I took a breath, and steadied myself. I wanted to give Courtney the strength she had given me, and I needed to be calm when I did it. "Hi Courtney. I heard you're having a tough day."

Courtney nodded her head, but didn't say anything.

"I know how you're feeling. This week's my last week too, and it's been the toughest week so far. I want to stay in bed all day too. But you know what's helped me? The picture you drew for me. I have it framed next to my bed."

"Really?" she asked, softly.

"Yes," I said, nodding my head. "Anyway, ever since you gave the drawing to me, I knew I had to give you something. And then I remembered what we talked about in the chemo room. Do you remember? About Stargirl?" She nodded her head. "And then I found this, and I knew that you had to have it." With that, I pulled the box out of the backpack.

Courtney's eyes widened a little bit, when she saw the picture of the Stargirl statue on the box. The statue captured Stargirl flying out of some clouds, her blonde hair blown back. Her right hand was extended, thrusting her gold "Cosmic Staff" upward and forward. She was wearing her blue mask and costume, a large white star on her chest. She also wore a huge smile.

Under Courtney's watchful eyes, I opened up the box, and gently pulled the statue out of the protective Styrofoam case inside. I set it down, on the table next to her bed. I felt that I needed to say more, and suddenly the words came easy. "Do you remember what I told you about Stargirl? About how she was a young girl named Courtney, and how her powers came from the staff and her belt?"

Her eyes still on the statue, Courtney nodded her head.

"Well, I didn't tell you how she got the staff. You see, she was a superhero before she had the staff. The belt she wore gave her powers. But one day, a superhero named Starman gave her the staff. Starman was retiring and he wanted Courtney to have it. He was amazed at how strong and brave she was, and he knew that, when she had the staff, she would make him proud, and that she would be a better hero than he had ever been. He knew that she would be magnificent. That's why I gave this to you, Courtney."

Courtney turned her head and looked at me.

"When we met, I was amazed at how strong you were. I was sitting in that room, feeling sorry for myself. And then you walked into the room. You've been through this twice, and still you were smiling, and helping other people. Do you know how incredible that is?"

Courtney gave a slight, almost undetectable shake of her head.

"Well, it is," I said. "And when I think about that, I can't help but think about what you will be like when you're older. Years from now, long after you gotten through this, there will be things that happen to you, things that would make other people cry. But you, you're going to remember how tough this time was, and you'll tell yourself, 'this is nothing; I had cancer when I was nine years old and I beat it.' You're going to be just like Stargirl, Courtney. You're going to be magnificent."

Courtney had tears in her eyes, and so did I. I wiped mine away.

"And if you forget how strong and incredible you are; and you could, because we can't be strong and brave all the time; well, you'll always have this statue to remind you. Okay?"

All Courtney did was nod her head. I swear, though, that I saw a glimmer of hope in her eyes. Maybe I saw it because that's what I wanted to see. All I knew was that I had said all that I could say.

"I should get going." I stood up. "Feel better, okay? And just remember, no matter how bad things seem, they can get better. Everything can change, Courtney, and for you, it will."

I looked from Mark to Barbara to Mom. Everyone was crying, to some extent. I started to walk away, and then I heard Courtney say, "Thank you, Jack."

I turned back to Courtney, and smiled, "You're welcome."

Mark and Barbara intercepted me before I could reach the door. Mark shook my hand, and Barbara gave me a tight hug, saying "Thank you," as she did.

Mom and I left Courtney's room, and walked to the elevator. I had forgotten about my IV bag. It was almost empty, and the pump read 1. The alarm would go off when it reached zero, which would probably occur before I reached the nursing station. Luckily, I knew how to turn it off.

Despite how I felt from the drugs in my body, my spirit soared. I knew that I had returned some of what Courtney had given to me. Before the elevator arrived, Mom grabbed me and gave me a hug. "I'm so proud of you." She let me go, wiping the tears from eyes. "You did a good thing, Jack. You were right. I think she liked the statue."

I wish I could say that the next day I saw Courtney, and that she was back to her old self, smiling again, as bright as she ever did, and that she never cried again. But that's not how life works. It takes more than one day and one person to convince you that things will be all right. The fact is that I didn't see Courtney again that week. Barbara did visit me once more, though. She thanked me again, and told me that, while Courtney was still in rough shape, she couldn't take her eyes off the statue.

⇒⊷ ⊶⇐

Around 4:00 PM, Emma arrived, having traveled directly from work. She and Mom hugged, as if they had known each other for weeks as opposed to a day. Emma then came to me and gave me a kiss. "How are you doing today?"

"Other than the nausea, I think he's had a really good day," Mom said, with a smile.

Emma looked at me. "What happened?"

"Mom, you look like you want to tell her. Go ahead."

Mom was eager to tell Emma about our meeting with Courtney, which she did, with some brief corrections from me. After all, it was Stargirl and Starman, not Sungirl and Sunman.

When Mom finished, Emma looked at me in wonder. "You did that?" She asked. I nodded my head, and she leaned over and put her hands on the sides of my face and kissed me. *I'm glad I remembered to brush my teeth,* I thought. Suddenly, I heard a knock at the door, and saw Mike Goldman standing there. "Is now a good time to visit?" he asked.

"Come on in, Mike," I said, sitting up a little bit. Mike walked in, wheeling his litigation bag in with him. "Mom, Emma, this is Mike Goldman, he's a partner at my firm. Mike, this is my Mom, and Emma, my girlfriend." Mike smiled, having seen Emma kiss me, and shook hands with Mom and Emma.

"Elizabeth wanted me to apologize," Mike said, "but she had to run back to the office to take an urgent client call on another case. How are you feeling, Jack?".

Who cares how I'm feeling! I thought. *What happened at the hearing?* "I'm okay. How did the hearing go?" A second later, I realized that Mom and Emma had no idea what was happening, so I provided the background on the hearing.

"It started out pretty scary," Mike said, picking up his litigation bag, after I had finished. "Can I put this here?" he pointed to an empty spot on the bed, and I nodded. He set down the bag and opened it. "Well, since it was our motion, we should have been the first to make our arguments. Instead, Judge Metron asked Weinstein, the plaintiff's lawyer, to begin. So Weinstein starts his argument, and a minute later, Metron interrupts him, and says, 'What about the Ramstein case?'" Mike turned to Mom and then Emma. "The Ramstein case was a case Jack found that said that people who brought the lawsuit against our client were not the proper people to make the claims they were making."

Both Mom and Emma nodded their heads, but looked like they had no idea what Mike was saying.

Mike continued. "Obviously, Weinstein had his answer ready, that Ramstein was not applicable to this case, and why. Metron interrupted him again, and said 'I don't know how you could say that, but go on.' It went like that for a while, Weinstein trying to state his position, and Metron interrupting him to point out the flaws in his argument. After Weinstein was done, I stood up, ready to add a few points, but Metron told me to sit down, he had heard enough. And then, right there, he said he was granting our motion!" Goldman's face broke out in a huge smile. "Weinstein asked for leave to amend the complaint, but Metron said no. He gave us thirty days to answer the remaining claim on the complaint, but we know that one is pretty small."

At the moment, I was ecstatic. I was tempted to jump out of bed, and do a jig, nausea and fatigue be damned. I had worked my ass off and battled cancer while doing it. *Fuck cancer,* I thought.

Mike turned to Mom again. "That may have sounded like a lot of legal jibberish to you, and it was. Essentially, we won a huge case that could have cost our client over a hundred million dollars. And we won, basically because of the incredible job your son did, not only finding the right cases, but writing two great briefs that convinced the judge that we should win. You should be incredibly proud of your son."

Mom did look happy. "I've never been more proud of him," she said, and she winked at me. Emma reached to me and placed her hand in mine. She beamed as well.

"The best news," Goldman said," is that National Mutual's general counsel was there. He was over the moon. He said they have two more class actions coming up, and they want Garrick to represent them. And they want you, Elizabeth and me on them."

The news thrilled me as well. Millions of dollars would be flowing into Garrick's coffers, and the lead partner was essentially crediting me for it. It was everything career-wise that I had ever wanted.

I turned to Emma, and then Mom. At that moment, I suddenly understood what Dad had meant when we talked two weeks before. Everything became clear, and I knew what I needed to do. I was wrong that I could have both my dream job and my dream girl. I remembered how miserable I had been over the past year, working on just one class action case with the rest of my caseload. If I wanted to be a partner at Garrick, I would have to work just as hard for the next four years. I knew that if I kept working the way I was, there would be now way I could keep Emma.

Even after I made partner, the workload wouldn't change that much. Mike Goldman, the King of Facetime, was proof of that. Months earlier, I had wondered how much time he spent with his family, but, at that moment, I knew that however much time he did, that would not be enough for me.

My experience with cancer and chemo had given me perspective enough to know that my "dream job" was no longer my dream. In the past week with Emma, I had been truly and utterly happy. That's what I wanted out of life, to spend time with the people I loved. I wanted to marry a great girl, maybe even Emma, make some kids, and spend as much time with them as I could, maybe even reading comics and watching sci-fi shows with them. I didn't want to be in an office night after night, wishing I was home to tuck my kids in bed or naked with my wife. I knew what my dream really was. It was was time to make it my future.

I turned back to Mike. "That's great, Mike," I said. "And I would be happy to work on those cases. But my workload is a bear. Heck, it was a bear before I went through all of this. I think I need to scale it back a bit. Maybe if I was transferred off of some of the other cases, like the King Industries case and a couple others, I could do it. Otherwise, I don't think I can handle it."

I knew that I could work that way at Garrick for three or four more years. I wouldn't make partner that way, but I could obtain more experience before I found another job that would work better for me.

Mike looked at me, with a brief, barely noticeable look of surprise on his face. Then, he looked at Emma, and nodded his head slightly. "I understand, Jack. When you get back to the office at the start of November, let's sit down and take a look at your workload. We'll see what we can do."

"Thanks, Mike," I said, relieved, "but I should be back in the office before that."

"Take a couple of extra days off to make sure you're fully recovered, and to celebrate. Speaking of which, I picked this up on the way here." He reached down into his litigation bag, and pulled out a bottle of Dom Perignon champagne. "When all of this is finally over, I want you to share this with your friends, and celebrate all you've done in the past five months. The work you've done on this case is the least of it."

"Thanks, Mike, for everything."

"It was nothing, Jack." He looked at his watch, and shook his head. "I've got to get back to the office, but take care of yourself okay?" He extended his hand and I shook it. After saying goodbye to Mom and Emma, he left.

"Congratulations, Jack," said Mom. I smiled back at her.

"It really has been a good day, huh?" asked Emma.

I nodded and lay back in wonder. A month ago, I had been at the lowest point of my life, with no hope or faith of anything changing. One month later, everything seemed different, and so much better than it had been, even five months before. *It didn't happen in a New York minute,* I thought, *but, damn, that changed fast.*

CHAPTER NINETEEN

I walked through the door to Pinnochio's, escaping the cold December air. There was no snow on the ground, although the temperature was just below freezing. Inside Pinnochio's, it was perfectly warm. Two of the tables were occupied with customers, but they had finished their meals, and their bills were lying on their tables. *Excellent,* I thought. The other tables had been assembled together to accommodate my dinner party.

Mark walked over to me, and shook my hand. "Jack, my friend," he said. "How are you tonight?"

"I'm fine, Mark. It looks like you're ready for us."

"Yes, we are. These two couples are almost finished, so in five minutes or so, we'll be ready for your party."

It was five days before Christmas, and I had rented out Pinnochio's to throw a party to thank my friends and to celebrate the holidays. We would spend a couple hours at Pinnochio's and then head over to O'Brien's. I anticipated that we would all have a great time.

"Excellent. Thanks for everything Mark."

"My pleasure," Mark replied. "Why don't I take your coat and I will get you your usual drink. You can wait for your guests at the tables."

"Thank you." I handed him my gray wool three quarter length coat, and walked to the tables. The party was a semi-formal one, therefore, I was dressed in a white button down shirt, red tie, black sports coat and dark gray slacks. A few minutes later, Mark delivered my Maker's Mark and Diet Coke. As usual, Mark had poured a stiff cocktail. I sat there alone for a few minutes, filled with excitement. That night was the first time that the group of people had gathered, and we had a lot to celebrate. I was also excited to fly home to see my family in three days for Christmas. As I waited, I rubbed my head to feel the stubble that was finally growing back.

Kyle and Rachel were the first to arrive, minutes after the last couple had left. I embraced them both when they came to the table. "Smalltown!" Kyle said, "Are you ready to have some fun?"

"Definitely," I said, as Mark walked over to take their coats and drink orders.

"Where's your beautiful girlfriend?" Rachel asked, after providing both to Mark.

"I'm not sure, I responded, with a shrug. "She said she had to run an errand. She should be here soon."

"Good," said Rachel. "We really like her. You better not screw things up with her. If you do, she gets Kyle and I in the break-up." Her eyes and smile told me she was only mostly kidding.

"Then, I guess I don't have a choice, do I?" I didn't think there would be any chance of that. In the past two months, I had fallen completely in love with Emma. We spent virtually all of our free time together, which given my reduced work schedule was pretty often. On most weeknights, I worked until 7 PM, and then met Emma for dinner at my place or at a restaurant. I would often work for an hour or two afterwards from home. I still worked on weekends and some nights until after midnight, but not as frequently as I had before. I knew that some of the partners weren't happy that I wasn't taking on as much work as others did. I also knew that I would never be considered for partner, but I didn't care. I was happier than I had ever been in my life.

At that moment, Barry and Rich arrived with their wives, so I excused myself to welcome them. Everyone was dressed formally, like myself, although Barry wore a Santa Claus hat. He justified it by reminding me that the cartoon *Santa Clause is Comin' to Town* clearly demonstrated that Santa had been a redhead. Rich's wife, Hope, was showing her pregnancy in her green dress. Two weeks after my last chemo session, Rich announced the news that Hope was twelve weeks along, and he never had to experience the joys of a sperm bank, like I did.

Jim and Donna arrived next. They too looked happy, maybe even happier than I had ever seen them. I embraced them both and waved the waiters over to provide some appetizers and to take their drink orders.

Sarah and Dan were the last couple to arrive, holding hands as they walked through the door. I walked over to greet them.

"Hey Jack," said Sarah, as she gave me a hug and a peck on the cheek.

I returned the kiss, and shook Dan's hand. "Hey guys, I'm glad you were able to make it."

"There's no way we could miss this," Dan said.

"I appreciate that," I said, seeing Mark wave to me from the bar area. "Just one second."

I walked to Mark, who had some questions about when I wanted the entrees served. As I gave him the times, Emma walked in. She took off her coat and I saw that she was dressed in a stunning white and gold dress. When she saw me, she smiled and my heart skipped a beat. I would never get tired of that smile.

While I spoke with Mark, Dan and Sarah went over to greet Emma. I had been nervous when Emma and Sarah met for first time during my last chemo session. I wasn't certain how Emma would feel about my being friends with an ex. However, there was no reason to worry. Emma and Sarah became fast friends, almost to the point where they were closer than Sarah and I.

"Hey Smalltown, do you know what just occurred to me?" I turned to see Kyle standing next to me, watching Sarah and Emma hug. "The only reason you met Emma at the Parker House was because you had been diagnosed with cancer. If that hadn't happened, you would have stayed in New York that weekend."

"Yeah, I thought of that as well," I said.

"Well, did you also realize that means that Sarah is responsible for you and Emma being together?" Kyle asked, with a sly smile. "I mean, if you hadn't had sex with Sarah, she wouldn't have found the tumor that night, and you wouldn't have found out that you had cancer. When you and Emma get married, you should thank Sarah for it."

"Ha ha," I responded, with my own smile. "Let's never mention that again, shall we?"

Kyle laughed, and I walked over to meet Emma.

"Hi there," she said, and then we embraced and kissed. When we separated, she caught her breath, and then fished out a box from her coat pocket, and handed to me. "I have something for you."

I recognized it instantly as a watch box from Tag Heuer. I opened it to find a platinum diving watch. "Emma, this is incredible."

"Turn it over," she said, in excited anticipation. I looked on the back of the timepiece. and saw an inscription. It said "*To my Starman, Love Emma.*"

"Thank you," I said, and kissed her again. I took off my watch that my parents had given me when I graduated college and put on my new one. It fit perfectly. "I thought we were exchanging gifts later tonight. I left your gift at home."

"Oh, I have another gift for you," she said, with a devilish twinkle in her eye. "It's not much bigger than the watch, but I think you'll like it when I'm wearing it tonight."

I suddenly wanted to skip the party, head home and exchange gifts. "I love you," I said, and kissed her.

"I love you, too," she said, when we parted. "Am I the last one here?"

"Of course," I said.

"Great!" Emma said. "Let's get this party started."

I told everyone that it was time to take their seats. I remained standing at the head of the table, and gestured to Mark. He brought over two chilled bottles of Dom Perignon, one of which was the bottle Mike Goldman had given me. Mark and the waitresses then began filling the glasses on the table.

"If everyone doesn't mind," I said, "I'd like to speechify a little bit. First, to my Jewish friends, Happy Chanukah, and to my Christian friends, Merry Christmas. I hope everyone has a great holiday and spends it with those they love most."

"Here, here" and similar other shouts filled the room.

"Next, I have some engagement news." Several shocked faces turned suddenly to look at Emma and her left ring finger. "Last week, my friend Jim proposed to his girlfriend Donna. She said yes." I paused for everyone to congratulate the couple. When they finished, I continued. "To Jim, knowing Donna, I can say that you're a lucky man. To Donna, knowing Jim, I'm not completely certain why you said yes, but I'm happy you did. To you both, congratulations." Everyone echoed my sentiment and toasted the couple.

"Yesterday, I was walking around the neighborhood, listening to my iPod, as I usually do, and Elton John's *Mona Lisas and Mad Hatters* came on. Now while it's not the happiest song about New

York City, it's one of my favorite songs, and it has one of my favorite lines, 'I thank the Lord for the people I have found.'"

"That's what I want to say to you." I struggled to contain the emotion in my voice, and a tear ran down the right side of my face. Several other faces at the table mirrored mine. "Because I thank God that I found the people, both inside and outside this room, who helped me the last six months." I thought of Mom, Dad, Jesse, Kara and my other family and friends in Minnesota that I would see soon. I also thought of Mike, Elizabeth, Dr. Cross, and Dr. Schnee. I also thought of Courtney, who, according to her mother, was in remission, hopefully forever. "If I hadn't found you, well, the best case scenario would be that I would be in a straight jacket in Bellevue right now."

A few people laughed and some had tears in their eyes. Everyone smiled.

"And it's because I found you …," my voice completely broke, but I didn't care. Emma gently clutched my left hand. "Because I found you, I received the news a couple of days ago from my doctor that I am cancer free."

Cheers and applause filled the room. I had already shared the news with Emma and my family the night before. I also found out a week earlier from the reproductive clinic that, based on a sample I had given them a week before that, I was able to have children. I didn't share that news with the group. No matter what *Seinfeld* says, yelling "I have swimmers!" in public is not appropriate.

"So thank you for everything," I said, when the applause died down. As I raised my glass, the others followed and we each drank much deserved champagne.

After my speech, everyone gathered around to hug and congratulate me. When we were done, I turned to Emma. "That was beautiful," she said, with a smile on her face and tears in her ocean blue eyes. At that moment, I knew, beyond a shadow of a doubt, that I wanted to spend the rest of my life with her. Realizing that fact, I suddenly saw my future in her eyes. It would not be a fairy tale, "happily ever after" life; I knew that there was no such thing. As the years passed, Emma and I would face hard times that would test us and our relationship. I knew, though, that, no matter how bad things became, and no matter how bleak they looked, happiness could be right around the corner. I was aware that everything can change, but I knew that, if I married Emma, the two of us would have a happy life together.

And so we did.

THE END

AFTERWARD

This novel is a work of fiction, but it is based upon events in my life. Like Jack, I was diagnosed with testicular cancer. Jack's experience and reactions to the diagnosis and the chemotherapy treatments virtually mirrored my own. Almost twenty years later, I am cancer free.

While the rest of the characters in this book are based upon people I have encountered in my life, all but one, Sean Kimerling, are fictional. As I described in the book, Sean was an Emmy award winning sports anchor on WPIX 11 in New York City as well as a pre-game announcer for the New York Mets. On September 9, 2003, at the age of 37, Sean died from testicular cancer. Following Sean's death, his family started the Sean Kimerling Testicular Cancer Foundation, the mission of which is fulfil "Sean's wish to bring awareness of testicular cancer to those most at risk, so that if a man hears that he has testicular cancer he also hears 'we caught it early.'" Please visit seankimerling.org to find out more about testicular cancer and how you can contribute to the Foundation.

ACKNOWLEDGEMENTS

This book was a long time in the making and a number of people helped me from its inception to the final product that you hold in your hands. While my name is on the cover, all of these individuals, who contributed to what is between the covers, need to be recognized.

To my wife, Mary Kay, who provided me with support, inspiration, valuable suggestions and love throughout the two years it took me to write this story. I could not have made it through this project without you.

To my kids, Maggie, Riley and Ben, who thought it was so cool that their Dad was writing a novel. Your wide-eyed pride gave me the drive to continue when I needed it most.

To my parents, Bill and Mary, for EVERYTHING. A long time ago, I chose a path for myself and you gave me the tools, opportunity and freedom to take that path. I know that it has not always been easy for you, but without you, I would be nothing.

To my siblings, Pat, Missy, Mindy and Kate, for being a great support group and displaying a lack of surprise that I would one day write a book. I gave Jack a great sister in Jesse, but she was a combined representation, and a weak one at that, of all of you.

To John Aissis and Tom Carlson, who listened to my ideas as I formed them and offered suggestions that made those ideas so much better. To Salvatore Romanello and Peter Kingam, who answered questions about law firm life and cancer treatment when I forgot (or never knew) them.

To Brad Budde, Kelly Donovan, Heather Greenberg, and Dale Neuschwander, who read the first draft and pointed out its flaws as well as its strengths. To Alison Stebbins Donovan, who edited the book. Any flaws or errors that remain in the novel are mine, not my reviewers'.

To Jeff O'Dwyer and Jennifer Romanello, who advised me on publishing the book. To Kyle Herges, who designed an incredible exterior for the book.

To any and all, who, upon hearing that I was writing a book, did not voice the statement that often went through my head during the process: *there is no fracking way you'll finish that book.* I thank you all.

ABOUT THE AUTHOR

B rian Kemper is a practicing attorney and a cancer survivor. He lives in central Connecticut with his wife Mary Kay and his three kids: Maggie, Riley and Ben. He is also, as his friends remind him, still a bit of a geek.